ANJOU

BRITTANY

TOURAINE

NONO
Love and the Soil
(NONO)

BY

GASTON ROUPNEL

LANGUEDOC

MAINE

Translated by
BARNET J. BEYER

CHAMPAGNE

LORRAINE

NEW YORK
E. P. DUTTON & COMPANY
681 Fifth Avenue

NORMANDY

PROVENCE

PICARDY

PREFATORY NOTE

M. ROUPNEL aroused a great deal of interest in the literary world of France in 1910, when *Nono,* his first novel, was published. Although there is something of the manner of Jules Renard in *Nono,* it is, nevertheless, one of the few contributions to contemporary French fiction of marked originality. The characters are vividly drawn, and they linger in the memory of the reader. Nono, a simple winegrower, the hero of this book, is instinct with vitality, and will remain a humble companion of the great characters of modern literature. He is so rich in pregnant expressions of rustic wisdom that he often suggests Gargantua; but he is more tender, more moved by human sorrow, and more sensitive to the beauty of nature than Rabelais' hero. In Nono we find the elements of poetic grandeur combined with the most sincere naïveté. He is a man of a single love attachment, and his whole life is moulded and frustrated by it. His moods, whether dominated by sorrow or joy, always compel our interest.

The author of *Nono* was born 23 September 1871 in Franche-Comté and has spent much of his life at Gevrey-Chambertin, near Dijon, the district which he uses as a setting for his novel. M. Roupnel has de-

v

voted his life to teaching and writing, and at present he is a lecturer at the University of Dijon and writes articles and stories for the leading newspapers and periodicals of France. Another novel written by M. Roupnel, *Le Vieux Garain,* appeared in 1913.

M. Roupnel has drunk deep of the springs of Burgundy. He seems to have imbibed the very spirit of that beautiful region of France; and he gives us in *Nono,* in direct and pungent language, not only richly colored descriptions of the country, but also realistic presentations of its vivacious people. In his descriptions of nature there is a certain mystic sentiment, which Burgundy, a hilly country, full of sunshine and good cheer, hardly suggests. This, M. Roupnel explains in a letter that he was kind enough to write me. He says: "I have inherited from my Norman ancestors (English perhaps) the soul of a mystic which strangely is little in harmony with the sunny vines of the hills of Burgundy and the hearty laughter of that jovial country. All I can say is that nature seems to have constituted my temperament of these two distinctly different elements . . ." These two qualities pervade M. Roupnel's absorbing story, *Nono.*

I wish to express my sincere thanks to my friends Professor F. W. Chandler and Mr. A. Miller for having read the manuscript and for valuable suggestions.

BARNET J. BEYER.

NEW YORK,
20 November 1918.

CONTENTS

PART I

PART II

CONTENTS

PART III

NONO: Love and the Soil

NONO

LOVE AND THE SOIL

PART I

CHAPTER I

WHEN one has the reputation of being "an uncouth and foolish Jacques" . . . there is really very little to be done! "Let the tongues wag! . . . Moreover, the world is large! . . . There are other places besides the plain of Rouvres! . . . There is many a Jacques here below! . . . And they are necessary! . . . A half decent world must have a little of everything: it must have the good and also the wicked! . . . Thus it is with a good vintage: there must be ripe and unripe grapes! . . . foul and sound! . . . And our forefathers didn't hesitate even to mix some white grapes with the red! . . . "

In this way poor Jacquelinet, nicknamed "Nono," consoled himself. As he spoke he craned his long neck towards his listeners, and thrust forth a long face, foolishly good-natured and cadaverous. Above his thin eyebrows rose the wrinkled forehead of a bewildered, simple fellow. His small, soft, and shriveled eyes had the enraptured gaze of innocence. Deep wrinkles fretted his entire face, mercilessly furrowing his hollow cheeks. Their sorrowful lines revealed the toil of the winegrowers, and told of the misery of tilling the soil. However, his turned up, flabby nose was a sign-post showing that the wine-shop was owned by a naïve, uncouth Jacques. But what a sweet smile on those lips parched by the sun! And Nono would raise his head and gayly jog it as if to breathe in the spice and good humor of the Burgundy air.

Nono's great pleasure was gossiping. During the day, alone in the fields or in the vineyard, Nono would confide in his little donkey. And the puny, pensive beast listened, drooping its dusty head towards the ground: "Fine weather, my chum! but the wind has changed its course, for the trains can be heard." Or else: "The oriole is singing, old pal! . . . that means rain." Nono would also, at times, venture to predict about the wine and the corn: "The soil is very rich . . . It's a sign of a year for wine." The donkey did not say no; and Nono, content to be understood, sharply closed his pocket-knife: "It's already past four o'clock, my chum! . . . We're going to fill up."

In the evening, surrounded by loitering and churlish neighbors, standing at the door of his wretched stable with the donkey's harness over his shoulder and in his arms, Nono would begin his interminable babbling, while the mule rolled on the hard ground and rubbed its back against the stones.

With a cheerful artlessness, he would reassure his

anxious friends, or calm those that were fretful: "You're wrong in complaining of your occupation. 'Tis the sun that ripens for us our grapes. It does three-quarters of the work; and the generous rain does the greater part of the rest. Besides, the wine is sown and the soil is full of promise. Nonsense, the bulk of the work is done. And then, if the wine is bad, instead of selling it, we drink it. But there are cranks who are never satisfied. They're full of groans, more so than rickety windmills."

The winegrower is particularly fond of grumbling about his meager fare: "The bourgeois eats what he likes. He fills up on fowl and chops, and stuffs himself with truffles, but if we want to have a taste of meat, we must kill a wretched pig which only yields some bacon and no roast joints."

To such complaints, Nono replied mirthfully: "Ah! my friends! . . . There's nothing better than bacon and vegetables. We children of the soil, we ain't proud. For us a good stew's the thing! And how varied the bacon is! . . . It's pink, white, fat and lean. The poor pig has always something to offer. It gives something from everyside: the back, the flank and the belly. After having squealed a while, it's put, from head to tail, into the salting-tub, and here is our pittance for six months preserved in salt, which owes nothing to the butcher, a vender of stale delicacies and of tough meat!"

Nono then concluded: . . . "That's how I am! Not too ill-natured, not too thievish, rather roguish, content with everything and especially to be on earth, happy to be well-settled in my little nook, and to work there to my heart's content, happy to make my friends laugh and to make no one cry."

And thereupon the friends would walk off jeering: "Confounded Jacques!" Now this Nono was really a good fellow, for he spent a good third of his year in doing favors. He would cart for those who had to fetch casks or gather in some sorry harvest. For such trifles it would not be befitting to disturb a big horse, they were just worthy of a little mule and of Nono.

Those who wished could pay him: Nono never asked for anything. He had his own way of thinking: "We must needs help one another, for we live together in the same world. Besides, we mustn't always work for money, but also at times for the sake of the spirit."

Nono had his slight failing. No sooner was he tickled by a light touch of drunkenness than the artless fellow would make queer speeches to much-amused crowds. From the very outset he would insist upon emphasizing two or three things: "I'm no impostor. I'm above all no Prussian. I'm no drunkard. I drink to please the world, but I can't get drunk. How unfortunate it is!"

Nono then spoke freely of himself, his life and his origin: "I'm a child of the soil. I've lived in the Baraques de Gevrey fifty-three years; but I was born at Villebichot, down yonder, half a league in the direction of Citeaux; but I don't recall those days. My old man used to talk of 'em: 'My Nono,' said he, 'was born in the gamekeeper's house. He was a tiny bit of sausage shriveled up in a cradle. To-day he's a stuffed monster.' "

"But that," added Nono, "was the way the old man bragged. What would you have? that old man spoke what he thought!"

When in another vein, Nono delighted in singing the praises of his province: "La Montagne is worthless; it's a barren and drab country. Le Pays-Bas is a country of misers. La Côte! . . . Yes, here's one for you—unspeakable! And then! . . . To the right of Gevrey is Mory: a habitat of wolves. To the left is Brochon: a city of beasts.

"Take even Gevrey! . . . The town ain't everywhere the same. . . . In the upper part, there's the Rue Haute, yonder behind the forest, almost beneath the cliff: wretched little hovels not rising a foot above the ground, and a pack of bears living within, as in caverns.

"In the center is the market-town; and there you find only humbugs, shops and cafés: a heap of chop eaters and lemonade drinkers. And all those pups are proud fellows who fear the ground will make the peasant's foot too yellow.

"All that is worthless stuff. But there are Les Baraques. . . . Quite near here, much below La Côte, on the real highway, are our homes. I'm a child of Les Baraques, and that's the pride of my life. Les Ba-

raques of Gevrey-Chambertin! . . . Ah! my friends!
One of the biggest highways in the world runs through
here without much ado. At least so I've heard. And
as a matter of fact Paris and Marseilles actually border
it for a short distance. Some say: 'The Baraques is
a wretched-looking place!' But every person who
comes along the highway sees well enough by our de-
meanor that we ain't shoemakers, but winegrowers—
independent winegrowers."

When Nono got tispsy in earnest the tone of his
speech changed, and he grew gloomy. He began to
lose faith in himself and in his tilling of the soil:
"After all the toiling peasant is hardly rich. There's
scarcely more than one way for him to become so:
that is, to have a kind aunt and to be her real heir.
As for me, however, instead of an aunt I only had
a wife; and even she was a low cunning harlot. And
yet she was a dear thing, and I'd have stuck to her.
But where is she at this very minute? I haven't heard
from her for seventeen long years. The world's large:
she's lost somewhere; and you can be sure that with
my vineyard work on hand I hardly have the time
to set out in search of her. And yet, I repeat it, she
was a very dear thing when you knew how to manage
her. But . . . the rest of the world is just full of a
gang of lewd villains. This isn't meant for you."

And Nono would then sadly allude to his unfortunate experiences as a husband: "I don't see what
pleasure one can have in living with a wife of a poor
man? Why just that woman, and not another?"

At other times melancholy inspired Nono with dismal ideas which condemned life entirely: "Look here! . . . If, after my death, the Creator talks to me of beginning life over again here below, I want to be a boarder of a rabbit-hutch, that is an animal, not a man; I want to have four paws and be full of hair. As such I'll be less plagued."

But at times Nono got even more violently drunk. He was often enough on Sunday evenings in a sad plight. For hours he would lie helpless in the wheelwright's yard, yawning and staring at the passers-by. Like a bruised worm he would feebly wriggle his lanky carcass. If anyone approached him, he drearily raised towards the onlooker his dry and emaciated face. His large ears limply protruded from his head; in his small dull eyes there was hardly more than the dim glimmer of an insect's eyes. He would swing his crooked finger before the noses of the people, and with a tremulous voice, gradually becoming more vehement and fretful, he would force each one to agree with him: "You can't be saying 't ain't so; for only a fool'd deny it."

When Nono would finally get home, he would find a sad place indeed, which was cheered only by the wildness of a very little girl—his grandchild. On seeing her, the drunkard would suddenly grow tender: "My little one! . . . A terribly long time ago, indeed many years ago, there was a charming little woman who resembled you very much. It was your grandmother. I was then a young chap. But since then, sorrow and death come together and laid waste: the one cut the harvest down, and the other trampled it to dust. Oh, the devil! And now we're both alone in life, you a mere bud and I laden heavy with years. Ah! We've nothing to brag about."

Less tender at other times, he would give his little girl such advice as he deemed necessary: "See that later on you don't also become a strumpet!" But the child, who was only five years old, understood little of this highly moral counsel.

Nono's extreme state of drunkenness would last only one night, however. The following morning he would become once more the simple fellow, everybody's boon companion. And thus he jogged along, dragging his listless feet made heavy by his boots, joked with incessantly, and ever an easy dupe, honest and good-natured to the core.

CHAPTER II

AND yet this dull and gloomy life had, like every other one, its days of happiness and sunshine.

About thirty years ago, when Nono was still a young man, someone entered his life to offer him his share of love. And this person—who was to be the joy and torment of his existence—had not appeared unexpectedly, and had not treacherously planned her part in effecting his doom.

When Jeanne Sirodot was still but a little girl, when she was yet Jeannou, Jeanette, Nénette, a baby in short . . . "Well! . . . we were already playmates and a pair of friends . . . We were in love! . . . "

"I knew her when she was hardly taller than a beetroot," Nono continued, "only, do you know? . . . all in all she was already somewhat of a bother . . . a real little beastly thing! . . . I was nine or ten years old; and I used to take care of her when her mother went to the wash-house or to do household work. Well! I had to be on the watch; her limbs were no bigger than the paws of a seven-pound rabbit, and she toddled along quicker than a little beast!"

Nono had to be in the right humor to relate this story. But Sunday evening, in the Caillot Café, after an afternoon spent in drinking, heedless Nono babbled willingly.   Then, betrayed by drunkenness and encouraged by the cruel obsession of an ever living reminiscence, Nono threw open to all, without shame and without rancor, his galled and battered soul.   He raked up mercilessly a beloved past.   He laid bare a bygone youth. . . .

" . . . After all a little dear one is charming!   That one you only had to take in your arms, and you were happy . . . I must admit that I was in a way her nurse: I saw to it that she blew her nose, and was clean and dry . . . Later I'd take her to school . . . Still later, she in turn came to work for us.   In exchange for some vines we cultivated for her mother, little Nénette did our household drudgery.   For my father and I were alone.   We had no woman at home. My old man wasn't often sober.   And then we knew as much about household work as a shoemaker knows about making medals.

"This Nénette was our joy, our support, our salvation.   You should've seen the little being animate the whole house.   Ah! she was clever and quick at household toil!   The cloth here and the broom there, and the stone floor was clean!   And now the beds were made!   I tell you that in no time the wretched hole of the Jacquelinets (father and son) assumed a princely and glorious air.   And, to top it all, the clever and lively girl would smile to you, give you a sly wink, thrust her skirt up and run off! . . . Quick-silver! A flash!   No time to see a thing! . . . No trace left! . . . The old man and I remained alone, staring open-mouthed at each other . . . Well, old man! . . . That's alive, eh? . . . That's youth for you! . . .

"The old man smiled: 'I knew one in Le Pays-Bas —a very old bird now—who . . . ' and then he would tell me a raw story: he didn't know any others.

"But that Nénette became very pretty, and I wasn't on my guard! . . . And yet those idle tramps blabbed enough about her:

"She has fine legs and an aggressive walk! . . . Her short skirts don't conceal that it's not bean-poles that hold her up.

"On hearing them so often blab in this way, I finally saw with their eyes . . . Oh! . . . so little and so young a girl, impossible! . . . a darting round tuft! . . . And you would have munched that pretty, delicate and brown face with as much pleasure as a sugar almond! . . . The young lads called her 'the Kabyl,' for her hair was curled and black, and everyone compared her to a wild little squirrel.

"But beneath her wild hair her features were small and cute enough to make you cry . . . yet fearless and forward . . . full of fine courage. And there was something funny too: the tip of her nose was pink like that of a rabbit's, and she had the smile of an urchin! . . .

"But has anybody here known her in her young days? . . . Has that charming face ever raised towards you its brown soft eyes? . . . Haven't they moved you? . . . No? . . . Well then! the very

Heaven which looks upon us from on high won't move you! . . .

"For me, you see, her soul was in those eyes which aroused my love. Therefore, I had only to let my heart loose, to have my fill of love and suffering. But, alas! . . . I was tormented with jealousy. Too many idle beasts prowled about and beset that skirt! . . . She had about her the web of a hornet's nest. I wasn't the most fortunate of the crowd, for I was neither the youngest nor the boldest. Besides, what could I do with that Renardin in the struggle, who was hotter than a live coal . . . Don't forget: he was watching the little darling for two or three years! . . . Ah! I suspected it! . . . Every time the child passed by— the big fellow was at his door! . . . his feet tucked in felt slippers . . . his hands in his pockets . . . his bald-pate uncovered—as graceful as a crag—his shoulders cramped in as far as his waistcoat.

"Who'd 've said, on seeing that thickset wretch, with the surly mustache of a beef-eater, his dark complexion and his darting eyes, that he was the blackguard of the province! . . . Oh! there is no use jeering . . . But you, Ganat! . . . and you, Lécuyer! . . . and then you, you fat one there! . . . You know it as well as me: years ago, when your wives would bring you some little vines—well, they didn't get the seeds from the official receiver! . . . You're laughing the wrong way! . . . That's true, however! . . .

"But if that blackguard had his day . . . I can assure you I had mine too! . . . That's what you were

driving at . . . eh? . . . You wanted to make me
speak of my glorious day? . . . Well, you'll see.
There was no harm done that day. We had a little
chat—that's all. We were in the same vine row; and
remember it was a row almost dead. I was digging,
and she had come to sharpen the vine-props. It was
rather a nasty, dim winter day with just a phantom
of light. . . . And the pruning ain't worth much,
when the vine ain't well propped and it's shivering
cold, under an overcast sky. . . . A sky that's as
smoky as a bakehouse. . . . How can you be gay,
when the weather reminds you of a funeral? . . . I'll
be frank with you: when everything's so out of joint,
I lose my good humor and become a tough fellow to
handle, too. . . Well, we were both having a little
bite in this row about four o'clock. . . . She was nib-
bling at a piece of bread I was holding in my hand . . .
And then it was the old story of kissing and coddling.
We were very close to each other . . . There was
some power gripping us relentlessly. Without pity for
me, it brought our faces closer and closer together . . .
It made our eyes sparkle and our mouths water . . .
My friends! . . . hear me! . . . I seized her in my
arms! . . . Oh! she was almost there already; I only
had to draw her closer to me . . . But when I felt
the little rogue! . . . when I felt on my waistcoat
her heaving bosom! . . . then my lips fell where her
own were . . . And do you know? . . . Well, that
day I also did my duty on earth . . . Do you know
what I did? . . . Well, I cried like a child! . . . And

I said to her: "Girlie, you mustn't cry! . . . There ain't a dearer thing in the world than you . . . As for me, when I earn three francs fifty for my day and two bottles of wine, I'm quite happy. Don't share with me, therefore, my bondage! And then, it's late: let's go home together.

"A short time elapsed, and her mother Clémence fell ill; and one fine morning the miserable doctor raised his fat red snout and slyly remarked: 'Ah! her neck is swelling! . . . Very well! Very well! I thought so: this woman has a cancer in her stomach, her condition is very serious. In fact, nothing can be done; pay me and I sha'n't see her any more.'

"Well, what could we do? . . . One night, Nénette and I were helping the old woman drink. I raised her head which was as yellow as ginger bread, and the little one held the cup to her lips. But the old woman turned her head away and said: 'Oh! I'm going to die . . . Something's pounding me inside! . . . I'm going to die! . . .'

" 'Oh! mother Clémence! . . . ' said I, 'perhaps not yet! . . .

" 'Yes,' she answered, 'I feel it; I'm going to die . . . Ah! It's about that little one that I'm worried! . . . I'm a very poor Christian indeed to have brought that good child into the world! . . . Ah! Jacques! . . . Ah! my boy! . . . don't forsake her! . . . Love her! . . . '

" 'Mother Clémence,' I answered, 'if only that is

worrying you, you can rest assured: I sha'n't be her enemy!'

" 'My boy! . . . My poor boy! . . . ' said she, turning her head in every direction on the wretched pillow. 'My boy! . . . Help her along! . . . '

" 'Mother Clémence! as long as I'll have my arms, and they'll not be worn out to the shoulder, I'll work for her.'

"Just then the old woman began to moan, and the little one caressed her; for she had a good heart . . . then. . . Oh! later it was quite another matter! . . . She became a slut! . . . It's easily said! . . . Ah! we're human beings, and yet our hearts are of stone! . . . But when you marry a pleasing girl, you must have thirty-one days of pardon ready every month! . . . Instead of that . . . I chucked her out . . . Ah! my friends! . . . Where is she now? . . . Where is she for the past eighteen years? . . . Is she alive? . . . Is she dead? . . . Ah! I hear she has returned lately to Dijon! . . . Ah! . . . if any of you've seen her, let him tell me whether she's still a pretty darling! . . . But what am I asking you? . . . You, a pack of drunkards and blackguards! . . . For you only want to make me talk, and then show me your hellish teeth . . . You want to make me weep and joke . . . But I don't give a hang about you all! . . . And you're only a gang of stingy louts and cobblers! And I'm going! . . . So-long! . . . "

CHAPTER III

BUT there are things that Nono never related. They were not known to everybody. He alone knew of their existence . . . they were slumbering within him. . . . In the somber refuge of his soul, holy memories were buried that could not be unearthed . . . But he knew that those memories were ready to come forth immediately at the strident call of his solitary despair, ready to weep with him, to relieve him from his distress, to save him from death. And at times he evoked them in the agony of sleepless nights . . . And they rose forth, ever vivid and fresh like things which never die! . . . At his invocation, they never failed to appear . . . the eternal visions! . . .

Nono would thus evoke his entire life of love, from the sad and serene evening when all that was to grow into joy and woe had taken root.

That evening Nono had just come home. He was busy in the stable putting in order the donkey's litter. Suddenly, on turning round, he perceived Nénette. She had come up noiselessly, and remained standing with her hands crossed behind her back leaning against the brickwork.

"Jeanne! . . . what's the matter? . . . "

"Mother's dead," she replied in a calm voice.

Nono put down his prong after having arranged some of the scattered straw.

"Poor little one! . . . " he muttered.

Nono leaned his lanky body against some faggots that were piled up between two vats. Both remained thus standing for some time facing each other, without uttering a word.

"My little Nénette! . . . " Nono at last said, "Come up to the house."

"No, Jacques! . . . We are quite well here. Here, I can tell you better what I've got to say. I've come over to say good-bye to you. I'm going where my mother is now. Jacques! . . . don't cry for me too much! I know what to do: I won't suffer. My mother and I almost agreed to it. We talked a lot together. During the night . . . as soon as I heard her toss about . . . I got up; I was up before she even uttered her first groan. I then waited until her fit was over. While she was suffering I held her hand: that was her only relief. Then, the crisis partly over, I remained, and we talked. At first I tried to reassure her. But as soon as she realized her condition, she became calmer. We then spoke of our life and death as very natural things.

"Nono, my friend, my older brother, in spite of what I'm going to tell you, continue to love me a little. Here I am before you with a broken heart for love of you. But honor ain't worth much. You

see, I dreamt I was your wife . . . to share all with
you . . . Ah! but there's something terrible separat-
ing us . . . About two years' ago, a man with his
head almost buried in his sweater entered the house.
I was alone ironing the clothes. My mother had gone
to the wash-house. You surely recall that day? . . .
As soon as I got up, I fled; I ran here, towards you
. . . And he dared follow me! He was standing just
where I'm now. I was standing where you are now.
And you were in the yard washing some wine-casks.
He and you were talking together quite indifferently.
But he, though answering you, kept on staring at me.
And I was trembling with fear. . . .

"My Nono! . . . I wanted to be your wife . . .
but I wasn't worthy of your dear kiss! . . . Now I've
confessed to the only man whom I love! . . . And
this is the last day of my life! . . . I'm going with
my soul at peace . . . Good-bye! my friend! . . .
Good-bye! my Jacquot! . . . It's getting dark! Go
upstairs. . . . I'm going to sit up by my mother. But
to-morrow, rise early so that it's you who will close
my eyes. . . . And since I'm only after all an unfortunate creature who leaves the world without having sinned willingly, when the undertaker will have
dressed me, kiss me, Jacquot! . . . "

Nono didn't answer; but walked over to Nénette. He
took hold of her, and raised her in his arms. . . . She
was as light as a feather. . . . She did not resist. . . .
He took several steps backwards, and sat down on

the heap of faggots, with his dear burden lying against his breast.

"Just lie like that a bit! . . . darling! . . . Don't speak! . . . Don't move! . . . Remain quiet . . . do, my little one. . . . Just for a bit! . . . "

She obeyed. . . . And they remained so, resting on the dry faggots, crouched like birds in a nest made rather hard by the pricking sprigs.

Quite near them, the young donkey was eating, and turned towards them his peaceful head. He looked at them tenderly with the pensive eyes of an old scholar. One could hear his jaws grind. In the opposite corner, the rabbits, which felt the presence of someone friendly, remained awake; and now and then, behind the trellis, a little shadow would spring up without fear. . . .

The animals breathed forth a mild kind of warmth. There was no seclusion, but an open-hearted intimacy among beings inspired with the same tenderness. For it is delightful to sleep or dream with friendly animals nearby. Their short, noiseless breathing fills, little by little, the stable with an atmosphere warm and soft like down. Their little obscure souls feel reassured, and gradually our peace becomes the same as theirs.

Nono remained motionless. Nénette lay stretched out in his lap with her head reclining on his arm. He was waiting. . . .

And the donkey turned towards him a gaze that almost expressed sympathy. One saw in the darkness his large eyes shine beneath the thick long lashes. The young companion of the roads and paths probably told Nono to wait a little longer in order not to disturb the sweet slumber of his dear one.

Now the moon shed her beams through the door: from distant, dead lands she brought a vermilion glimmer; and one perceived above the poor roofs, a rose-colored corner of the starry world—of the sky all in motion.

Nothing any longer disturbed the soft stillness. Not a straw moved beneath the springing rabbits. The donkey's tail hardly wagged; it was as quiet and friendly as smoke from a cottage roof. In the lowly stable there reigned a humble and tender peace. . . .

The regular breathing of Nénette asleep descended and caressed Nono's hand. When he was certain that her slumber was profound, he rose with his darling in his arms, and walked out without a noise, cautiously moving his heavy boots. He tiptoed up to his room almost without making the stairs creak, and placed Nénette on his bed. He picked up the sheet, covered her with it, and then covered her feet with the feather-quilt.

While he was busy with these attentions, the head of his old father appeared, through the half-opened door. Old Francis had his cotton bonnet on. It was a huge mass of white beneath which one could just barely see two little sly eyes.

"What's this? . . . Big beast! What are you doing with that child? . . . You must have her in your own bed now? . . . "

"Stop your shouting! . . . Don't make a noise: You're going to wake her! . . . Her mother's dead. . . . "

"Ah!"

"And she's asleep, the poor child! She's tired out! . . . She's been up these twenty nights! . . . She fell asleep as soon as she lay down . . . at once . . . like a musket shot! . . . "

"Yes, she's sound asleep! . . . "

The father and son bent their attentive faces over the young girl.

"Do you know? . . ." said old Francis. "She's graceful like that! . . . Look at her, with her little arms stretched out, her pretty little head turned sideways! . . . And look at her curled hair: it's like the mane of a wild lion! . . . And beneath it such a sweet little face. . . . But what'll become of her now? . . . the poor child! . . . "

"Well! . . . Do you know, old man? . . . I'm going to marry her. . . . "

"Ah! . . . If you have a mind to! . . . "

"Yes."

"Well then! . . . that's easy."

The old man added after a moment's thought: "She's hardly plump! . . . If you have a mind to . . . it's all right! . . . As for me! . . . I know that when I was a postman in Le Pays-Bas, I had to have women who were built differently from that one! . . ."

"Old man! . . . Dress yourself! . . . You'll remain here! . . . You'll see to it that the little one

don't wake up . . . and if she wakes, see that she
don't run away . . . she might take it into her head
to throw herself into the well! . . . I'm going to
watch by the dead woman."

Nono spent the dreary hours of the night sitting
in front of the grim face and closed eyes of the corpse.
These eyes were angrily sunk in her black and blue
flesh. Now and then, they seemed to open and stare.
. . . Her lips looked furious, her arms ready to
rise. . . .

"Ah! . . . Mother   Clémence! . . . "   thought
Nono. "She struggled hard before she departed this
life! . . . One can see it! . . . It's hard to die. . . ."

And Nono gave free course in the irresistible
thoughts that loom up in one's mind when near the
dead. Even to the simplest soul, the life of a dead
person seems like a path in the plain, a narrow stony
path which runs from the horizon of dawn to the
horizon of night. . . . And all along this path, there
are numberless days, like imperceptible cold glimmers,
little gray sparks, without warmth and without love!
. . . Throughout this path misery is plentiful. . . .
There is a world of human woes! . . . It is an entire
existence bent over the untilled soil! . . . The pitiless
task ends only when the human being lies down never
to rise again, and crosses over his breathless chest his
arms without life. . . .

. . . Nono was thinking of the mother . . . and
he was also thinking of Nénette. The life of one had
been that of a hapless woman. What would be the

life of the other? . . . whom he had just taken upon
his own hands. She would be what he would make
of her.

. . . And Nono's eyes tried to penetrate this darkness, to follow with his gaze a tender little phantom
walking courageously by his side, hand in hand, along
the paths of the future, in the dim glimmer of days
to come. . . . But would he be able to guide the steps
firmly along the path seething with the iniquities of
man? . . . Nono had till then only known the necessary duties of a rustic life. Never yet had his soul
foreseen the severity and nobility of a duty that comes
from on high. . . . And now in the darkness where
the dead woman slumbered . . . his eyes perceived the
grave rays! . . .

But the poor winegrower was still hopeful despite
this gloomy darkness. He felt within him the resolutions both of love and courage. Courage? . . . He
has plenty of it: he has strong arms, and he is no
stranger to work in the fields! . . . He already sees
before him those fields quivering with barley and
wheat! . . . the vines recovering their old bloom! . . .

And then, there is one other thing. . . . Nono!
. . . You will show all the rancorous people that true
love can forgive an involuntary wrong! . . . and can
nobly raise the eyes till then downcast! . . . and can
infuse into the heart, in which it lies tenderly, the
pride of honor! . . .

After a creaking of springs the clock struck four.

At the last sonorous stroke the door suddenly opened and Nénette appeared.

"What? . . . Father let you out? . . . " said Nono.

"The poor old man is asleep! . . . And I left without making any noise. . . . "

"Little Nénette! . . . Since you're here, let me tell you that it's too late. It will soon be morning. The birds are already waking. Instead of closing your eyes . . . let me take your hand and open my heart to you."

"Have no fear! Nono! . . . My mother has sent me to sit by your side, I look at the dead face without sorrow, for I've just seen her spirit. While you were watching by her. . . . I was listening to her in a dream. But how shall I tell you? . . . I wanted, in this dream, to accompany her on a road; and she continued gently to push me away from her path. . . . This dream has saved me! . . . Now I'll continue to live alone in this world! . . . "

"Alone? . . . Darling! . . . And I? . . . Am I dead? . . . Ah! I too have just been dreaming of many things! . . . But I was dreaming awake. . . . It seems to me I was still a child yesterday. . . . And yet I'm five-and-twenty! . . . But to-day I've ideas worthy of my age! . . . Darling! . . . I hesitated a long time before letting you know; for I'll never be anything but a poor winegrower. But for want of delicacy, I feel I have the heart and courage necessary to give you the happiness due a good woman. . . .

Dear Jeanne! Let's get married, and love each other dearly! . . . "

"O my Nono! Do you forget what I told you to-night? . . . " And little Nénette covered her face with her hand. "Do you forget so quickly? . . . Ah! my mother said to me: 'You are impure, my little one! . . . Your marriage will be a falsehood. . . . ' "

"My little girl! . . . Look at your poor mother! . . . Do you see how much she has suffered? . . . She must have lived through terrible days to have such a face! . . . I can see all the misery she has suffered: her sorrow has left its traces. . . . And here we are, both of us, saying: 'What a pity.' Well, my Nénette! Would it have been so, if one day your mother had found someone to say to her: 'Clémence! . . . You are as pure for me as the angels. All the respect a man can have, I have for you. The wretch, who trampled on you, has left no trace. Your soul and heart have not been befouled. . . . Will you give me them? . . . I need them! . . . If you don't want to have the death of a man on your conscience . . . . . . well! . . . You must be mine! I must have you, I tell you! . . . You must be my young companion; and later on, when I'm old and you still fairly young, your hands must warm mine!'

"Do you know? my Nénette! . . . If someone had talked and acted so to your mother, everything would have been different. Her end wouldn't be so heart-rending. . . . Instead of death, there would be happi-ness in this house! . . . You would have brothers and sisters who would laugh, in the evening, in all the corners. . . . And the old husband and wife would almost be in the humor of laughing along with them. . . . But her life is ended! . . . Let God have the pity men haven't had! . . . But you, darling! . . . you're still with us . . . alive! . . . And I haven't searched for you. You came to the old vineyard. . . . You offered me what I didn't dare take. . . . But now. . . . I've got you and I'll keep you! . . .

"Look up at me! . . . Ah! that's right! . . . My dear innocent girl! . . . But how should I tell you what I feel in my inmost heart, and for which I find no words? . . . Look at me again! . . . You're fresh like the morning dew! . . . Darling! . . . Don't slander yourself any more! . . .

" . . . Where do you come from? . . . My dear girl! . . . You just happened to cross my path! . . . Little angel! who told you that you must come and share the life of this poor fellow . . . to make of him the happiest and richest of men! . . . "

. . . Little Nénette is kneeling at the side of her mother's bed. . . . It is not in vain that the living die. . . . When the silent darkness has entered forever beneath our eyelids . . . then the soul opens its spiritual eyes. And it sees into the unknown. . . . The poor beings who remain in the merciless world are still weeping. . . . But all around them, in the darkness that the funereal candle hardly dispels . . . a phantom without form, a freed spirit, tenderly brushes by them . . . warns them. . . . Nénette feels

it: the hand she is holding in her own is growing cold
and hard . . . the face she is contemplating is lifeless
. . . but it is in her soul now that she finds the well-
beloved presence. . . .

Her mind goes back to distant memories, and she
looks at the pleasant face of the one who rocked her
cradle! . . . And that face grown young again smiles
. . . and shows the path leading onward.

" . . . My little girl! . . . The day is come! . . .
Rise now! . . . The neighbors will soon be here. . . . "

"Is it morning already?"

"Why, yes! . . . Look out! . . . "

They went to the window where the sky was
brightening, the dawn scattering everywhere its many
rays.   The open road turned in front of them, and
beneath the long shadows of the lime-trees, it descended
towards the light. . . .

CHAPTER IV

THE love of Nono and Nénette began in the midst
of sorrow; and the first conversation of the lovers was
solemn. Death, which had just visited their house,
still encompassed them with its lingering shadow.
Their startled life as yet did not dare set up any fresh
hopes. Their love wakened gradually, uneasily, from
the ruthless horror of the night.

But time continued its course; the days grew longer;
March had come.

And little by little, on these hearts which abandoned
themselves gently to fate, love came and shed its blossoming rays, and spring arose with its fresh dew and
soft sunshine.

One evening in March, Nono was still washing the
few dishes after dinner, while old Francis was out
on the balcony sneezing and enjoying the fresh air.

The old man called:

"Hey! Jacques! come and see!"

"What?"

"A very little birdie crouching at the foot of our
wall."

"Oh! little birdie! . . . It's a young one: spring
has made it dizzy; it has no wings; it flies awkwardly.
A little wind or rain terrifies it; and it alights at once,
anywhere at all. We mustn't hurt it."

"I say! Come and see it, instead of babbling in that way. You'll tell me later whether she just alighted anywhere."

Nono went to see. On bending over, he perceived a vague slender form near the wall. She was sitting half-way on the tub of a rosebay, fidgeting there like a shy child that is restless on a chair. She raised towards the window her bright face, and on it one divined a sweet smile.

"Well, hey!" said old Francis. "What do you say of this little birdie? Did it fly here unintentionally? Answer, eh? . . . Look at her . . . holding to the wall like a frightened animal. She moves just enough to be seen in the dark. . . . You bandit! . . . She's looking for you now! . . . "

Nono's voice descended softly from above: "Little friend! . . . "

A soft coaxing voice arose: "Jacques! . . . "

Old Francis was shaking his head and gazing at the many pointed roofs that could be seen in the distance. A heavy sky poured darkness over all; and below, across the earth, spring was quickening the trees and plants to life. The dark air was as fragrant as the fumes that rise from a plowed field. A gentle breeze blowing from the mountains brought with it the sweet scent of the forest oaks and of the fallow land.

"Come on, little one! Come and bid us good evening."

"Come up! little friend!"

A furtive step sounded on the stairs; and Nénette soon entered. Old Francis asked her: "Well! . . . Here you are, little one! . . . Why didn't you want to come and say good evening? Hey! . . . naughty creature. . . . Ah! you rascals! . . . What are you doing there in the dark near the woodstack? . . . Squeezing hands, eh? . . . See that you don't go too far! . . . Have a bit of patience, and don't go quicker than the curé; give him a chance to set things in order with God Almighty regarding your marriage. . . . Ah! I hear a noise that sounds more like kissing than the ticking of the clock! And now you're moving your chairs together. I suppose you can't hear each other. Go right on! . . . Act as if you were in your own home! . . . But since you don't bother about me, and I seem to be talking to the air, I'll go to bed."

The two lovers continued to speak for a long time in a low voice. Their free hearts whispered to each other sentiments of devotion and tenderness.

The flames of the fire disappeared, the embers died out beneath the ashes. The words of Nono and Nénette gradually became less audible, and sank into murmurs and kisses.

The month of March is still but the very beginning of spring; all is yet premature and bare: the earth is still ungarnished and the branches are dry; this early spring brings with it only scant flowers and sunbeams.

April is the month when the earth bedecks herself. It is moistened with dew, perfumed with fresh moss,

and decked with periwinkles. The days grow brighter,
and there awakens a fresh easterly breeze that caresses
us tenderly in the mellow sunshine.

On Sunday after Easter, on one of those radiant
April afternoons the two lovers were walking together
towards the wood of Caillée: The wind brought them
a breath of verdure and of fresh water. A green mist
spread over the trees of the forest. The slender
branches of the peach-trees were strewn with blos-
soms. The peaceful almond-trees were already covered
with their fragrant snow-white mantle. And because
of the host of things that begin to bloom and love on
the coming of the spring sunshine, because of the
waking of the wings of all that lives, there was in
love-intoxicated nature a murmur of sap, a sweep of
lapping water and of waving grass, a rippling of
brooklets.

The two lovers hearkened to their divine hymn of
creation, spring murmuring like the love which was
making their hearts beat.

They were sitting near the outskirts of the wood.
. . . Stretching out a little, they were beneath the
blossoming branches. Their nest of love and care ses
lay beneath a hawthorn-bush. Surrounding nat .
rocked them with her song and sheltered th .. with
her wings, and fired them with a sense of mystery and
exultation. Their lips uttered love's universal language. . . .

. . . A soft, breathless whisper could be heard. It

was like the low imperceptible rustling of an April breeze over the young rye. . . . Nénette suddenly started up, pushing Nono from her; but her conquered lips yielded a hopeful promise.

"Yes. . . . Yes . . . to-night."

"Ah!" exclaimed Nono standing up. "My joy is worse than pain . . . it brings tears to my eyes . . . it makes my flesh creep. . . . "

And now the evening is come; the promised hour is approaching . . . the two lovers are waiting for the night to advance. . . .

Here is at last the silent night which shrouds like a forest the love of man, a night with a blue darkness, warm like a well-clad being. . . .

In front of their little house, beneath the spreading vine, the two lovers are sitting on a stone bench. In the distance can be heard the trembling of the trains. Still further, beneath the poplars of Boïse and the willows of Mansouse, the croaking of the frogs. The simple frogs are celebrating their paltry loves in the mud. The blue night is filled with their tender croaking.

Dim lights appear one by one along the roads. The moon glides towards the crags of the mountain; and, from its livid and death-like face, a light descends upon the living earth. . . . The two lovers search in vain for words that will reveal their inmost feelings. They have no other language but that of the eternal murmur which has united their lips, and which makes the heart babble like a spring. . . .

. . . Everything they feel—this silence where one can almost hear the limpid expanse breathe—this sublime and noble sentiment which penetrates them like water pure and cool—all that descends into their hearts with ecstasy and kindles the magic life of love. . . . And love comes and adorns the wild rose-bush with flowers. . . . It brings forth the fresh-blown eglantine. . . .

. . . They do not speak; but their eyes and their caresses sing beneath the spreading vine, on the coming of night, the supreme hymn. . . .

. . . Hosts of unsatisfied desires awaken in them. An intense, rapturous chill comes over them—a breath of great delight and agony—under which their bewildered souls tremble. And they are like many others in the power of the eternal law; they call for the master before whom all flesh tenderly yields and trembles for joy—the relentless master who tears asunder, one by one, the heart-strings of his slaves. . . .

He pleads with her: "Come! my darling Nénette. Let us go to your house . . . in your house, yes? . . . You promised. . . . "

She does not answer . . . she no longer hears . . . the moments of silence have come. . . .

Nono rises softly, and takes Nénette in his arms. Without saying a word, she puts her head on his shoulder, and he carries her noiselessly thus, up the

dark staircase.   He climbs softly the wooden steps.
In the darkness he holds aloft his light and loving
burden bearing it towards that old ancestral bed of
so many births and so many agonies. . . .

"Old man!" said Nono to his father.   "Old man!
You must hurry and clamber up to town.   Go to the
mayor and try to have him advance our marriage a
fortnight.   Dress up well; put on your new blouse,
and your gamekeeper's cap. . . . "
"Ah! I understand! . . . Overgrown blackguard!
Big rascal! . . . Ah! so that's what you're at! . . .
You couldn't have waited? Eh? . . . I thought so.
. . . I was saying: 'They're going to pair off some
night in the moonlight; we must hurry to the parish
priest and have him arrange matters in accordance
with the Christian sauce . . . have him bless your
rascality as if it was the Host's bread. . . . Hurry,
eh! . . . Ah! how people will laugh at you, if they'll
see a beardless recruit appear in this world, clad as
a nurseling, whom they expected six weeks later . . .
at the very least. You'll both be in a fine fix . . . Ah!
it'll serve you right! . . . Little rogues! . . . After
all the season had its share, too. It's spring that's the
blackguard. . . . I know it! . . . Long ago, when I
was a carrier in Le Pays-Bas. . . . "
"Go ahead, and put your new blouse on!"

CHAPTER V

AFTER the wedding, old Francis gave up, as it was customary, the rooms of the first floor to the young couple; and he would clamber to the garret every night. From the very first morning, it was he who waked the young couple after his own manner.

"Hey there! what's the matter? . . . Aren't you getting up any more? . . . Eh? . . . The mule has its snout at the door, and it has nothing to put in its mouth except its braying! What are you waiting for? . . . Eh? . . . And then the little one? . . . What is she doing? That's right, little one, hide your little face under the sheet! . . . I can see you, just the same. . . . Big lazy fellow! . . . You must take care of these little ones. They're tender: they need care and gentleness. Remember you're a great big hulking man! Lazy-bones! . . . Get up! . . . I'm thirsty! . . . "

"Are you going to make this racket every morning? Can't you leave us young folks alone, old fool? Get away and let us dress."

The married couple got up. Nono lit the fire, and Nénette prepared the soup. While she was doing her house work, old Francis continually kept staring at her with his little sharp and pert eyes. Sitting in

35

the corner of the fire-place, he languidly shook his
long face, thin, freckled, and fretted with squalid
wrinkles. He opened his large toothless mouth where
his tongue was rolled up like a spiral shell.

"Well! you see, my Nénette," said Nono, "that's
my old man! He makes the same racket almost every
day. . . .

"Every morning he crouches near the fire, and
starts his endless preaching: he predicts frost, hail,
the Prussians in France, the death of the mule or of
the pig. . . . And then he sneezes and blows his nose
in the fire. All that is in the bones of an old drunkard.
In the morning, he must spit and bawl a bit!"

Old Francis shook his head, and continued in the
nasal and solemn tone of old men: "In Le Pays-Bas,
when I was a postman. . . . "

"All right, old man, enough! . . . Come and eat
your soup. . . . "

Having eaten his soup, the old man drank a glass
of wine, filled his pipe, and began to hold forth: "Ah!
. . . Jacques! . . . Do you recall? I said: 'There's
wood in the wood-stack, bacon in the salting-tub, and
wine in the cellar: we can laugh at everybody. Well,
no! . . . The principal thing is wanting: a house without a woman is like a fire without a flame—just
good enough to smoke a sausage. . . . In fact, look
at this little rogue! . . . How she turns and twists!
. . . How she flutters about! . . . Worse than a
butterfly! . . . Just look at that curly head and

the pert little white petticoat, and the knavish little
waist. . . .

" . . . She gracefully affects to be furious. But
all that, it's the old story of wheeling and spinning
about, to show her impetuous youth. . . . It's the
trick of the flirt, and of the little knave! . . .

"Oh! I know a thing or two in the matter of
women! I've had my fill of all those poor creatures!
·. . . I was a hot one. Yes, I was quite a knave in
my days. Now I'm an old rogue; but I've petted so
many round cheeks that I'm not at a loss in a fair
of women. So listen to my warning, Jacques; take
good care, Jacques! . . . "

"Take care of what? . . . You old fool, you hardly
have faith in your daughter-in-law and son. . . . "

"Look here: you should've married a simple girl,
not mischievous, one well set up, with strong limbs
and solid hips, a sensible girl, but not too brainy.
That's what I think! . . . When I married, I got the
kindest and most stupid girl of the surrounding country. And therefore I was happy. . . . "

"Look here! . . . Have some pity on the child:
she's my wife! . . . she's your child . . . and now
you're making her cry. Old fool, you don't seem to
realize that our love is quite old, and seems as if it
was born with us. My Nénette! My darling sweetheart! . . . Don't cry!"

And Nono gently bent over his young wife, and
his long swarthy face leaned tenderly over her charm-

ing forehead, covering it with his breath and his shadow. . . .

"Father Francis!" said Nénette, turning to the old man, "against whom have you got a grudge?"

"Ah! Little Jeanne!"—gravely continued the old man swaying his old head up and down—"little Jeanne, you've a good heart and you're my worthy child. But what I'm saying is inspired by the wisdom of the aged. The truth comes out from old people; and she's pitiless. She is a knave that doesn't scrape too hard the old barks, but she lops off the young trees, ransacks the young birds, and, in a word, hardly fancies youth."

"I don't understand you," said Nénette in such a resigned and soft tone of voice that Nono rose suddenly.

"Now! . . . I'm going. . . . I've got enough of it. . . . I've a mind to say: 'Let the old people croak!' But it's hardly Christian. I'm off. I've my work elsewhere. Good-bye, my Nénette."

When Nono had left, old Francis, both hands crossed over the crook of his stick, began to take snuff, sneeze, and noisily clear his throat. . . . Raa. . . . Raa. . . . Raa. . . .

"Father!—asked Nénette—why do you say my husband must be careful? . . . Of what, or of whom? . . . "

"I mean you must be careful."

"But why?"

"Because a married woman who's too pretty is like

a thoroughbred horse in shafts. He's a fine sight, and dandy for driving; but at his very first whim he throws his driver into a ditch and that breaks his neck for good."

"I'm not a pretty girl; and you know quite well that I love my husband very much."

"That's true; your heart is sincere, and you've never given it to anyone but to my blockhead. . . . I know it. . . . But if the heart never belonged to anyone . . . the leg was more liberal. . . . Eh! little one! your face is as red as a cherry now! But I don't want to hurt your feelings, I want to warn you, my girl. . . . No more such affairs now. . . . We'll never talk of it again; but see that you have no more fancies—of the heart. . . . Remember you have an old shark that sees, and who knows many things about you that Nono ignores. . . . "

"Father! I told him all. . . . "

"Oh! . . . little one! . . . Let's not say that!"

"Yes! . . . I told Jacques that Renardin once. . . . "

"Once! . . . Once! . . . Go on! . . . Go on! . . . That's strange! . . . but when girls affect to confess to a man—they go as far as the nail. If the man is not stupid he guesses as far as the finger; but as a matter of fact it reaches as far as the hand. . . . And upon my word, if it doesn't reach as far as the arm . . . it ain't usually her fault. . . . "

"Oh! . . . Father! . . . Grandfather! . . . "

Nénette hid her head in her apron and cried.

"Well! . . . little one! . . . Despite all your charm and cunning, I had but to say two or three words to my big Nono . . . and you'd never have shared his hearth."

"Yes! . . . I would! . . . "

"No! . . . You wouldn't! . . . " replied the old man with a doleful firmness.

He then continued in a gentler voice: "No, I tell you! . . . If you had told him everything, he wouldn't have married you. That fellow. . . . I know him better than everybody else. I haven't borne him like his mother; but I've seen him live and work. I know his soul. I see it as if it were in a glass before me. He's proud. He doesn't look it. He won't eat anything someone else nibbled at. He'd croak of hunger rather, than force into his miserable empty belly the rest of another's feast. . . . "

"Oh! . . . Grandfather!" said Nénette, raising towards the old man her tearful and distressed face. "Oh! . . . Grandfather! . . . What will become of me? . . . Don't do me any harm. . . . If you knew! . . . I've changed entirely now. I was quite little. . . . I didn't know anything. . . . I've been wronged in a house . . . but I had no one to defend me. . . . "

The frail young woman looked up to the motionless old man with an imploring face and clasped hands. The little shrewd eyes stared at her without harshness.

"Don't do me any harm, Grandfather! . . . Don't say anything to Jacques; let me live my humble life

here. . . . I'm so happy here. . . . I promise—you'll
see: I'll be good."

Old Francis stretched out his wrinkled hand, twisted
like a root, and caressed the young curly head which
was bent towards him.

"Ah! little Jeanne! . . . I think so too. But let's
come to an understanding. Let's try and be friends.
The old people, who've done and seen everything, are
more indulgent than a young man can be. . . . Don't
cry, little Jeanne! . . . I'm not your enemy. I love
you and know you, believe me! I know you've a good
heart. . . . But your head is a little fanciful, and the
flesh is ever knavish. Well! . . . You must reconcile
all that. . . . You mustn't give this to Nono, and that
to others. . . . But try and put all in the same hand."

CHAPTER VI

Two months after her marriage, Nénette, one evening, was coming home all bent beneath a large truss of hay and grass for the rabbits. She was carrying it in her arm, rolled up in her blue linen apron. Now and then, she straightened her heavy bundle with a blow of her arm that exerted her entire delicate body. She took off her white hood, and her black curls wantoned in the breeze. Her short winegrower's skirt was beating against her ankles. She nervously turned in every direction her little sharp face, tanned by the sun, looking merrily for some friendly cheerful greetings.

But there were no friends; she only met with a hostile group of four winegrowers. They were of those who are the first to go home, and who stop and gossip at crossroads. With a gaping mouth, impertinent eyes beneath grayish lashes, the cap over the ear, they malevolently stare at the passers-by and at the entire universe.

Flon-Flon, one of them, was a big fellow, rather stoutish and badly shaved. He held with both hands his empty basket which was hanging down his back. He was slowly turning his large uncouth frame towards the four horizons. He perceived Nénette first.

42

"Ah! look: the cracked woman is coming, with her hair fluttering in the air. Watch her cut along; she's very thin, but she's as fiery as live coal. She's nervous and cracked. Why, she's a bundle of nerves and whims. She's not French. Her mother brought her here from heaven knows where. She must have negro, Tartar or Gypsy blood."

Nénette passed by, however, rapidly, in a flurry, casting a naïve, coaxing glance. In her light chattering voice, she greeted the group. Flon-Flon, the tall uncouth wag, insolently fixed upon her his two little sly and stony eyes, deeply sunk in folds of scarlet flesh.

Beside this portly peasant, bubbling over with health, triumphant with flesh, and whose veins were full of rancorous blood, Briquet appeared like a poor cadaverous being with a little crouching dark head, and keen eyes, distended like those of a suffering cat. But he began vehemently:

"She's playing for us a pretty fine comedy; and her love affair is the grossest nonsense we've ever seen across the vines. Why! she and her blockhead of a husband do nothing but lick each other in the vineyard! I've never seen a bigger idiot than that big Nono trying to put on sweet airs and make graceful faces. He's certainly changed, that confounded ass! He gave up his friends, the café, skittles. . . . All the time he's with his little wild beast. . . . And besides, he's working himself to death and he's happy

. . . With his silly look and gaping mouth, the idiot parades his happiness before everybody."

"Eh! . . . Eh! . . . Listen, friends! . . . " said Fumeron—another little fellow, stunted, nervous, with a greenish complexion, and whose yellow icy eyes cast sharp glances—"Listen, friends! . . . I've seen many a lover: some are hot, others cool, still others proud, and many are stupid. . . . When a woman has in her grip the tip of a man's nose, you can never tell to what tune she'll make him dance . . . whether it's the polka of the old folks or the quadrille of the young rabbits. . . . But remember what I tell you: Nono will soon dance a triangle with Renardin, who is very clever at that sort of thing; and the farther he'll go the more complex will the music become; there'll be fiddles, clarinettes, trombones and perhaps a church choir."

"Never mind! . . . let things take their course, friends! . . . We'll have our revenge. Renardin knows a great deal about the saucy creature. He had the first draught of the pretty one. And our Nono, content and not proud, is drawing at the dregs with gusto. But he'll soon lose his breath drawing in that way. And when his first heat is over . . . beware! . . . The day for the friends will come."

"And one fine morning—I speak my mind—Nono on walking will turn his dull little eyes sideways and smile sweetly to his wife . . . but he'll find nothing . . . neither fire nor smoke. She'll be off with a

paramour. Ah! on that day, the village will laugh.
. . . But will you have a pinch of snuff, friends? . . .
Flammêche! . . . stupid beast! You're not saying a
word! . . . "

Flammêche said nothing because he thought of nothing: a poor drunkard with a dry face and a long,
dirty red beard, and large, round, tearful eyes emitting
an unfocused wild gleam.

And the four slanderers dug into the open snuff-
box, staring at the delicate and slender form of
Nénette as she disappeared in the distance.

The evening, sweet-tempered like an old friend who
comes from a long journey and places his staff at
the threshold, descended—with a melancholy and
human gravity—from the mountain towards the vale.
It was an evening in August. The upper atmosphere,
purified by the sun, was as limpid as pure crystal.
The warm earth sent forth fragrant vapors. Before
all who returned from the plain or from the vineyards, the mountain stood like a huge black mass; its
unswerving, solitary summit soared gracefully in the
sky. The crests opened on their flanks their gulfs of
darkness where the woody slopes and the first shades
of night trembled. On high were the forests, the
hosts of oaks, the craggy rocks, and the precipices
where the frantic blasts of the wind blow. Below, at
the foot of the hills, were the lit-up villages, buzzing
like beehives.

"Jacques! . . . " said Nénette on coming home that

night. "I don't know what I've done to your friends; but every time I meet them, they eye me up like a ferocious beast."

"My friends! . . . What friends?"

"Flon-Flon, Briquet, Flammêche, Fumeron. . . . "

"Oh! they're not my friends. They've served with me in the army, that's all. We'd go out together when we were young; but now I've other things on my mind."

"But you did associate with them, and now they're angry because you've left them. And they're not the only people: there are other winegrowers here who don't like us. . . . "

"Oh! . . . that's true. Some of the winegrowers are good-natured: but there are also others who assume strange airs, indeed, in these parts of the country. They're a pack of cracked beasts, blacker than roots, with bald pates, and no more lashes than rats. They're ever fretting, steeped in gall, envying Tom. . . . Dick . . . conspiring against their neighbor and ready to bring about his misery; they're cursing the earth, the heavens, the rich and the poor.`. . . And by dint of ever spitting and being galled, they become as dry as old hoofs.

"Only Flon-Flon has a round paunch and enjoys fine health. He's also a member of the municipal council. His name is not Flon-Flon; he belongs to the Claudiot family. He hates me more than anyone else. I know it, believe me. He begrudges me my happiness and my industry. But he can only talk, that's all. He's such a toad-eater and coward that he was once called Bootlicker; but Flon-Flon is the right name for such an idle boaster and braggart.

"You mustn't think all winegrowers are bad. There are many who're good. And Briquet has a good wife. It seems they'll soon be our neighbors. They've taken Bressan's lodgings from Martinmas day.

"Yes. . . . That's right. . .. . Briquet is only a poor, mad fellow. But Fumeron is the worst of knaves. Faith, he was long enough in prison. He always thinks he's forgotten something when he hasn't stolen anything. . . . Flammêche, however, ain't more wicked and cunning than an ox or a rock."

"Yet you can talk to them and persuade them we're not their enemies."

"Persuade what?" said the ungracious Nono. "They've nasty pates, and they can't be persuaded. They're hopeless. Don't you see that it's all mean jealousy. They hoped to make of me a buffoon for their amusement; and they're enraged because I'm leading, thanks to you, an honest simple life. . . . My poor Nénette, to make them grunt in peace and put on friendly airs, they'd have to see, you and me, dying of shame and sorrow. Then . . . they'd like us again."

CHAPTER VII

FIVE years have elapsed. Their days, as numerous and light as leaves, have fallen to the ground. Five times already have they bedecked the earth and gathered in the fruits of the indefatigable soil. The love of Nono and Nénette has been gratified. Little Laurette was born about one year after the marriage. She has grown and is now a very graceful child.

"She'll be five this Midsummer, my friends!" said Nono, raising her in his arms and showing her proudly. "She is heavy and chatters already worse than a Parisian. Her tongue is somewhat wild; but she already copes with me in reasoning."

Happiness is never enduring, however. There is a very ancient law, which seems to be inspired from on high, that gradually transforms the souls of men. Within them, it builds and destroys repeatedly its frail edifices. Man yields to destiny his lowly heart in which happiness and sorrow in turn mercilessly hold their sway.

"Old man! . . . " said Nono to his father; "don't you think Nénette has changed? For three or four years she was as merry as a lark; but during this last year or two she got to be very queer; and, for that matter, during the past few weeks especially, she's pitifully sad."

It was early in the morning, and Nono was getting ready to go to the vineyard. He greased his boots and affected to appear and speak indifferently. Old Francis shook his head and remained silent for a moment, holding his pinch of snuff in the air at the end of his thumb. Then he decided to talk, at the same time making many grimaces and shaking his head slightly but with force.

"My boy! . . . You ought to have married a kind, simple woman . . . with a strong body . . . who could wield her wash-bat easily. . . . But you wanted sparkling eyes! . . . Now you have 'em. . . . And yet all women are a swarm of fleas. Strange to say, each man wants one in his house! . . . Being mangy or married is about the same: it itches and galls for life. . . . Yours is not the worst."

"Old man! . . . I'm not asking you for any clap-trap speeches. Don't pretend to be an old simpleton. You're old and you've got good sense. You love me a bit. . . . This is perhaps the moment to do me a good turn . . . for my eyes can see, and my heart suffers. But I sha'n't say any more. . . . I'm off to the vineyard. . . ."

Nénette appeared a moment later; and the old man seized the opportunity at once. As she passed near him with a bundle of dry linen, old Francis put out his arm and struck her skirt slightly with his stick.

"Raa. . . . Raa. . . ."

"Oh! . . . You! . . . What is the matter with you?"

But the old man, in a merry and brisk tone of voice, had his fling: "Eh! . . . little one! . . . Will your nasty little affair last a long time yet?"

Nénette turned round, and at once understood.

"What do you mean? . . . "

"Oh! . . . you needn't put on that grim face, and thrust terrible glances at me. I say again: is that going to last very long . . . your nasty little business of a loose wench?"

Nénette looked at the old man with anger, quite ready to cope with him. She wished to reply, but she lacked the assurance of the true criminal. She flushed. Her bare soul, trembling with shame, could be seen through the light tint of blood—that pure blush of youth. She sank into a chair, and turned her head away. . . .

. . . The silence was rather long. The young woman sobbed softly but bitterly; she murmured words of despair; it all sounded like the murmuring of a brook.

" . . . Go on, my birdie, chirp your story. . . . What do you say? . . . I can hardly hear your murmur: talk louder. . . . You say it ain't true? Yes, it's true. . . . What! . . . . What do you say? . . . it's a long time ago? . . . an old affair? . . . Oh! it ain't as old as the vines in these parts. . . . Ah! Ah! . . . a stroke of madness, you say? . . . Well, when I was a postman, more than one bold, plump

wench came to share a bit of this madness with me.
. . . None of these fibs, little one! . . . Don't tire
yourself telling me that your offense goes further back
than eighteen months . . . that nothing happened
since. . . . Tell me, last November, last December
. . . and not to involve the entire calendar . . . let's
come down to the Sunday of three weeks ago . . .
did you go to read the Lives of the Saints at Renardin's?"

"Eh! . . . That stops your tears! . . . Now you're
calmed. . . . And look here a moment: I don't say
you return to Renardin as tranquilly as a curé goes
to his Low Mass. . . . With you it's High Mass, and
even bawled out loud. Of course, you make a fuss
at first; but you soon get used to it, don't you? And
then there's no more fighting. It's all the man's fault,
isn't it! Do you know what's bound to come of it
all? I wonder! . . . Well, I've put my foot in your
household affairs."

"Ah! . . . " exclaimed Nénette who ceased crying,
but pressed her eyes convulsively with her hands. "Ah!
father Francis! . . . what are you saying? . . . For
after all, I'm too unfortunate! Just when I've given
up everything . . . when I'm turning a new leaf. . . .
You come and attack me! . . . Ah! if you knew all
. . . you wouldn't be so harsh. . . . "

"Eh! . . . Eh! . . . I know all about it already.
An old man is a monster. . . . He roams about, and
leans on his stick. He walks on half dead, broken
up, using his stick as a crutch, with his nose to the

ground and his neck hanging down. . . . They say: 'He's a dotard . . . an old beast. He's as deaf as a post and as stupid as a mule.' . . . I laugh when I hear that; and at once I pretend to be deafer and more stupid than ever, I look at no one, and I listen to no one; but I hear and see everything. . . . A cursed fellow . . . an old man . . . eh? He roams on staircases, in garrets, in poultry-houses—he pokes his nose everywhere. . . . He sees at a little window a curly head that's hiding. . . . He hears the boards of a garret creak. . . . He hears a voice in the cellar unlike that of the cooper's . . . sometimes slipping along among the vines, quite bent with age . . . he sees a young couple . . . but he's not a nuisance, and so goes off. . . . "

"Ah! stop, father Francis! . . . Don't talk so much. It's useless, believe me! . . . "

"Speak up, then! . . . "

"Ah, what should I say? . . . There's a curse on me . . . You don't understand. I don't either."

"Yes, I understand. The poor creatures gone astray ever return to the one who led them astray. They always go back to the knave who made of them what they are. There's anger . . . even hatred . . . but also pleasure: they go well together. Besides I can still understand that a little wench should have wanted to get a smack of Renardin when he came on furlough for two months, a year and a half ago, for the grape-gathering season. You did it. He was a handsome fellow, indeed. He was a sergeant in a new uniform

. . . irresistible.   But you've gone back to him after
he had left the army, last September, and once more
put on his leather cap: that's mean and knavish.   He's
playing the blackguard once more, the amateur pig-
merchant, that good-for-nothing wretch. . . . "

"Oh, yes! I'm a guilty woman, a great criminal.
But my great offense, my real crime. . . . I committed a year and a half ago, at those fatal grape-
gatherings. . . . All I have done afterwards was an
attempt to defend myself, to go and see . . . try. . . .
Ah! . . .   At times I wanted to kill him.   I ran to
him in a rage. . . . And then! . . . what shall I tell
you? . . . What power has he over me? . . . Ah!
I want to become again a good woman, but I can't any
more. I'm lost, believe me! . . . Oh! I'm tired of life.
My girl has kept me back; but, faith! now it's all over.
I must do away with myself. . . . You have just
given me the last blow! . . . How good of you!
. . . "

"Come now! . . . calm yourself, little one! . . .
I'm going to settle matters up."

"You! . . . Ah! poor old man! . . . What do you
want to settle? . . . The blackguard has my letters.
I wrote to him two or three times during his last year
of service at Toul.   He's threatening me with those
letters: 'Yes,' says he, 'I'll read your little notes to
your lanky, stupid husband; and if he doesn't break
your ribs with a pruning-bill afterwards, he's a coward.'   Ah! . . . I'm going to throw myself in the
well."

"Ah! . . . One's hardly comfortable at the bottom. . . . Is that the only remedy you've found?"

"There's no other."

Nénette was holding her hand on her pale forehead, and spoke in a low and dry tone of voice. She continued: "Yes! . . . There's no other! . . . But that's dying very young and in despair."

"Ah! yes! . . . There's no other remedy, you say? Well, go and fetch Renardin. Tell him I want to buy the little pig he showed me last night. . . . "

"Oh! I won't bother any more about anything. . . . Go and see whom you like. I don't care about anything. . . . Good-bye! . . . "

"Look here! . . . Just wait a moment before you go to dream at the bottom of the well. . . . "

"Oh! . . . I'm not interested enough in life now to do anything. I'm disgusted with myself and with everybody else. I'm a mad woman and a criminal. . . . "

"Hey, there! . . . Wait a minute and listen. . . . If you don't do what I'm telling you to do for the sake of your life . . . do it at least for the sake of the honest man who has married you. . . . Go, my girl! . . . Go and fetch the man who is destroying your life. . . . Go, my girl! . . . "

"Oh! why do you look at me in that way?"

"This look is for you . . . it's my tenderness. . . . Jeanne! . . . "

"Don't say it. I'm a criminal. Your poor boy

had no luck. He's so kind-hearted. . . . Jacquot. . . . "

"He's right."

"He's so unhappy . . . the dear boy! . . . "

"Poor girl!"

"Why do you say 'poor girl?' . . . I'm weeping, father Francis, but it's not on my account. . . . He's very unhappy. . . . Jacquot . . . isn't he?"

"Yes, if you like. . . . Call me 'grandfather'."

"Grandfather! . . . Do you remember what you once told me?"

"Yes . . . Don't cry so much, little Jeanne. Your little one comes from school at four o'clock. She'll say: 'Mamma has cried.' Don't tell her it's on my account, for she'll scratch me."

But Nénette did not listen to him. She put her face in front of his and pleaded: "Do you remember, grandfather? . . . Do you recall what you told me one morning?"

"Now come! . . . Jeanne! . . . Don't cry."

"Do you recall? . . . I didn't do anything worse, because I couldn't. . . . "

"Calm yourself, and don't cry. Go and call the fellow. . . . Little Jeanne! . . . "

"Poor old grandfather! . . . "

"Go, little Jeanne. . . . "

" . . . He's more powerful than we, believe me!"

"Perhaps; but go and call him anyhow, I'll see that justice is done him, little Jeanne! . . . Oh! . . . a poor kind of justice! . . . the justice of an old

man! . . . But it will be justice.   Then faith! it'll
last as long as possible.   Go and call the fellow . . .
my little Jeanne.   Go in peace and come back
to me. . . . "

CHAPTER VIII

NÉNETTE departed without saying a word. A few minutes later, she returned with Renardin. As is customary in these parts of the country, she filled two little glasses of pressed grape brandy; then, she sat down quietly near the window and looked out on the street, seeming not to hear anything. The thick-set, stocky boor thrust himself comfortably into a chair. The old man and he clinked glasses and began to talk.

"What's new hereabouts?" asked old Francis.

"Pooh . . . nothing much."

"Is there no business? Don't you sell any wine?"

"No. There are no wine merchants to be seen. The knaves are all buried somewhere! . . ."

"It's like every other year. . . . They wait until we haven't a sou, a piece of bacon, or a log of wood . . . until we stand before our cellars full of wine to be sold, with our tongues hanging out of our mouths ready to die of misery. . . . Then they rise from their graves; and, after having looked at our helpless mien, they offer us, smilingly, a miserable starvation price. And we must say 'yes,' if we want to regain use of our tongues, eat, and not croak. . . . But that's business! . . . You too, a hog-merchant, have these tricks, eh? . . . And how about your love affairs? . . . "

"Oh!" said Renardin evasively.

"You're still after women? . . . eh! . . . monster!!"

"Well, I manage to get on."

"Ah! . . . Blackguard! . . . I'd like to see you play your pretty tricks!"

"Pretty tricks? . . . Oh! . . . that's not my strong point. There are some who beat about the bush: they kiss and mutter soft, tender words. . . . What can be done! . . . Caresses and such other foolish nonsense! . . . That's not my way. As for me, nothing softens their stubborn hearts more than some good round kicks; and I add the finishing touches with my fists. . . . That's the way *I* do! . . . "

"Ah! that's right! . . . that's quite right! . . . Ah! you monster! . . . Believe me, I know something about it, too! In my day, I was also a boy. . . . A long time ago, when I was a postman in Le Pays-Bas. . . . "

"Ah! I don't want to brag, but I can tell you I know how to handle women. More than a few of them have already passed through my claws! Quite a bunch of them! You'll find them among the households of La Côte. . . . I visit that section when I care to."

"Ah! you big scoundrel! . . . I know it quite well! . . . But you're my exact double! I've been so. When

I was a postman I had them all: vine-dressers, cow-
girls, woodcutters, all the young ones, all. . . . "

"But what do I care about your cow-girls? . . .
Why don't you talk to me of a dashing little dressmaker, or of a rustling bourgeoise, all rolled up in
silk and laces like a little fish in flour, all decked out
in finery, powdered, furbished with mignonette, perfumed with violet . . . quite ready to be fried and
munched . . . eh?"

"Ah! . . . the scoundrel! . . . Ah! . . . the blackguard! . . . What a devil he is! . . . "

And old Francis snorted and yawned as he looked
at his interlocutor with a kindly simplicity.

"And then! . . . old man! . . . I've still to find the
woman who'll cope with me. For I'm a beastly stubborn fellow; and I've always ended—even when it
seemed almost impossible—by making them knuckle
down and yield. . . . There are some who've fought
very hard! . . . Well! . . . I've had 'em all, just
when it pleased me. . . . They began by putting on
airs and making a great fuss, but they've finally come
around to my way, and fallen like wounded
doves! . . . "

Renardin threw up his hands, stood erect and thrust
out his chest.

"Ah! you confounded cur! . . . confounded cur!
. . . " said old Francis, as if he had exhausted all
his admiration. He remained with his eyes and mouth
wide open and in so comical a posture that Renardin
burst out laughing: "Ah! old scoundrel! . . . old fox!

. . . " he repeated, slapping the old man's knees un-
ceremoniously. Old Francis chuckled in his senile
manner. Renardin winked sardonically, and shook his
finger mockingly near the corner of his eye. . . .

"There's a little fool at present who is rebelling.
. . . If there's one that belongs to me, it's surely that
one. Her husband is getting only what I've left
over. . . . "

"Is she married?"

"Yes."

"Overgrown good-for-nothing! . . . Blackguard!
. . . Knave! . . ."

"Oh! there was spite in this marriage. She was
aiming at me in this business. . . . I was too brutal,
it seems, for that graceful child! That dainty creature had to have a gentle angel. She took advantage
of my departure for the army, and married. . . .
Otherwise! . . . Poor little chicken! . . . She thought
it was enough to see a mayor and a curé in order to
escape me. . . . But as soon as I returned, I showed
her of what stuff I'm made. . . . I told the pretty
thing what I thought of all that. . . . I hinted to
her that she'd have to take up again an old habit.
. . . "

Renardin suddenly left off his purring and mocking
tone, and began to roar furiously.

"Ah! . . . damn it! . . . There's one woman
whom I told that I loved her sincerely. . . . That's
the one! . . . I went at it with all the frankness of
my youth. . . . And what was the result? . . . For

once in my life I was sincere, and the pretty creature
had to throw me aside because she found her bargain:
a good-natured mollycoddle and an excellent idiot!
. . . Ah! hang it! hang it!. . . I had no luck. I
had to draw lots and be knocked on the head with
five years' service just then. . . . She took advantage,
the creature! . . . She patched up her bargain in a
few weeks. . . . Well, let's forget it. . . . But now
I'm home again. . . . Here's the fellow! . . . Look
at him well! . . . Here he is with a full blown chest!
. . . Approach, my pretty child! . . . He's ready to
attack. . . . He's going to be reckoned with. . . .

"Ah yes! . . . these past few weeks the little one
has been struggling hard indeed. . . . I scent a little
revolt . . . a very tiny one. . . . We'll see what the
pretty one will gain by it! . . .

"Poor brat! . . . She's as light as a flea, and she'd
like to grapple with Renardin! Poor chick! She comes
to make a row in my house. . . . I let her shout for
a while; and then, I get hold of her. . . . Oh! the
struggle doesn't last long. . . . Ah! that little one can
wriggle and writhe! . . . But I have her and hold
her finally. . . . Ah yes! she can struggle, call and
yell! She can bounce from the ground to the sky
. . . great God! I'll not let go my powerful
hold! . . . "

Renardin rose and puffed with anger. His red-
flannel girdle loosened, and every now and then he
raised his trousers to his hips with a frantic kick.

"But do you care much for that woman?"

"For her? . . . I don't give a hang! . . . "

"Then it's to spite her."

"Yes."

Renardin sank into his chair again. He remained seated for some time leaning over with his elbows on his knees and his jaw in his palms. His furious eyes were riveted on the ground. But his anger suddenly began to choke him; he breathed heavily; and, springing up with fury, he threw his cap on the table and burst out:

"Ah! . . . the knavish little wench! . . . I offered to be her husband! . . . I, Renardin! . . . I who have more than ten thousand francs in the bank, and more than a hundred rows of vines! . . . I, the powerful Renardin! . . . Ah! you little wretch! You didn't want to be my wife. You'll come back to my hovel anyhow . . . you'll come back. . . . No, I'm not a gallant fellow who can be overthrown. . . . Hang it no! I've my rights! . . . "

"Well, my poor fellow, you surprise me. . . . You say she didn't want to marry you? . . . Could she have wanted a more handsome fellow than you? Don't get into a passion. But that poor woman is in a very sad plight. It serves her right: how could she refuse a handsome fellow as gentle as you are! A stupid child, believe me! . . . But I'll bet you I can guess who that woman is!"

"You don't know her."

"Ain't it Etiennette Commarin."

"No."

"Is it Verrier. It can only be that one."

"Hell! . . . Besides, don't try to guess. . . . She's from another region: otherwise, I wouldn't have talked of her as I did."

"Oh, why didn't you tell me that at once? That's all right: yet I'd like to know who she is. You know, an old man is cunning!"

Renardin rose and began to laugh. He tapped the old man on the shoulder mockingly: "Yes, you're one of the foxy fellows. You're wily and shrewd. . . . But what about the pig: do you want it or not? It's sixty francs for someone else; for you it is fifty francs."

But the old man, still merry and good-natured, cleared his throat: "Raa. . . . Raa. . . . " He stretched out his arm and with his stick gave Renardin a friendly tap on the leg: "Scoundrel! . . . big scoundrel. . . . " This he muttered in the bantering, amiable tone that is used when talking to animals and children.

" . . . But you can well say that you gave me much pleasure. I like to hear the young folks talk. I've spent a pleasant afternoon listening to your stories. Nénette had already told me the details of the affair. . . . But you've treated it with more spirit, and it interested me much more."

"Who? . . . What? . . ."

"Nénette," said the old man tranquilly. "She told me as best she could all about your naughty affair."

Renardin sat down again, and riveted his stony

little eyes upon the old man. He searched silently, with his base, gnawing look, the tranquil face of old Francis. The latter opened wide his toothless mouth, and winked with his sharp little eyes. The boor, settled on what he had to understand and do, raised his head, pushed his cap down over his ear, and began to whistle with indifference.

"The little one and I have been talking for a long time, almost since half past twelve. She spoke for more than an hour without a stop. . . . She simply had to give vent to what was in her heart for some time. She emptied her bag on me without warning. I didn't say a word. . . . I listened to her. When a woman is off at such a gallop, you might as well try to stop an express train as to stop her. . . . Ah! I've learnt about your exploits . . . nasty pig! . . . And to think that I've never noticed anything at all! . . . I'm cunning, however. . . . But when one is old, one's mind doesn't work in that direction. . . .

"The little ones aren't so. A little one is very queer. She amuses herself with everything about her. She's a child after all. Then, one fine morning, when she realizes there's danger beneath the rock where she tried to play, she wants to begin to yell in everybody's presence. 'What is she going to do?' thought I as I listened to her. But when I realized that she's going to tell all, this very night, to Nono. . . . I calmed her a bit: then I sent her to fetch you in order to talk the matter over peacefully. I said to this little one: 'Ah! let's hear once for all what Renardin has

to say, before he'll have his jaw cracked.' . . . It's
for your sake, big monster!

"Your story and Nénette's are about the same.
Moreover, you have the same idea! . . . You, also,
want to use the boots of my big Jacques as a confes-
sional! . . . Funny idea! . . .

"The little one says its your baseness that eggs you
on. I think it's rather one of the turns of remorse,
and it comes from your noble soul, for you've a very
noble soul, decked out with benevolence, and stuffed
with kindness, sweet repentance, and all sorts of chari-
table things. There's, to be sure, a little baseness at
the very bottom; but there must be some crust beneath the tart, and bone beneath the meat. . . . "

"Old demon! . . . What the devil are you bothering me for? Is that all you wanted to tell me? . . .
I'm off. . . . "

"But, my boy, I'm not going to hold you back. . . .
Perhaps you've some important work on hand. . . .
Off with you quickly! My big Nono will call on you,
to-night, to conclude the conversation you haven't the
time to bring to an end now."

Renardin began to puff and shrugged his shoulders.
Then, he put on an indifferent air and feigned to be
absorbed in the cracks of the wall. But it was the
sheerest semblance, for the chubby nose of the boor
began to sniff noisily.

Old Francis was quite calm now and took his time;
he still continued to clear his throat gayly and then
helped himself to a pinch of snuff.

"Off with you . . . if you're in a hurry! . . . Go ahead! . . . You have some letters from the little one that you wanted to hand over to Nono. . . . You needn't bother, my boy! . . . He'll go and fetch 'em a little later, as soon as he returns from the vines."

"I don't give a hang about those letters. Here they are, take 'em! . . . "

"Ah! you had 'em with you! . . . " and the old man put out his hand and took the package—"ah! ah! . . . that's how they are, the lovers! . . . They always have with 'em their darling's letters. They waste their time rereading 'em, kissing 'em, and caressing 'em. . . . Renardin, you can well say you're a fond lover! . . . But you'll get over it. You'll also become an old hoof like me."

Changing his tone, the old man said: "Jeanne! . . . Throw that into the fire!"

The young woman came forward and looked at the two men as if she had not seen them before, staring at them with hard and sunken eyes. Finally, she seemed to understand.

"Father! . . . Keep these letters and read them. . . . They're short; I simply ask him to let me alone. . . . Read them so that you won't think me more guilty than I am."

"Little one, strike a match and throw that into the flames—and do it quickly so that they'll be no more! . . . "

He spoke in an unusual tone that sounded very strange. Nénette obeyed. After a moment of silence, a crackling was heard in the fireplace; then the flame sprang forth with a start, grew bigger and gradually died away. . . .

Nénette walked over to old Francis; they looked at each other in silence, and on the young face, big silent tears began to roll down. The old man had, as usual, his hands crossed on his short stick, but a grave tenderness adorned his features. He looked like one of those ancients of bygone days who was at the same time father, judge and patriarch, who would sit on his curule chair with his hands crossed on his ivory staff, hard by his little domestic altar, his eyes on the holy embers of the hearth, the severe guardian of its flame and honor!

"Do you see this little Jeanne, Renardin! Repentant tears are rolling down her cheeks. For three weeks this dew has been falling to the pitiless ground. . . . It's enough. Let's stop it! . . . This Jeanne is the delight and support of my old age. Yes, I love her dearly! I told her so once. . . . She hardly believed me. . . . But we're friends now."

Renardin played the part of the indifferent person who does not listen. He pretended to look at the course of the clouds in the sky. In order to see them better, he bent his dark head spotted with black hair.

"What! it's raining? . . . Hang it! We're going to have more pools of rain from the mountain!"

"Never mind the clouds! . . . my boy! . . . Let's end our business. . . . Well, what about the pig? You said forty francs. That's very high. But what's the use of haggling? All right, the bargain is struck."

"Forty francs! . . . You're jollying me! . . . Why, it's worth twelve sous a pound."

"Yes, forty francs. Ah! that's what you said. Besides, that doesn't matter. . . . It's very generous of you to want to confess to Nono. . . . It's a noble idea to cleanse one's soul. . . . But I laugh at it. . . . I'd like to see you carry it out. . . . My Nono would open his mouth wide, and gape at you. But hardly anything surprises him. . . . He'd act like a true-born judge. . . . I've a notion he'll make your bald pate sink into your knavish neck . . . one of those blows of absolution that sends you direct to paradise. . . . Ah! I know him. He's the worst brute hereabouts. That big good-for-nothing never warns anybody. The left fist cries: 'Kill!' the right one answers: 'Fell!' You'll have hardly begun to explain your business than the big fellow would already be at you. He wouldn't listen very long. . . . All he'll know is that he must destroy a pair of shins and break a handsome jaw. . . . We'll hardly have the time to hear the cries and run in . . . when everything will be over! the big one . . . gaping . . . flurried . . . very much annoyed because he has nothing more to do. . . . Beside him . . . you! . . . as much of you as will be left, limbs broken, carcass a mass of ruins, jaw dashed to pieces . . . and in that whole mass of ruins there'll be no more life than in a boiled chicken. . . . Well then, you silly fool! . . . But let's stick to

the point. If I should undertake to talk to my
Jacques. . . . Ah! I'm not very clear, and yet you seem
to understand very well. . . . Let me tell you something worth while. . . . Jean Antoine Renardin's skin
is hanging in the balance; therefore, hurry and take
it home, and leave it there under cover . . . and make
sure never to let it rub against Nénette. . . . Just one
wicked word let loose and your skin will be in strips.
It would be a great pity, for it's a rare skin—well
weathered and browned! . . . And what will the poor
wenches do who'll have no one to catch their kisses?
. . . For they like to throw 'em into the dung-heap.
. . . They've a base taste! . . .

"By the way, my Renardin! . . . You say the girls
are very fond of you; but here's one who falls at my
feet, confesses all, and would throw herself into the
well rather than return to you one more time! . . .
You disgust her! . . . And I imagine she's not harder
to suit than the others. If I were you, I'd look into
the matter and visit those households of La Côte where
your chicks are scattered. My friend! . . . also
change your methods. The true-born cock doesn't
bray: he sings very clearly. I've heard you once, and
I thought: 'Hang it! . . . how the fashions change!
. . . Where's his delicacy? . . . This looks more like
a battle with a pack of wolves! . . . '

"But your taste is just as bad if you're going to
keep that little pig: it would be a good bargain for
both of us. Let's not make a knavish price. We're
friends. Forty francs is a good price. But I'm not

bargaining. Go and fetch that pig. Now be careful!
. . . The life you're leading. . . . Ah! I hear my
Nono has come home. . . . "

Nono entered with a grim look.

"What's all this noise about? What's that beast
doing in my house? . . . "

"He came to sell us a young pig. . . . And I
bought it."

"For how much?"

"Forty francs."

"If the pig is very young, it's almost twice the
amount it's worth."

"No. It's a good-sized one."

"Ah! . . . then it's all right."

While they were talking, Renardin had muttered a
"So-long!" and quickly disappeared.

Nénette was crying, her chest flat on the table and
her head in her hands. The old man, with a wink,
silently called his son's attention to her.

Nono sat down near his wife and took her in his
lap.

"Ah!" said old Francis, "there are beings who have
the souls of angels, but whose flesh is vile. Poor little
ones. . . . My boy, if you see something is out of
gear don't begin to kick and pout. A mere trifle may
have upset many things. You must very gently speak
your mind, and they'll be set right. . . . But I'm
thirsty . . . Jacques! . . . "

CHAPTER IX

THE two following years were for Nono and Nénette two years of happiness. They had, however, their share of anxiety. Indeed all the winegrowers in La Côte were in despair: phylloxera began to devastate the vines; and the barren spots not only grew more numerous every day, but they threatened to spread everywhere. Old Francis prophesied the direst misfortunes: "I always said so: I knew it would happen. In four or five years we sha'n't reap grapes enough for wine even to say mass with. . . . I merely want to warn the young folks, for I'll be busy elsewhere. . . . The jackals are already barking at me."

In that alone was the old man's prophecy true. His years had already passed. He began to cough in the very first month of the winter of 1884. He was never to see again the trees covered with leaves and the earth in full bloom. He was really not sick. Nono only became anxious when the old man refused to drink his glass of grape brandy, and declared that he no longer liked wine. Nono and Nénette then begged him in vain to abandon his truckle-bed in the garret, and sleep in a good bed on the floor below. He insisted on climbing to the garret.

One night, Nénette heard him cough. At daybreak

she brought him a bowl of hot milk. Sitting on the bed, she raised the old man's head with one hand, and with the other she put the bowl to his lips. But the old man, instead of drinking, turned his head away. Nénette had but time to place the bowl on the floor and bring her hand back, when the old man gently let his cheek fall into it. On these little trembling fingers old Francis breathed his last.

On coming home from the funeral, Nono and his wife sat down, facing each other, with heavy hearts. They remained thus for a long time, lacking the courage to change their mourning clothes, which made them appear strange to each other. Nono, who resented this uneasiness, made an effort to speak:

"My Jeanne! . . . They're laughing at us. They think we're mourning entirely too much for an old man of eighty-seven years. . . . We might as well continue with our work. . . . But I say we've had a great loss. . . . In a home, there are no better guardians than these old men: they have an eye on the door, and misfortune dares not enter. Their old, withered hands mete out peace and friendship in a home. . . . The old man was very much loved. We must love the aged, for they've been upon earth before us. Besides, we're told: 'Honor thy father and mother.' "

"Yes, Jacques! . . . that old man loved us very much! . . . the dear old man saved us! . . . "

"That's right; there was something indeed between

you and him, but I wasn't aware of it. But now we're alone in this great world! We've lost our old friend. . . . We must come closer to each other, my Jeanne, so that we can cope with life."

The sad evening peacefully came to an end. Then the days began to set slowly once more.

Nono, absorbed by his hard work at the vines, felt less keenly his loss; but his silent little companion continued to grow sadder and sadder. Her sorrows were manifold: her heart bled for the lost affection of the old man, and death seemed to have left something of its stupor in that frail and nervous soul. Poor Nénette was terrified by darkness, slumber and dreams. In all that there was also mingled a vague anguish of mind, a fear of the future, a presentiment. A misfortune seemed impending. Old Francis had spoken of it. Formerly his sprightly eye had destroyed these spells. But he was no longer with her. Nénette's poor tormented soul could hardly now recall this beloved image. Was the spirit that watched in the darkness the kind soul of the shrewd old man, or that of the grim old corpse that Nénette had seen stretched out on the funereal bed like a dreadful stranger?

The gloomy shades of melancholy gradually enwrapt the young woman. She awoke with terrible nightmares: then, sitting up in bed, she listened with anger to the peaceful breathing of Nono, while the cold gusts of the northwest wind filled the house with voices of despair.

Nono was alarmed to see that steady gaze, that pale, terrified face. Several months elapsed. . . . There was no change for the better. Was it madness? melancholia? . . . or some unknown curse? . . .

And upon the young couple, along the road they anxiously followed, there descended, little by little, all the inevitable woes of their destiny. . . . Their sorrows came in turn, at their hour, just as old Francis had foreseen in the past. . . . He had had a glimpse of them, hidden yonder as in invisible ambush, in the distant shadow of days and years.

Nénette had, without justification, some terrible fits of ill-temper. Nono tried in vain to calm her. He even sent for the doctor—a stocky fellow, square like a bull, with a pink bald head, a heavy drinker and a fiendish manilla player. He treated his patients in a rough and ready way, without any attempt at delicacy, and without tormenting his mind to learn the new discoveries. He prescribed, with an easy-going authority, to his patients—chiefly drunkards and peasants—blisters, laxatives, cupping-glasses, and leeches; this mingled with gross remarks gave him a popular reputation of frankness.

"Your wife is cracked," said he to Nono as he entered his carriage. "At Chartreux and at Dijon there are some who aren't as mad as she taking the cure. If she had half a dozen brats to clean, she wouldn't think of standing on her head to see whether the sky was flatter than the earth."

Then he added, taking the reins in his hands: "I'd treat that with a good hard kick: it's only a question of forcing down and then out, without ceremony, the bilious matter of the stomach." Thereupon he cracked his whip and departed.

Nono, standing in the middle of the road, was quite nonplused by the doctor's advice. Then he grew angry. "Confounded crank! . . . Old jackal! . . . Miserable leech huckster! . . . "

But Nénette continued to be ailing. In the spring of 1885, the doctor came again and advised that she be diverted.

"Divert her!" said Nono, "that's easy to say! . . . But what can I do? . . . The fairs seldom take place. We can't have feasts every day. . . . " Then he added: "Darling! . . . Do you want to go to Dijon with the donkey? . . . You'll see the shops. . . . There's a basketmaker in the Rue du Bong. . . . I've perhaps seen there the finest work the hand of man can make."

But Nénette shrugged her shoulders. She consented to go, however, to the village festivals where she danced at the balls. And then a wonderful idea occurred to some of her neighbors. . . . To have Nénette serve at weddings! . . . She's comely, handy and clever! She'll be really useful. Besides, she sings like a darling; her songs and her high spirits . . . why that'll be the gayety of the wedding! . . . Especially now that we can no longer count on the men: they're drunk even before the curé has blessed anything!"

The advice was good, and, therefore, it was heeded. Nénette soon became the indispensable little queen of all festivities. To every wedding and every parish feast Nénette brought her roguish gayety, her lively songs, her round ardent face, and her passionate eyes.

Then she seemed to have come back to life. Her dark, soft eyes grew still larger. Her face, once thin and with somewhat angular features, gradually became round and beaming. Beneath her sensitive nostrils, her charming lips were like blooming red roses.

Nono, however, did not share in this rejuvenescence. This new vitality, on the contrary, seemed to have been drawn in part from Nono's own life. Two deep furrows fretted his hollow cheeks. In his gloomy eyes, there was a cold, nervous gaze. Still steady, and with his neck craning, he walked in silence from vine to vine. His long inexpressive face looked like a rough carving in wood.

This sadness had come over Nono since Nénette had returned one night from a wedding in Le Pays-Bas, and threw herself on his breast, weeping like a terrified child. All night she had wept in his arms. . . . They had agreed that Nénette should never serve at weddings. . . . She returned to her former amusement, however.

So great was her haste to leave for the festivals that she even forgot her foremost duties. To all intents, Nénette had abandoned her home, never looking after anything. When Nono returned from the vine-

yard, he was obliged, in spite of his fatigue, to hunt
for a candle, the sugar, the flour, wash the dishes
and at times even make the beds.   And little Laurette,
sitting on a stool, watched him cook, with an instinc-
tive uneasiness, his extraordinary combinations. . . .
"Poor little one! . . . All that will hardly be good, but
I didn't even find an onion. . . . Is there any butter
in the cupboard?   Go and see.   . . Ah! 'tis a miserable life, my poor child! . . . "

When Nénette came home, he still had the heart
to kiss that ungrateful forehead.   "Little friend," said
he.   But he could not add another word, and, with a
gesture of complete distress, he covered his eyes with
his hands.

Some of his good friends did not fail to jeer at
him: "Well, 'tis about time! . . . Nénette has turned
out to be a jolly woman! . . . She's getting plump.
She's filling up like a little rabbit.   Besides she's all
fire and flame.   You're lucky to have a pretty wife.
Now one can see she's got the work she likes."

"Yes, that is right," answered Nono in a quiet tone.
"Let her be well.   I'm glad to see her happy, healthy
and respectable."

"Oh, as to that! . . . my Nono! . . . you said it.
. . . As to being respectable, that woman is the gem
of the land! . . . She deserves the pink top-
knot! . . . "

And Nono feigned not to see the evil faces of those
friends, not to perceive the ferocious joy that made
their chubby noses sniff, and their stony eyes twinkle.

He did not see the big fellows wink to one another
and rub their faces with their heavy hands to hide their
hideous smiles.

But once alone, in the vineyard or in the fields,
Nono changed his expression. He worked like a mad-
man. He gave himself entirely to his strength and
his courage. He threw himself into his work as into
a sea of oblivion. Standing flat on his feet, his forehead close to the vines, he would dig with a regular
and desperate eagerness. He swung his pickax with
rage, and tore up huge lumps of moistened earth which
he threw between his legs.

. . . In those sad days, Nono found his real peace
of mind in the Marais fields. There he was surrounded
by a vast plain, with green fields, narrow paths and
invigorating silence. In the east, there was a long
stretch of pensive and ruddy woods. The nearest
village is Saint-Philibert with its gray walls, thatched
roofs and bare trees. It was the village of his grandfather, and the native place of his poor family. Nono
found again, in these fields, where the elders of his
race had toiled, the courage which is that of the eternal
man. His humble and gentle soul of a man resigned
to his fate rose in peace towards his supreme dreams.
His eyes wandered toward the distance: his gaze would
lose itself beyond the woods, far off where all blends
into one.

. . . Yonder, towards the east, in a fog of colorless
mist, in a vague mingling of sky and air, the human

paths terminate as in a dream. On the blue hills, their traces hardly visible and stippled with trees, rise and then disappear like beings set free who at last find peace.

CHAPTER X

But Nono's sorrow was bitter indeed. One afternoon in March, he was busy digging in his garden, getting it ready to plant some vegetables. Nénette and he had just had a heated dispute. The young woman had been asked to serve at a wedding of two hundred guests. Nénette was at first elated. But Nono stamped his foot and exclaimed: "No! this time it's impossible. Renardin will be at this wedding in Epernay. Have nothing to do with it."

Nénette grew angry and decided to have her own way. There were no good reasons to stop her from going where she was asked: "Besides, I want to go there . . . that's all! . . . "

Nono replied indifferently: "Well then, go where you like."

This calm answer exasperated Nénette, and she burst out in a rage: "All right! . . . All right! . . . I won't go. But don't put on that stupid helpless look, for it just makes my skin creep! . . . Yes! . . . Look at me! . . . What are you going to do about it? What can you see with your bleared eyes?"

Nono had let her shout, and walked out. Having reached his field, he had at first wanted to work; but he soon thrust his spade aside, and sat down in the

furrow muttering to himself: "Ah! great God! . . .
This time I think I'm done for. . . . I've borne meekly
a heavy load of sorrow and shame. But I'm about
to sink beneath the yoke! . . . I feel a terrible madness coming over me. . . . And it's coming at a gallop, too. . . . "

He reflected a long time, holding his head in his
hands. And suddenly he cried out: "But there's
something still worse! . . . She doesn't even love her
little one! . . . Oh! it's certain! . . . She doesn't love
her! A week sometimes passes without her paying
more attention to the child than to the merest trifle
at home. . . . I must look after her. I must put her
little stockings on. . . . I must see that her wretched
little dress is mended. . . . And during that time, she
—the other one—sings! . . . And then suddenly—
without any warning—she paws over the little darling
like a hungry beast. You'd think she was going to
smother the child with kisses. . . . Oh! she'll make
the child mad, too! . . .

" . . . Ah! hang this life! . . . No! I can't work!
. . . I must go home. This is the first time that I
must give up a task! . . . It's cowardly! . . . But I
can't help it. Besides, hang it! . . . as Nénette says."

The clock struck four when Nono entered his house.
As he walked up the stairs, he heard a sudden movement of chairs . . above . . . in his room. When
he reached his door, he stopped short—petrified with
stupor. Nénette was standing with her eyes cast down.
She was ironing some shirts. But in front of her

Renardin was leaning on the table, covering his face with his large hairy hands.

"Get out of here—you! . . . " said Nono quietly.

Renardin left without saying a word. Nono sat down and watched Nénette move the iron to and fro on the breast of a shirt.

"Look here, you! . . . " said he. "I never want to see that man in my house again!"

Nénette raised her head and flushed.

"But he didn't do any harm."

"I didn't do him any either."

"Hasn't that man a right to watch me work?"

"Yes, if you worked as hard as you do now, it must have been interesting to watch you. In the meantime, don't tear that shirt by rubbing it with an iron that's as hot as hoar-frost! . . . "

And with a sudden outburst of anger, Nono rose, wrested the iron from his wife's hand and threw it into the ashes of the fireplace.

"Oh! . . . " said he, calmed all of a sudden, "it's not surprising: before you can make your irons hot you must at least have some fire! . . . And it has been out for some time! . . . There was some other work on hand!"

And without bothering about Nénette, Nono went to the woodstack and took some fagots. He then began to break them and arrange them in the fireplace.

Nénette watched him. She was so terrified that her mind was a perfect blank for a time.

What was he going to do? . . . Wasn't he going

to kill her? . . . She deserved it. Besides, all was done for. Love and happiness had just been dashed to pieces in a few seconds. Nothing but ruin was before her. . . .

But suddenly a rancorous rage arose in her against that big, gross, ungraceful peasant, who was gnawing, without violence at her delicate heart, who humiliated her because of some trivial evidence. Ah! if he had only insulted and beaten her! . . . But no! he was standing there stupidly, with his clumsy knee in the air breaking the fagots. He hung his long, veined neck down like a big horse; he did not deign to look at her, insult her or cry; he just let her remain there like some inanimate object. She was in turn humiliated, in despair, and exasperated; and all that . . . in silence! . . . in vain! . . .

She then felt a shudder of contempt and hatred pass through her body: it made her blood run cold. And, in spite of herself, almost unconsciously she muttered: "Blockhead!"

Nono heard it, but he did not turn round. He finished filling the fireplace with wood; then he looked in his waistcoat pocket for a match. He raised his leg and struck the match with a straight powerful blow along his entire thigh against his velvet trousers. From his habit of lighting matches in the open air, he quickly enclosed the flame in the hollow of his hands. When the fagots began to blaze, he sat down on a chair with his head drooping on his chest.

After a quarter of an hour of silence, during which

there was no other noise but the crackling of the fire,
Nénette approached and said in a low voice loud
enough to be heard by Nono: "If I didn't have my
child, I'd hang myself."

Nono raised his small gray eyes: "Oh! don't let
that stop you. I don't want to brag; but, with an
honest father like me, she can always do without such
a mother as you. . . . She even deserves something
better; go right ahead then. There's plenty of rope
in the garret, and in the woods you'll find some very
strong branches. There's the staircase; creep right
up, and go and hang yourself to your heart's content."

When little Laurette returned from school, she
found her father sitting in front of the fire, his legs
crossed beneath his chair and his long back bent like
an arch. She walked up to him to kiss him; but she
stopped and contemplated, with an astonished look,
that drooping, soulless face with its distended, gaping
mouth and blank, fixed gaze. She then looked at her
mother, sitting near the window and sewing in silence.
Her mother nodded to her amicably as she wet the
thread before threading the needle. The little girl
walked over to her mother on tip-toe: "He's drunk?"

"Yes. Don't make any noise."

Laurette sat down on a stool near her mother. The
mother and daughter spoke in a whisper. They seemed
to watch a dead person. The clock continued its
monotonous ticking.

Nénette tried to shake her thoughts off by speaking.

Her voice sounded like a deadened murmur; but never had she been so motherly in her gayety. She put many questions to her daughter, spoke to her of her tasks at school and of her little friends. The talk was very friendly and the child was delighted. In fact, it was the mother who, having become quite young again to please her child, spoke of the most trifling things with a happy, childish charm. But it was also an involuntary effort to tear herself away from the torments of the present hour; it was a way of returning to the distant past, of fleeing from woeful age to reach once more the serene purity of childhood.

And gradually indeed, amid these distant shadows of time and conscience, faint glimmers loomed up; the devastated space was soon full of memories and prayers. And soon it was no longer possible for the poor soul to escape from these visions: her entire past seemed to be reaching towards shattered dreams and disappointed love. All the past days of all the bygone springs had come in vain to cast their flowers upon the ruined soul; that which came back and shrieked in its torment was the entire life of the young girl—of the child! . . . She had been a charming housewife and a courageous little woodcutter. She had loved with all her soul. Beneath the wretched flesh, the heart had perhaps remained murmuring and pure like a spring which is only for a time befouled. . . . It is this murmur that she hears now; it is to this faint voice of bygone days that she is listening. And now she hears once more the humming of the bees and the call of the titlings in the hawthorne bushes, when they kissed. . . . "O my dear friend! . . . O my darling! . . . "

Little Laurette looked at the tears that rolled down her mother's face. Nénette tried to hold them back, and her features were distorted by the violent effort. Her mouth, with the lips closed tight, had convulsive fits. The poor face then was fretted with sudden wrinkles, and the tears filled the shriveled features as if they had come from everywhere. The little girl was sitting on her mother's lap, and also cried. The mother pressed the child close to her bosom, rocking her violently as if she were going to lose her. And in this exasperated rocking could be seen the sorrow of a supreme moment.

The little one said suddenly: "Let me go, mamma! . . . I want to go to bed."

"You didn't have any supper!"

"I'm not hungry. Let me go. Remain with papa." Laurette looked at her mother as if to say: "I understand. You must remain alone."

When her daughter was in bed Nénette lit the lamp and sat down near the table to sew. Her husband was still sitting in the same place. She was waiting for him to get up. She waited a long time. Finally Nono rose from his chair. "Hm! . . . Hm! . . . " he muttered as if he had come from a dream. He passed by his wife, turning his head away. In vain did Nénette raise towards him her eyes where her soul lay prostrate in the dust.

Nono went into his room. Nénette heard him drop his boots and go to bed. A few minutes later he snored.

When alone, the young woman, in despair, hid her face in her hands. She was in such agony that she could hardly breathe. She thought that the terrible weight that lay on her breast was to remain there forever. And a chill came over her, like a cold night that follows a warm day.

She was sitting and thinking for a long time. Hours had perhaps elapsed. Then she stood up, raised her hair and rubbed her eyes. She breathed as after a fall from a great height. It was over now. Prostrated at the feet of her faithful companion, she was going to confess everything. She would open to him the depth of her soul; she would reveal without any pity all her sins; she would make her supreme confession as when in the pangs of death; she would be like the poor soul that rises from the ground never to fall again; she would be before her husband as before death.

And afterwards whether he would forgive or not, she would have expiated her sins. There would be no more coquettish toilettes, no more bonnets trimmed with knots, and no more dresses trimmed with flounces. She would have become again a vine-dresser with hobnail shoes and a striped hood. She would destroy her flesh with the hard work of the

fields. She would toil until her soul should have found
again a kind of fierce health.

Nénette entered the room where Nono was sleeping.
She walked over to the bed with the lamp in one
hand, and with the other she covered the flame so
that the light should not wake her husband. . . . She
watched him sleep. . . .

The tall winegrower was exhausted with fatigue.
He was sleeping with his mouth open; his lips drawn
back and his gums exposed, gave him a horrible grin.
The eyes seemed to have been closed with violence
as if after the detonation of an explosion. And on
these two lids, under which slept the former gaze of
tenderness and love, there were numerous wrinkles
crossing one another like the cartruts in a muddy
hollow.

Nénette was terrified at the sight of this grimacing
slumber. She recalled the man with his straight face
when he stood close to her little body. She remembered
that long face so thoughtful and honest which she
had tried to reach on tip-toe, her heart in a flutter
and her soul uplifted.

This is what had become of her noble husband.
Oh! how much he had suffered to have changed thus!
. . . During ten full years he had worked like a mad-
man. . . . It was for her. For her his arms had
toiled. But perhaps also for her, because of her
frivolity, did the wrinkles of care fret his face. These
scattered memories thronged in her mind. She recalled his equivocal remarks, that air of wishing to

ignore all, and that gesture of great sorrow, when, after having caressed her, he passed his hand across his care-worn forehead. . . . Ah! each of her sins had left there a trace or a wrinkle. . . . Each of her criminal pleasures had withered a little more that beloved face! . . .

Nono, disturbed by the light, turned on one side, Nénette went to place the lamp on the table and came back. She knelt down at the foot of the bed. She stretched her arms out towards the sleeping face, and in a whisper she murmured her prayer. She prayed to be taken back again, to be forgiven with kisses, to be clasped and loved once more! . . . She murmured a long time. But her lips gradually tired, and her eyes soon closed. . . .

In the morning when the dim light of the refreshing dawn penetrated the mist, Nénette was still lying, at the foot of the bed in a half slumber in which the world of dreams and reality was mingled. . . . It seemed to her that her prayer was heard: Nono sat up and held out over her a hand of forgiveness. She lowered her head beneath that blessed gesture. But what a heavy hand, however! . . .

Suddenly she started up, for Nono rose and had just roughly thrown the linen over her. His abrupt movement had cruelly brought to an end and transformed her happy fleeting dream.

When Nono was on his feet he was a sad spectacle. He scratched his arms, craned his neck and muttered:

"Hm! . . . Hm! . . . " The ludicrous lappets of his shirt dangled over his crooked knees and thin hairy legs.

Nénette contemplated with terror this long face, bewildered, dull and cold.

"What are you doing there? . . . Stop your look-ing at me in that way! . . . "

Nénette rose slowly, dried her tears with the back of her hand and burst out laughing. And yet she was still crying! . . . Her sobbing and laughter at first mingled nervously. The struggle was coming to its close, and the trembling, little woman rubbed her eyes with the rage of despair.

"Will you stop cutting up like that? . . . I've just about enough of these hysterical farces! . . . I know what's behind 'em all! . . . Cut those grimaces out or I'll kick you down the stairs! . . . "

Nénette's little eyes at once became fiery and in-solent; she smiled bitterly at her husband. Then she began to hum, and affected to get busy with her house-work. She went to fetch the wood from the garret, the water from the well and the wine from the cellar. . . . She did not stop singing as she worked. Her exasperated joy filled with laughing murmurs the stair-case, the garret and the entire house.

As for Nono, he dressed and had his breakfast. He took from the cupboard the bread and a bowl of strong cheese. Seated at the table with a pig-headed and brutish air, he chewed in silence. With the point of the knife he pushed huge pieces of bread into his mouth; then he placed his fist at the edge of the table, the blade of the knife pointing straight up in the air. In the meantime Nénette grew calm. But the storm soon burst out anew.

"Are you really going . . . to that wedding? . . . " said Nono as he was getting ready to go to the vines.

"I don't know yet," answered Nénette in a soft voice.

"You better decide then, so that I can know whether I must come back at eleven o'clock to give the little one something to eat! . . . "

Nénette reflected. Then, with a timorous tenderness she said: "Oh! I want to stay home."

"All right. Stay home then," grumbled Nono roughly.

The young woman looked at her husband. She had never seen him thus. She could hardly recognize that wornout brutal face, and that sharp, violent look. Despair seized upon her soul: she trembled with rage to see her repentance and tenderness shattered by his stubbornness.

"Oh! . . . Oh! . . . What a fool I am. . . . Of course, you must really be stupid to try to make up with such a beast. . . . Yes, I'm going to that wedding! . . . And I'm not leaving two hours later, but at once . . . at this very moment! . . . "

"Well then! . . . clear out at once! . . . "

Nénette had already taken off her apron and thrown it in the corner. Without saying a word, she went to the wardrobe and threw the light door open with a bang; then she ran to the chest of drawers, pulled them out with violence and began to throw the clothes on the chairs in a huddle as in the distraction of a fire. . . .

Nono stood and watched her silently. Then he shrugged his shoulders and descended to feed the rabbits. When he returned, he found Nénette dressed looking at herself in the mirror. She was arranging with her fingertips the dainty curls on her forehead. She turned her head in all directions in order to get the proper light. She fluttered like a swallow before taking wing. A large, greenish net cravat gave her the appearance of a graceful little boy.

"Yes! . . . You can look! . . . " said Nono. "That's great! . . . "

"What's great?"

"With these ball clothes you're going to help in the kitchen, besides the six kilometers you must walk in the mud! . . . You damn madwoman! . . . And yet, after all I don't give a hang! . . . "

"And I give a rap, eh?"

Nénette's voice trembled with anger: "How stupid of me to let him yell at me in that way! . . . I'm an angel to be so obliging. . . . "

"Oh! . . . an angel? . . . perhaps when you dream! . . . but otherwise you're a dirty wretch! . . . "

Nénette could no longer control her anger, and her insults soon calmed Nono. He was, like all peasants, deliberately gross in his language; but the habitual tone in which he spoke effaced the real meaning of his words. Nénette's insults were different both in tone and choice; and Nono saw those lips which he had so often kissed sink in mud forever.

" . . . But go ahead quick! . . . My poor child! . . . " said he in an almost doleful tone.

And this very tone exasperated the unhappy Nénette and made her furious. She would have wanted blows, a violent anger, an uproar, action, something in fine which would have dispelled this nightmare, dissipated the stupor of the air, driven away the spell which was about to link her destiny. . . . Or else, let everything come to an end! . . . let everything totter down with the house! . . . bury the beings! . . . annihilate life and the pangs we suffer! . . .

"Yes, I'm going," she yelled, "but never to return again. . . . I've enough of it . . . enough of your wooden face, your shabby hovel and your greased boots! . . . Enough of you, blockhead! . . . Yes, I'm clearing out . . . forever! . . . "

" . . . Well," said Nono calmly, "while you're at it, you can set the house on fire, and throw the little one into the well! . . . "

Nénette no longer listened; she ran like a mad-woman. She was looking for her hat . . . for the pins with which to hold it. She had one between her teeth; the other she furiously thrust in her hair. As she ran on, she grabbed her gloves here, a handkerchief there, and a little farther her purse. Then she dashed to the door, opened it and threw it back to the wall, and rushed down the stairs. . . .

Nono had hardly had the time to look about. He remained there, and gaped before the open door. But he heard a noise behind him. He turned round, and saw his little Laurette in her shirt.

"What's the matter, papa?"

Then, in a sudden flash of tenderness and understanding, Nono perceived the enormity of what had just happened: "Why, your mamma is leaving! . . . my child! . . . "

Little Laurette ran to the staircase and cried: "Mamma! . . . Mamma! . . . "

"Go out on the balcony rather, if you want to call her," said Nono in a hoarse voice.

The little one ran out on the balcony and bent over: "Mamma! . . . Little mother! . . . "

"Cry louder, little one! . . . She forgot something! . . . "

"Little mother! . . . Little mother! . . . "

But the wind blew in the opposite direction and carried these feeble cries away with it.

"Papa! . . . Why did mamma go away so quickly? She doesn't hear me."

Nono hurried in turn to the balcony. He was about to utter, with all his might, down the road, in the hostile wind, his supreme cry. . . . But he stopped short: about thirty paces away there was Renardin standing near the gate of the house! The big fellow exulted in his triumph. Nono saw him rub his hands joyfully. Nono was silent.

He and his daughter saw Nénette walking on without turning back; then she almost began to run and quickly turned at the corner of the Café Caillot. . . . She disappeared there.

The father and the little girl entered the room. Nono closed the glass door of the balcony, and sat down despondently. The frightened child looked at him.

"Papa! . . . Why did memma go away so quickly? . . . She didn't even kiss me! . . . Is she late? . . . Tell me! . . . "

"Yes, my child."

"Is she going to Epernay?"

"Yes, my child."

"But she'll come back after to-morrow? . . . eh? . . . papa! . . . "

"Of course, my child."

The little girl was silent a moment. She looked at her father and thought. She bent down to scratch her knee, and she raised her shirt above her little naked legs, charming and round as if they were made of ivory.

"Papa! . . . It's already raining a little, and mamma hasn't taken an umbrella! . . . Why not? It's too bad! she's gone very far."

"Yes, my little Laurette."

"Papa! . . . last night mamma suffered very much! . . . "

"Yes, my child."

"It was your fault, eh? . . . Did you get drunk? . . . "

"Yes, my child."

"You won't make her cry any more, will you, my dear papa? . . . "

"No, my little darling!"

"You'll be good to mamma! . . . She's so kind! . . . "

"Yes, my child.   But go to bed now, because you'll catch cold. . . . leave me alone for a while. . . . "

PART II

CHAPTER I

THE news was spreading everywhere. Early in the morning, the poor bandy-legged newsman had shouted at every door the event, and blew at the same time his cracked horn till his lungs almost burst. The winegrowers questioned one another about the news as they were walking, with their baskets on their backs, to the vineyards. The village was filled with the murmur of contented voices. It buzzed like a bee-hive. And from a distance, perhaps this very quiver-ing of human happiness resembled the imperceptible creaking of an ant-hill, which works and constructs fearlessly beneath your feet, which animates with its generous toil every nook and corner of the land.

Nono passed by again and again in the midst of this gayety. He would walk off with long strides raising his feet as if he were clambering up a moun-tain. He stopped in the middle of the crossroad of Les Baraques; and there he stood agape with his head stretched out, his arms dangling at his side, eagerly gazing with his dull eyes on the distant roads. But he could only see, beneath the trees afar off, the long carts of Le Pays-Bas, and the yellow cart-tilts of the stage coaches.

The inhabitants of Les Baraques were all in the street. Every eye watched closely the poor face of the unhappy Nono. Flon-Flon, more puffed up than ever, cheerful and red like a ripe spreading vine, approached with a sly good-natured look:

"Hey! . . . Nono! . . . Are you waiting for anybody?"

"Yes," said Nono who was not in the humor of saying much.

"Whom are you waiting for?"

"My wife."

"Your wife? . . . Ah! Hm! She isn't come back yet from the wedding. . . . Ah! . . . Perhaps there's some mean trick in back of this . . . Women, when the deuce takes them at their worse . . ."

"Look here," interrupted Nono.

But a little later, a certain Lardoisier, called Calfat, with the abrupt boldness of a sly, thick-set poacher, succeeded where others would have failed:

"Well, you big noodle! . . . What the deuce are you doing here? . . . Jollying the world, eh? . . . Are you looking for someone to have a drink with? . . . Well, I'm ready. . . . Firmin Fausset is going to give you some fresh news that'll interest you."

"Ah! . . ."

"Yes."

"All right! . . ."

"Come on, let's go in!"

The two men entered the café. The other wine-growers gradually came to join them, and grouped themselves amicably around them. At first they spoke seriously so as not to anger Nono. They also drank likewise. Then their talk became more lively, and little by little they managed to slip in a few jokes. When it grew dark, they laughed heartily in the Café Caillot.

. . . There he was, the lanky Nono with his tormented, gloomy face, quite contentedly drunk! . . . He laid bare before a jeering crowd the gentle mockery of his unhappy love. ·. . . Briquet, in very high spirits led the party:

"But see here! . . . My poor Nono! . . . Only you saw nothing of what was going on! . . . That woman was the wench of the village! . . . We couldn't give you a hint, because you gave us up and looked down on us. . . . But, poor old chap . . . that affair was going on a long time! . . . Why, Renardin, as far back. . . . "

"Well, see here, anyhow. . . . I didn't watch her very closely," said Nono placidly shaking his absinth. "I never thought her a harlot! . . . "

"Ah! . . . Well, you should 'ave seen her last night in Dijon, you'd 'ave been sure at once."

"In Dijon?"

"Yes. The wedding-party went there in a jaunting-coach. The old folks wanted to go to the theater: but the young ones went for a good time to the

Brasseries-Rennies. . . . Hey! Firmin! . . . Tell the details of the business!"

Firmin was a stout, pale and peaceful fellow who spoke lazily:

"Ah! . . . I saw yesterday what I've never seen. Since I'm a musician and since I have tromboned at weddings in Le Pays-Bas, I've seen many women drunk, but never one as much as yours. . . . Jacquelinet! . . .

"Ah! Renardin took good care of her! She was in good hands! . . . When I saw her come in, holding on to Renardin's and Martin-Boiteux's arms. . . . By Jove, some jag! . . . And pretty, too! . . . and what a luscious, little pink snout! . . . And besides, where necessary, she was plump and dimpled to make your mouth water. . . She was glad to be hugged. . . . And you ought to hear her shout! . . . It wasn't a sermon she was handing us out. . . . And you ought to see her slip down glasses of champagne! . . . Ah! that fixed her right! . . . At last, she began to slobber in her glass and to bawl merrily, while the fellows were pulling her about hither and thither. She made a hellish racket. . . . She could hardly be quieted. She stamped like a mad creature! . . . When I left she whined like a cat, for the fellows were rough with her. . . . I'll tell you only that much. . . . "

"Well, you see," said Nono calmly, "I was never aware of it. I never thought her as bad as that."

"But, after all, my poor fellow!" said Flon-Flon,

"you knew the kind of creature she was, why did you tie yourself up for life with that slut? . . . "

"Ah! . . . What shall I tell you? . . . Do I know? . . . you're always fooled with any woman. You're often fooled when you buy a cow: but if you're wise you can get out of it. But with a woman! . . . This is one whom I've seen grow up, so to speak, between my boots. . . . Well, look at her! . . . You see a little face that smiles at you. . . . You think you're seeing the tenderness of the whole world. . . . You go at her with your soul and life. . . . And then! . . . The best is like the worst: she isn't worth a damn! . . . They say: 'I've a little angel in my house.' Yes, an angel! . . . The worst sow ain't the one that rolls about in the pigsty. . . . "

"Well, let me tell you something. You get rid of her now for good."

"That's sure. I'm rid of her."

"But look here, Nono! . . . Let me warn you of another thing. . . . You have a creeping thing in your house who is quite a tomboy. . . . She's ten, and she's cursed already! . . . Take care, nothing good will come of her."

While speaking, Flon-Flon raised his finger to stress his warning. And Nono, sitting sideways on his chair, one elbow leaning on the back, scratched his head as if to unravel the possible truth of the remark. He shook his long anxious face and said: "Why! that may be very possible! There'd be nothing queer about that."

"Ah! do you doubt it? Why, my poor fellow, you have only to look into that little one's eyes to be convinced. . . . Why, she'll be worse than the other one! Look here, does that little creature resemble you? . . . Say yes, if you dare to make a jackass of yourself! . . . "

"Indeed, hardly. But I'm going to look after her."

"You'll be right. . . . Keep an eye on her, old chap. Don't make of her what you made of the other . . . by treating her daintily. Ah! If instead of having kept your mouth shut, you had raised your paw. . . . "

"Ah! you're dead right! . . . I was too stupid and too good. I realize it. I can't do more. I see it now. But you want to look out, too! . . . All women must have a cudgel. . . . I'm going to train this one! Leave it to me! . . . They don't know me here. They laugh at me. Well, they'll see that I'm perhaps one of the most terrible! . . . I'm going to make her act uprightly, that little flea! . . . I'll straighten her bones! She'll see whether the fist at the end of my sleeve is made of lamb's wool! I can see it now. . . . She'll be vicious, eh? Well, you daughter of a harlot! . . . you'll get a taste of my boot! And then, the other one . . . her mother. . . . I'll revenge myself. Tell it to your wives. 'He swore in the café before all of us. Beware! . . . Surely, sooner or later . . . in ten years . . . in twenty years . . . but it's sure and certain; some day a murder will be committed, and the daughter of old Clémence will be the victim! . . . ' Now that's what I'm telling you, and I won't

say it again. . . . But you're not drinking. . . .
Tienette! . . . Let's have our rounds! . . . What'll
you have, you there? . . . Have what I'm having:
go on, a good absinth! . . . There's nothing that
makes the blood run so well! . . . Let me have one
more. . . . Tienette! . . . "

A great many winegrowers were there, sitting in
silence, in the thick smoke of the café. With their
elbows on the table, they smoked their short pipes
like old sailors. They relished Nono's speeches with
blithe and contented faces.

"But what's going to become of me! . . . I was
too happy! I wouldn't have given my hovel for the
warmest place in paradise. Well, in a few days, everything has gone to the dogs. Last Tuesday, at this
very moment I was sitting in my house and having
my supper, with the charming little pink creature, there
in front of me, she who was the companion of my
days and the darling of my nights! . . . What
pleasure have I got now; here I am bottled up with
the worst drunkards of the village! . . . "

"Well, Nono! you're a fine fellow!" said all the
winegrowers in a chorus. "That's right, go right on!
. . . Be agreeable! . . . "

"But don't get angry! . . . I'm just joking. You're
my friends. I like you all. And that's quite true;
I neglected you too much; I thought you were too
rotten. . . . That's wrong! . . . You must forgive
me. . . . You're my friends, my true friends, the fin-

est chums of the village! . . . Flon-Flon! . . . my chums! . . . I insulted you one day. . . . "

"Ah! poor old chap! you remember! . . . I forgive you. Besides, I knew it wasn't your fault."

The two friends shook hands; Nono, who could hardly hold his long face steady, rocked his head to and fro with emotion.

"My good old fellow."

"My poor old chap."

"And you, my old Briquet! . . . "

"Ah! Nono! . . . Old chum! . . . "

"And you, Fumeron! . . . Hey Flammêche! . . . Hey, friends! Ah! my poor old Tiennete. . . . Pierrot, why don't you show yourself! . . . Old Bonaparte, why don't you cheer up? We're celebrating! . . . I neglected you, they say. . . . Forgive me all! . . . I'm repenting. You know, it wasn't my fault. It was that creature who didn't like you! . . . And then, I hardly cared for the café. That doesn't mean that I couldn't drink, but I can't get drunk! . . . I'll even go one better; I could never really get drunk. I've tried it on every possible occasion. . . . Well, nothing doing! I wasn't more drunk than before; never more than now! . . . People say we feel good when drunk. . . . Ah! that's a pleasure I never enjoyed! It's a great misfortune; greater than anything else! . . . I must weep! . . . Yes! . . . Yes! Yes! . . . "

Nono added in a heavy voice, wiping his face with his sleeve.

"Look here, friends! . . . I'll pay for another round! . . . This is a holiday! . . . Let's celebrate my freedom! . . . I'm free! . . . Drink, friends! . . . I'm glad to see you. If there's some fresh meat I'll pay for your supper. . . . Tienette! prepare supper for this whole damn gang! . . . "

"You better go home," said the good woman. "Your unhappy little Laurette is waiting for you."

"The little one! . . . She's a harlot! . . . I'll kick her out! . . . Prepare the supper; I still have forty francs. My slut kept 'em for the little one's clothes. I'm going to spend 'em, and all these knaves are going to share 'em with me. . . . For I'm happy, and glad to be rid of her."

Nono came home at midnight. In the room a dim light permitted him to see a little shadow furtively creeping out of bed, and noiselessly coming to him. The drunkard extended his fist with all his might into the air, and struck with a dull sound the delicate features of a wan face. . . . Then he went to bed. . . . There was no sobbing; everything remained silent.

CHAPTER II

A NEW life had begun.

From the very next morning, the relations between Nono and his daughter had become clear and settled. When he came home, at eleven o'clock, after the express had passed by, he found little Laurette standing near the woodpile.

In two days she seemed to have grown amazingly! She had become thin and pale like a withered leaf. Her dilated eyes showed that she was terror-stricken. In the dark, one could only see her dismayed glances which followed timidly Nono's movements and gestures.

On coming home, Nono threw his muddy apron and cap on the drawers, where the pure relics of the little family were lying! the marriage bouquet, the photographs and the lockets with the hair of the dead.

"Here you are!" Nono shouted brutally to his daughter. "What are you doing there? . . . Couldn't you have set the table? . . . Would that have inconvenienced you? . . . Do you think you're going to do nothing? . . . that I'm going to give you your mess for nothing? . . . "

Nono went down the cellar to draw the wine; then he ate some cold bacon. The little girl did not stir, and continued to stare at him.

"Aren't you going to eat? . . . Must you be fed? . . . Well, that's your business. Eat or don't eat, do as you please, and croak at your ease! . . . "

At night, Nono came home, almost as late and as drunk as on the previous night. This continued for two days. During these two days, Laurette did not go out. She crawled about the house like an insect with broken legs. She moved from place to place silently, in an almost lifeless manner; she was incessantly raising her pale curls; that was her only gesture.

Little by little, however, by dint of constantly watching in the dark, furtive rays of light glided into this distressed soul. What these rays exactly were no one could have divined; but they hastened her soul into a precocious self-consciousness. . . .

The following day, when Nono came home for his midday meal, he found the fire burning, the table set, the wine drawn and the food ready. Henceforth, little Laurette rose every morning earlier than her father and slipped out of bed very quietly; Nono would only get up on hearing her little bare feet patter on the floor. And then it was that the lowly life of housekeeper began for Laurette; everything would grow animate beneath her light footsteps and feeble hands.

The little girl prepared and lit the fire, got everything ready, and warmed the soup. After her father left, she washed the dishes, and then it was time for her to go to school.

At school, however, the little one was a poor pupil. She learnt her lessons very badly: she had, indeed, so much to worry about! She attributed to herself constantly the importance of an anxious housekeeper who thinks of the meals, the provisions, the washing and the mending. Her friends did not like to play with her. She would walk along the road to school alone, with a large, unshapely basket under her arm.

The other little girls had warm winter clothes, black woolen kerchiefs, and cloth hoods. With their school-bags under their arms, their work-baskets in their hands, they would greet one another and bow like ladies. One might think them maidens of a northern land. But little Laurette had not her proper share in the eyes of her schoolmates. She was poorly clad in a black dress and a velvet waist, green and faded.

Nor was Laurette exactly a pretty girl. A cold uneasiness exaggerated still more her unusual slender body, her large limbs and her nervous gait. Her long, narrow face was marked with freckles which were especially noticeable near her projecting cheek bones. Her mouth was too large, and was tightened by a constrained expression. When embarrassed, she lowered her little soft and pensive eyes of grayish hue. The delicacy of her face lay in her finely arched eyebrows, penciled as if by a holy hand. She also had beautiful golden hair, which hung down her back in a thick, wavy plait. And that was enough to give the little being a deal of charm, a legendary grace.

Nono grew more stupid than ever in his sorrow and drunkenness. The villagers saw him pass by, taking long, heavy strides, as he plodded on. He held out his dull face and bent his body forward, as if the spade on his shoulder were weighing him down.

The first few months were the worst, for spring had come. Oh! this month of the Lady-day with all its bushes white! . . . The forest drowned in periwinkles! The young leaves streaked with little drunken wings! . . . And those bright nights, smothered with kisses and penetrated with the light breath of the zephyrs which seems to descend from the starry heavens! . . . Oh! how hard it is to plod through this burning and delirious world, so full of passion and caresses, with a heart turned to ashes and dust! . . .

"Ah!" said Nono, "how bright and happy everything seems to be in this beautiful weather! . . . But I! . . . There's no use talking, my end is near. When you only have your shame to swallow, you might as well give up! . . . "

But when autumn came, these moods of despair were almost unknown to Nono. When the water in the ditches, under the long grass and pointed leaves, became motionless and dark like the dead; when the sky ceased to be bright and clear and became a dull and opaque expanse, a sea of moving mist—only then was Nono's heart in harmony with nature.

Often did he stop while at work to contemplate the fields that had changed into a barren, marred stretch of land. As far as his eye could see, the ground was bare and the branches dead. In the marshes, one felt the deadly odor of the stagnant water and the decayed leaves. The vultures of the north walked on the stubble as if on a land of their own. In the dim sky, triangular flocks of strange birds flew by.

Nono stared, with his lifeless eyes, at the gloomy horizon and at the undulating ground below the mist. His bewildered mind ever returned to the same thought with a stupor, overwhelming and ruthless like the night.

"Well, what can be done! . . . She may be dead; but I'd be happier than I am! . . . There's no shame in thinking of the dead."

Unhappy Nono! Indeed, they are happy who have a tomb before which they can pray! . . . The vague images of their beloved do not forsake them. Everywhere about them, in the air, there are imperceptible tenderness and disembodied smiles. But what can be said of those who are at the same time dead and alive for us? . . . Ah! when we know that the being dear to us is always beyond, somewhere at the very depths of the soil . . . and we shall never see her again! . . . that she is no longer a friend or enemy! . . . not even a memory we cherish! . . . not even a dead being we mourn! . . .

"But where is that Nénette, in this vast world?" . . . On this ruthless earth, beneath a sky without a

God. . . . "Where is she?" . . . Where is she during the night? . . . "In whose arms? . . . "

There was much rain towards the end of autumn. All these dreary days Nono spent in the café, and, at night, went home drunk with absinth. He would stop at the doorstep, leaning forward, ready to tumble down, his arms dangling at his side, and his mouth wide open:

"Well! . . . What's the matter with you?" said he to his daughter in a heavy, indistinct voice. "Yes, what are you looking at? . . . You little creature! . . . "

He sat down and extended his long legs under the chair. While the little girl was getting the supper ready. Nono ludicrously affected a thoughtful air. With gaping mouth and looking at the ceiling, he seemed to calculate: "Yes . . . that's right. . . . However, let's see! . . . But sure . . . that's it!"

Laurette interrupted him: "Father! . . . Eat. . . . Your soup'll be cold. . . . "

"All right! . . . Let me alone! . . . I'm trying to figure out how many vineprops I'll need. . . . "

After he had decided to have his soup, he at once went to bed. Little Laurette remained alone. She had quickly done her housework, and now she could dream in peace. Her thin pale face grew animate then, with a sad tenderness. With the gentle grace of a little bird that smoothes down its feathers, she ran her fingers through her pale golden curls. And at the movement of her own caress, she drooped her head softly, as if she had wished to think of the caress of another hand, of the blessed hand that had once rocked her cradle. This was a dream, but it was only for this dream that the soul of the child still craves.

. . . Where is her mother? She knows someone has gone off with her. Her older schoolmates have talked enough of it. The cruel children have told her all that their precocious perversity allowed them to understand. . . . "But where is my mamma when the dark night comes?" . . . Wherever she may be, no matter in what place or shame, the pure and innocent soul of the child is ever with her.

. . . But here below, only those who can raise their eyes towards heaven are not forsaken.

One evening in November, however, her father gave her a happy surprise. He came home drunk, but he was loud and merry.

"Well now! . . . " he shouted at the very threshhold. "What's the matter, little one? I see you've set the table and cooked the soup! . . . Well, that's good. . . . Very nice! . . . Your father says so."

Standing near the threshhold, his face wearing the broad, silly smile of drunkards, he waved a grotesque gesture of welcome with his hand.

"You know I'm really not hungry. . . . I had something at four o'clock at M. Rogout's. He handed up some good wine! When we keep some good stuff for three years, we think it great. . . . But it is really hardly the proper time to begin to drink it. . . . We're too much in a hurry. We like to drink too much: I always said so. But you're a good little darling! Come now! . . . Come and sit on my lap. . . . What's the matter? Don't cry! I don't like it. None of that nonsense? . . . No faces now! . . . Won't you come to my lap?"

Laurette sat down in trembling uncertainty on her father's lap, and her arms enlaced the long, veiny and hard neck on which she hid her quivering face.

"You're loving! . . . I like that. You're a good little darling. . . . You do a great deal in the house. . . . Oh! I can see it, believe me. I have a keen eye: I see everything. This I have from my old man. He, too, was very cunning. . . . To do him justice, he was somewhat knavish. But you're a good little girl! . . .

"Ah! but you ain't so loving every day. . . . You usually look disgusted when I come home. . . . But it's me who is disgusted by such manners. I don't like that. . . . But don't cry. . . . I'm not scolding you. I'm simply letting you know that, after all, I'm your father, and that you mustn't be so particular with me! . . .

"You're a pretty girl! . . . Do you know it? . . . You're my little pink angel! . . . But see that you don't become later on a slut like your mother! . . . But what's the matter? . . . Ah! Heavens! you're choking me. . . . You little wretch, loosen your grip, or I'll land you a blow! . . . Don't start that business

again, because I don't like it. . . . You little slut!
. . . Look here now, don't cry! Come now! smile to
your father. . . . What a funny face you're making! . . . "

The drunkard burst out laughing. He bounced the
child on his lap, as if she were still a baby. With
nervous grace, Laurette held on to his neck. Not
daring to speak too loud, she mumbled on his cheek
some indistinct phrases. And the drunkard smiling,
drooped his head and listened to that unknown
murmur.

"What are you saying? I don't hear. Now look
here, talk louder! . . . You ask whether I love you?
. . . Why, of course. You want me to kiss you when
I come in the evening? All right; but don't put on
your disgusted air. . . . Yes, I'll kiss you if you like
it. . . . I'm your papa. . . . Only don't squeeze my
neck so hard, or I'll get angry! . . . "

Nono soon wanted to get up. "There's something
wrong with me! . . . I don't know what's the matter
with me. I'm going to lie down near you. Go and
fetch the bedmat. . . . That's right! . . . Put it
down near the fire. . . . That's good."

The drunkard lay down then, stolidly on the floor,
and soon fell asleep. He awoke only very late at
night. When he opened his eyes, he perceived the
child sitting near him on a chair. She was sitting
beside him, and feeding the fire.

Nono got up in a bad humor. "Now! . . . Great
God! What's the matter? . . . I fell asleep! . . .

How stupid! . . . Couldn't you wake me! . . . Ah!
good heavens! I'm all broken up. Help me rise. Come
now! Hurry! . . . You confounded little slut! . . . "

Laurette led him to his bed, and helped him un-
dress and lie down.   Then she came back and wept
near the fireplace.. . . . The following day things continued as before: Nono began again to get drunk with
absinth, and the evenings at the house were sadder
than ever.

CHAPTER III

On Christmas eve, Nono invited a number of his friends for a midnight supper. Among them were the frequenters of the Café Caillot: Flon-Flon, Fumeron, Briquet. Flammêche was not there, but Grêlé was there instead. Nono thus invited another wag, lanky, and round-shouldered, with a bony, reddish face seamed with smallpox and with alert, churlish eyes. He was a merry boon companion of the café. He had lately returned from the army, and had fought in Tonkin. Two other winegrowers of the Rue Haute and a mountaineer had joined these habitués of the Café Caillot. No one knew how they happened to join this group; but the fact is that they did not leave Nono and his friends for a moment and did not miss a single drink. While the men were eating the sausage and drinking the white wine, little Laurette sitting near the fireplace, notched the chestnuts before putting them into the grillpan.

. . . They soon began to tackle Nono, however. The poor fellow was tracked and surrounded. It was a question of who would deal the most bitter blow. Their subject of mockery was ever the same.

"Your wife is at Besançon," said Grêlé. "I'll give you her address whenever you like."

"All right. But what is she doing there?"

"She works with taste, it seems."

"Is she still with Renardin?"

"Ah! . . . that depends. They're together, they leave each other, and then they come together again. . . . "

"But what work is she doing?"

"She unbuttons suspenders."

"That's no kind of work. . . . You're laughing at me. . . Tell me whether she's working in a factory, or doing piece work at home? . . . "

A vulgar reply caused an outburst of laughter, but did not irritate Nono.

"You're laughing! . . . But, believe me, I saw your point very well. I play the innocent fellow to make you laugh a bit, but I understand very well. . . . I know what I must know. . . . I'm no novice. Besides, I was two months in the army! I was a soldier for only two months, because my old man was more than seventy. . . . I can assure you that these two months have taken the rawness out of me! . . . Oh! I treated myself to it! . . . What a time I had! They hardly believed it here; I had left with forty-two francs. . . . Well, do you want to know how much I had on my return? . . . Sixteen sous! . . . Ah! but my old man rubbed it into me! 'You big lout! . . . You lazy boor! . . . And during that time I ate rotten bacon! . . . ' Yes, but the old fellow didn't say . . . that during that time he had emptied thirty-two liters of grape brandy. . . . "

The conversation was about to digress, but the fel-

lows saw to it that it should not deviate from their
favorite topic.   They set Nono on the right track;
and all, finally, had the pleasure of hearing him rail:
" . . . First of all, love! . . . it should be settled
just as a matter of appetite. . . . Neither the
heart nor the head must bother about it. . . .
You might as well dry drenched lambs in an oven,
as hand over to a woman your heart and soul!
. . . Ah! the devils don't hesitate a moment to tread
upon 'em. . . .

"A woman is only just good to milk you! . . . You
don't have to laugh, Fumeron! You can also wear
the chocolate medal of cuckolds. . . . The fat ain't
a whit better than the lean ones! . . . Mine was thin
. . . yours is fat; but you're not paying for it. . . . "

"You damned idiot! . . . My wife, at least, didn't
run off with Renardin! . . . "

"Oh! that's all that's worrying you. It is she, indeed, who gives you your soup, and even the bread
over which to pour it. Once she's gone, you'll have
nothing at all! . . . Come! my little one! Either let
your belly pinch, or work. But these are two things
that a glutton and a lazy lout hardly likes. . . . "

"You damned fool! I, at least, don't give a hang
about my wife; and I laid her aside when I had my
fill of her. I didn't pamper her up for ten years,
like you, with sweets. Nor did I coddle and cajole
her the way you did yours. . . . And even now all
your speeches don't stop you from sweetening the
milk of a Renardin. . . . "

"Oh! that's possible. I don't want to criticise the thing. . . . The little one is here: that's true.   But as soon as she grows up, she'll get out of here! . . . Let her just reach the age of sixteen, and I'll tell her to pack up and go. . . . 'Well, little one, the cuckoo has brooded long enough over another one's egg! . . . Go and look for shelter elsewhere. . . . The world is large: travel through it, and make in turn some little ones to give it a bit more life.'   That's what I'll do and say, Fumeron! . . . And, in the meantime, don't you be too cunning! . . . Your wife and your three children will not only some day prune your vines, but they'll beat you, too . . . For they haven't much respect for the paltry brute who happens to be their father."

"These children are, at least, mine!"

"Oh! Fumeron! . . . These are certainly pretensions! . . . I've a notion, and nobody here will deny it, that you're altogether too certain about that. . . . The first one, your oldest . . . he's big, fat and has fine color. . . . Do you mean to say he doesn't suggest to you the fat butcher next door! . . . As for the little girl. . . . Is it M. de Maraudon who has given her that turned-up nose.   That's what happens when a real good-looking woman washes for the bourgeois! . . . And the second boy . . . why! he's the double of Variguard, Jr! . . . To be sure, my friend, there's plenty in the pantry, and there's lard in the salting-tub!   But you paid dearly for it."

As he finished these words, a noise interrupted Nono. Little Laurette was crying. Nono said no more. The poor beast remained open-mouthed failing to understand anything.

"Well now!" said Fumeron. "What's the matter? . . . What! . . . she's crying! And what next! . . . ha! ha! . . . "

"Leave her in peace," sneered Flon-Flon. "If we look at her she'll think she's interesting."

Then all those around the table shouted: "Yes! Enough! Nono! . . . send her to bed, and let her not bother us!"

"Do you hear?" cried Fumeron. "You confounded Renardinette! . . . To the kennel! Go to bed! . . . "

The child stood up, and sobbed bitterly. . . . Suddenly, she rushed at the man who was insulting her. The attack was so sudden that Fumeron was thrust back on his chair. The little girl struck him with the convulsive rage of a child; and the man, taken by surprise, protected himself awkwardly with his elbow.

"Hey there! you rotten little beast! . . . "

The other winegrowers rose, and seized Laurette, who was struggling to get away. Now she cast ferocious glances at her father; silently, she called him terrible names. In the midst of this uproar, Fumeron got on his feet and struck the child down with a blow.

"Why, the cursed beast sprained my thumb!"

He howled as he showed his thumb. Laurette calmed

down at once, and the drunkards pushed her into the bedroom and shut the door.

They had hardly sat down again, when the mountaineer rose: "I'm going," said he quietly.

The others looked at him with amazed faces: "Well, here's a fine customer for you!" cried Flon-Flon. "Now that his paunch is full, he goes away!"

"I ——" and the stranger blurted out a very vulgar expression.

"Great heavens! don't get angry!"

"Look at this now!"

"Does the company displease you?"

"Oh! it hardly pleases me," the man replied.

He was ready to withstand all of them. His legs were not very steady, but he was a strapping fellow. He had a square face and hard, strong features, tight lips and little hollow eyes, stubborn and pensive.

"Ah! you're like all the mountaineers: a lot of difficult creatures who always have something to find fault with! . . . "

"I don't know about that! . . . I can't find fault with everything. There's a good little child here; but her father is a damned idiot. I'm going. So-long!"

"Ah! . . . " muttered Nono who seemed to wake up. He arose noisily. But the man was already on the staircase. Nono followed him: "Hey! look here! Hey there! . . . "

. . . The mountaineer waited for him quietly in the middle of the street. Nono ran up to him.

"Hey there! I don't know if I caught what you

said. . . . But I'd like to have you repeat what you
said about me. . . . "

"What?"

"A while ago you let slip a word I don't like. . . .
You ate my sausage and drank my wine; and then
you insulted me by way of thanks! Understand me
now! I don't reproach you for what you've had, but
for what you've said."

"I won't recant nothing."

"Listen, then, my chum! . . . I'm not more of a
coward than any other man. . . . If it suits you, we
can start at once."

"Oh! I'm game. You're a big fellow. . . . So am
I. . . . Go ahead! . . . "

The mountaineer took off the muffler that he had
wrapped round his neck. Nono, his face in the air
and his nose puckered up, was unbuttoning the collar
of his shirt with both hands. Both men were alone
in the street. The air was soft and the night was
clear. Now and then could be heard from the nearby
houses the laughter of children and the bustle of feast-
ing; the rays from the merry windows brightened the
whitish road. In the sky, amid the dark abyss, a pale
moon reposed in a soft vale of white clouds.

"Are you ready?" said Nono.

"Yes. Here I am! . . . Only a moment ago you
weren't in such a hurry!"

"When do you mean?"

"When they insulted your good little girl, and you
said nothing."

"Oh yes!" Nono reflected. "Yes indeed! Well, let me tell you that I don't care much about fighting with you. It's very queer. Only, you know, I'm not a coward!"

"Yes, I think so. And you're perhaps not so bad."

"Yes! What you say is indeed true!"

"You're the least rotten of the whole gang."

"Yes! . . . that's also quite true! . . . "

"Oh! you're a poor fellow, that's all. . . . "

"Well then! . . . Mountaineer! . . . That, too, is right! . . . Yes, I'm a poor fellow. . . . One of the unhappiest hereabouts."

"Really!"

"Do you know of my misfortune?"

"No."

"My wife has gone off ten months ago with a neighbor, and left me a little one. I weep when I'm alone. . . . I laugh before the others. . . . It's just rending my heart to pieces."

"That's possible."

"That's possible! . . . That's possible! Why, I'm telling you so."

"It's because you want it so."

"Ah! perhaps. My fate is doing it."

"Oh! It lies with you to be almost happy, for you've a very good little girl. . . . Oh! I wouldn't give a damn for that wretch, for she hasn't even pity for her suffering little one."

"Look here! . . . Man! Tell me exactly with what you can reproach me. . . . I don't care whether you talk in the tongue of the mountain or in the dialect of the plain, but talk like a Christian. . . . "

"I saw in your house what I hadn't seen in fifty years, whether on the mountain or here below on the plain: a gang of sods insulting and beating a good little girl; and a blockhead of a father letting 'em do it. . . . "

"Yes! . . . That's so! . . . Enough! . . . Don't bang away as if you were deaf, I've got enough. . . . Now I'm sober. . . . Mountaineer! . . . Listen! . . . Well, I don't deserve entirely your reproach; but what you've said was right. . . . Are you going, after all? . . . "

"Yes."

"I say! I go sometimes to the mountain for a cart-load of wood. . . . What is your village?"

"Ternant."

"Ah! You're of Ternant! . . . Oh! I know it. . . . I've brought wine enough there. . . . But what is your name? . . . "

"I'm a Thevenin."

"A Thevenin! . . . Where is your house? One moment! Is it the upper part of the village?"

"I don't remain in the village. I'm in the woods. I'm a woodcutter. You'll find me: I'm in the Government woods. I must go: I have still to cross the mountain and the fields. Good-bye! Farewell!"

"Hey! . . . Farewell!"

Nono remained in the middle of the street, and watched the stranger till he disappeared.

"What's the address of the customer? . . . A tim-
beryard in the Government woods! . . . One hundred
thousand acres of forests! . . . "

There was no sound in the street save the low
murmur of the water in the fountain nearby. . . .
Nono was reflecting. . . . The cold air had made him
feel much better. The bright moonlight heightened
his spirits. The arrows that the pure stars of crystal-
like clarity launched, penetrated Nono. He raised his
eyes towards those glances that no distance can tire, that
the infinite cannot overcome, which are here below,
to all those of the night, a constant light and call. . . .

. . . Finally, Nono entered his house.

CHAPTER IV

THE sudden departure of the mountaineer had stupefied the winegrowers.

"Well, that's a customer for you!" murmured Flon-Flon, who was looking towards the door distrustfully.

"But where does that creature come from?" asked one of the two winegrowers of the Rue Haute. "Did you notice when he joined our party?"

"No," answered Flon-Flon, "but you know . . . that's one of the tricks of a mountaineer. When he sees a party of friends celebrating, he often sneaks in, and makes himself one of the party without being asked to join. . . . "

"That's quite true!" Briquet affirmed energetically. "On Thursday you must be on the lookout. . . . It's court day, and they come down in packs; for a week doesn't pass without their having some dispute. . . . They fight hard before the judge, and then they drink together. . . . But we have to pay for it! . . . "

"As for me," said Grêlé rolling a cigarette, "the mountaineer doesn't bother me: he makes me laugh! Saturdays, I watch them pass by when they go to the market, to Dijon, with their laden carts. The outfit contains everything: wine in bottles and casks, beets, straw, vegetables, and an egg-basket, a sack of potatoes, and besides, to make the load full, one or

two sacks of coal. Those bandits turn everything to
account! With their bits of ground, their wretched
stables, their poultry and their bits of forest . . . they
exploit their rocky land full of box-trees, worse than
pirates! . . . Besides, they can get cash out of
stones. . . . "

"And he certainly has his way of filling up his
paunch!" added the crabbed Briquet. "He himself,
chooses the house. . . . He comes round just as it
strikes half past eleven and places his big carcass in
front of the door. It's just as if by chance that the
housewife is setting the table, for the fellow hears
from afar the clinking of the plates. . . . The poor
woman looks annoyed at the sight of this being ap-
pearing from underground. . . . She sees the trick at
once; someone is coming to eat her food. . . . And
he, too, pretends to be annoyed. . . . 'Ah! . . . ' he
says, raising his face that's as graceful as a stump.
. . . And a moment later, he is seated at a corner
of the table, and digs into the plate as if he was
breaking up a field! From one end of the table to
the other, he stretches out his arm and has his pick
of the dishes and meats."

"But that serves us right! . . . Why must we buy
wood from those blackguards?" interrupted Flon-Flon,
who had been a timber cutter in Le Pays-Bas and
who was preaching for his master. "They're all timber merchants. . . . But what merchants! . . . Look
at 'em on September first, when they all come tumbling
down the mountain, to go to Dijon at the timber sale.

Seven or eight of 'em crowd together in one cart. Ah! you can see those carts laden with blue blouses, felt caps, and snouts raised in the air that are as friendly as pruning-bills. . . . They chew upon their buying for months; and the entire mountain doesn't sleep for a week, but they spend their time in calculating their knavish prices of thieves. . . . You're robbed when you buy from the mountaineers. My boss, who's a true man of Le Pays-Bas and who's very cheap told me so. . . . "

"Ah yes! Go right on!" exclaimed Grêlé. "He seemed to be outraged, but it was only to boost his friends. Who of you ever saw a man of Le Pays-Bas who was cheap? . . . Old chap, you flung this at us without even any warning! . . . "

"Le Pays-Bas!" howled Briquet. . . "they're all blackguards! . . . "

The little fellow was on his feet. Pale and drunk with wine, he gesticulated, talking like a prosecutor who uses his eloquence against the accused.

"Listen, friends! . . . There aren't no worse people than those of Le Pays-Bas! . . . But let me talk. . . . By heavens! I've much to say on that matter. . . . They made me writhe enough during harvest time. The man of the plain is a boaster, a bawler and a thief. . . . He always robs you, wild pigs and old seeds! . . . When we sell him wine: he never pays for it! . . . If you buy a cow from him: it croaks! . . . You marry his daughter: she's a harlot! . . . Ah! what base creatures! . . . "

"Oh! cursed Briquet!" shouted Grêlé. "Enough!
. . . He's gone! hold him back! . . . There isn't a
more terrible creature than that little fellow! . . .
Once he's at work, he can fell the whole of France!
. . ."

. . . The company laughed heartily when Nono
entered.

Nono had hardly opened the door when Grêlé
shouted to him: "Hey! Nono! . . . Where do you
come from? You've a fiendish look. . . . Have you
been tampering with a petticoat? . . . "

"Well, friends! . . . " said Nono quietly, standing
at the threshhold of the door and rubbing his head
with his cap. "I see you want to start me off again;
but it's too late. To-morrow morning I've some dung
to carry off. . . . You've drunk all the wine . . .
eaten all the sausage. Well, you've nothing else to
do here. Go home, let me go to bed and let's remain
good friends. . . . "

"Here's another customer for you!" howled Briquet,
still standing and ready for another speech. "Here's
a rotten cuckold whom we're trying to amuse, and
who, by way of thanks, is kicking us out! . . . "

"Ah! little Briquet!" replied Nono in a brisk tone.
"Your talk is too insolent for a lean little creature
like you! . . . Eh? . . . What's that? . . . When I
see long ears like yours, I'm very eager to pull 'em."

Nono took hold of one of Briquet's ears, and pulled
it briskly without much ado. Briquet lowered his

head, looked at Nono from head to foot with round anxious eyes.

"Well, little Briquet! why do you look at me so with your little squirrel eyes? Don't be so terrified! You're rotten! . . . But you're a poor creature, sallow, a mere weakling, frail as a leaf. You've a right, then, to be wicked. . . . Besides, your wife is a very good woman. . . . Go home in peace! . . . Poor worm of this cursed earth, creep into your mud! . . . Only, this is a bad place for you. Don't you ever come back again! . . . "

Briquet escaped sideways. . . . He remained standing with a sheepish look, his arms hanging at his sides, his head sunk between his shoulders, rolling his bewildered eyes. . . . They all laughed and jeered at him: "Hey there! . . . Briquet! What's the matter? What have you seen? . . . You look as if you had escaped from a trap! . . . "

"You must have little courage, indeed, to stand for that!" blustered Fumeron, brushing his huge mustache with the back of his hand. "Fancy me letting such an idiot pull my ears!"

He had hardly finished his sentence, when a powerful blow almost felled him. He straightened up, seized a chair by the back and turned it up as if to throw it; he stamped and yelled: "If I didn't hold myself back! . . . by heavens! . . . If I didn't hold myself back!"

"Hey! . . . Hold yourself back, I say!" said Nono peacefully. "My old man has often told me: 'The

man who restrains himself has a certificate for a long
life in his bag.' "

But the whole pack of winegrowers were in fine
spirits. Flon-Flon, a Flon-Flon as amiable as possible,
approached Nono very gently: "Well, old chum! . . .
You've a mighty good fist! . . . "

"Get out, you foul beast, shut up! . . . Look here,
friends! . . . You must go, even if you don't care to."

"Ah! confounded Nono!" replied Flon-Flon.
"We're going. . . . But you must come and have a
drink with us. . . . If you won't come, we'll think
you don't like our company. . . . "

"Well! . . . Listen, friends! . . . I'm going to
talk openly to you. . . . Your company is agreeable;
and yet it doesn't exactly please me. . . . You can
think whatever you like! . . . I've nothing against
you, and I don't look down on you. . . . But I say
things in my own way. . . . Only, look here! . . .
I'm not going to continue this business of drinking
and doing nothing. . . . I've no income like Flon-
Flon. . . . He's inherited his father's money. He's
but to dig into his chests: that's his hardest work.
We, on the contrary, must sweat for every sou. . . .
And at the death of his brother, the knave was happy:
his five franc pieces doubled. . . . But I must buy
vine-props, sulphide, and I've no wine in my cellar.
. . . I haven't a sou. My wretched wife has left me;
but that's no reason for me to abandon in turn the
shanty and the little one, who's a good little girl. I
warn you, therefore, that from to-day on, I'll stick

to my work: the tilling of the soil. . . . Know then!
This is a last farewell I'm giving you. . . . I've suffered: you diverted me, and I've done likewise. . . .
We'll each go our way: you all together in your way,
and I in mine, quite alone, happy, without a murmur! . . . "

"Come now, Nono!"

"Nono, old chum! . . . Come!"

"Old chap! . . . "

"Now that's enough! . . . Behave yourselves!
Come now! Off with you! . . . "

"Look here! . . . Nono!" said Flon-Flon in an
easy-going friendly voice. "Come and have the last
drink with us! . . . Come! . . . And then you'll
leave us. . . . "

"Well, all right! . . . I'll go."

But at the door of the café, Nono changed his
mind: "Ah! . . . Excuse me! . . . I'll be with you
in a minute; I left the trap-door of the cellar open."

In reality he was walking back towards his house,
not to close his cellar, but he was impelled by an inner
feeling, an awakening of tenderness in his soul and
body.

. . . There was a dim light in the window of his
little house. Nono did not dare walk up. He stopped
at the foot of the stairs and heard Laurette's footsteps: she was replacing the dishes and setting the
room in order.

With a heavy heart, he went out and sat down on

a low wall several paces from the house. He saw the window open, and the little one sweeping. At times the shadow of the child stretched across the road, in the space of yellow light which came from the window. The little girl, herself, then appeared and shook her broom on the balustrade of the balcony.

"Well, a girl of twenty couldn't do any better! . . . And she's only eleven! . . . Ah! here's one who's happy here below! . . . Poor child! . . . Ah! how I've acted to-night! . . . Didn't I say I'd kick her out later? . . . And yet you're working, little darling! . . . My child! . . . My dear one! . . . Your big brute isn't worth much, eh? . . . "

Thus was Nono talking to himself. But the light of the little house was soon extinguished, and Nono was alone in the night, surrounded by a profound stillness.

The moon filled with its beams the world of space, and adorned the earth with a bright gleam. The glowing night was azure tinged with rose; there was also almost a feeling of spring in the atmosphere. The moist glitter of the stars filled the night, too, and, their shafts like pure rays of fire, shot through limpid space.

Suddenly the sound of a bell rose in the night. It was a thin, shrill sound, befitting a poor country church-bell. The midnight mass began at Brochon. Nono was familiar with the tinkle of this old bell-tower standing out above the vines. He had often

enough imitated that shrill, distinct tinkling. And suddenly the bell-tower of Gevrey in turn awoke; but
soon all the belfries of the plain and of La Côte
mingled their ringing far and near. Then, when the
ringing had started everywhere, all the sounds joined
and produced one continuous peal, a tender and powerful murmur of bronze which shook the solid ground,
and moved the deep night.

Nono is thinking of his forsaken daughter, of the
young child deprived of tenderness, who is sleeping
now, guarded by eyes that are all-powerful and unknown. . . . And in the heart of this unhappy man,
a sentiment is born to lift him above nature and
death! . . . Is there someone who is the master of
the infinite and of silence . . . whose ears hear the
imperceptible murmur of every conscience here below
. . . of those who fall . . . of those who meekly seek
their way?

CHAPTER V

THE following morning at the eleven o'clock meal, Nono had much to say to his daughter: "Darling! . . . I didn't know my own good-fortune. . . . A companion like you . . . why, what can be better? My little friend, my pretty darling . . . we're going to try not to make each other wretched. . . . Only, to do that I must stop drinking. But I've some good ideas upon that head. . . . Do you know? to-day I'm going to help you clean up, and then we'll go for a walk together."

Just as they were about to leave, it occurred to Nono that Laurette was badly dressed. They looked in the wardrobe; Nono threw about some pieces of bright-colored cloth, waists and ribbons. . . . And from all these things there escaped a delicate perfume, a scent of lavender and faded lace . . . and something still more subtle. . . . It was not so much a delicate perfume: it was a reminiscence that remained with the things and in the air: an almost palpable reminiscence of the fingers and hands, and of the young face . . . and of his former love . . . and of days gone by.

. . . At last they found what they wanted: a long cape with a hood of plaited cloth. Clad in this, the child had the smiling, oldish appearance of a grand-

mother.   Her father put on an air of great gayety:
"Oh! ha! ha! . . . Oh! great heavens! . . . What an
old grandmother! . . . Oh! . . . there's granny Mi-
taine! . . . "

They left the house, and descended towards the
plain along the Crais Road.   That was the road that
Nono usually followed.   On this narrow, stony path,
which ran from the mountain down to the plain, Nono,
from his early youth, had not stopped descending and
climbing, going and coming incessantly to the work
of the fields, with the same gait mornings and evenings. . . .

Under the bright, warm sun, Nono and his daughter
were walking along slowly.   Nono pointed out to
Laurette the unpropped vines, some still covered with
the autumn green, others raked up by the crude digging of winter, which tears the soil up in big clods.

"Do you know, little one? . . . Well! we'll see to
it in spring, believe me!   The vines dressed in winter
will be much easier to dig. . . . They'll have the soil
fresh, the leaves green and the grapes sound. . . . The
others, if a good frost doesn't mellow them, will re-
quire mighty hard work. . . . And no matter how
madly we toil, it'll be of no use; there'll be wanting
that healthy and bright air. . . . . "

Laurette raised towards her father her thin, happy
face.   Beneath her black hood, one could see her little
golden forehead and the cheekbones that the cold air
brightened.

"Hey! . . . Little one! . . . you're happy . . . eh? . . . And me! . . . This is my first happy moment in a long while indeed! . . . Just to look at your pure eyes makes me happy. They're pure enough to plant water-cress in. But . . . child! . . . that's only a way of talking. . . . Ah! but look at the beautiful fields! . . . That's what gives more pleasure than everything else! . . . "

They had gone beyond the vineyards, and around them there was now a stretch of fields already green. Everywhere the grain was springing up on the long and narrow bare fields; for in spite of the December cold, their courageous life had continued: they coped with the severe winter.

"Darling! . . . Doesn't this view affect you? . . . As for me, it's my great pleasure. . . . "

When they had reached the crossroads leading to the Deux-Rentes, the father and daughter stopped.

"Perhaps we've gone far enough? . . . Aren't your little legs tired? . . . "

She shook her head.

"Now look here, can't you talk? . . . You wasn't that way at one time, eh? . . . I keep on talking and you never say a word! What's the matter? Tell me frankly: your father handled you too rough, eh? Don't be afraid: It's no more the big brute who's with you."

A shadow appeared suddenly and covered the green fields with a dull hue. In the middle of the glade lay Saint-Philibert with the steeple of the village lifting

in the center; bare stretches of land, black plowed
fields, and green wheat fields, rolled up on all sides.
The plain was filled with a shapeless mass of trees.
The melancholy approaching night stole over those distant dead masses.

"Look! Do you see, little one, that poor belfry
which rises above the woods, hardly bigger than a
needle? . . . It's Epernay. Your great-grandfather,
the father of my old man, came from there. He
worked the iron of those forests. . . . There are still
holes under all those thickets. . . . But they have disappeared. . . . Do you see the Broindon Castle, a
little farther? It's almost hidden by the mist. . . .
Little one, I know all those regions like the palm of
my hand. Yonder, in the mist, above the ponds, are
the Saulons; and very far off—but it can hardly be
seen—that's Noiron, the soil is very good there; then
there's Corcelles. . . . Tavonges, where I went to
balls and ran after the women. . . . And then still
farther, why, that's the very end of our little corner
upon earth; for that's the real forest of Citeaux. . . .
We'd like to push forward there anyhow; we'd reach,
after having crossed some woods, the countrysides of
the Saone, where there are meadows and large water-
ing-places. . . . But all that is too far away; it's no
longer ours!"

Beyond the forests, there rose some clouded stretches
of land, dim barren hills, crowning slopes that disappeared in a vague dotted line. . . .

"Well, Laurette! . . . Here is one of my great

pleasures. Ah! here's a corner I like to look at! . . .
Believe me, Le Pays-Bas is beautiful; one's happier
here than on La Côte.   Here, we've cattle, fields,
forests and water. I like it. My old man often said
to me: 'Seek your friend on the mountain! . . .
Plant your vines on La Côte! . . . Build your house
in Le Pays-Bas! . . . ' For that's the country of our
forefathers.   We've relatives in all these villages.
Even as far as Onges and Citeaux there ain't a village,
where smoke can be seen, where there ain't people
related to us. . . . As far back as the old folks can
remember there were Jacquelinets in the glades and
forests of these parts. . . . We're from here! . . .
My old man often took me for a walk thereabouts
where you see the night coming. . . . In those low-
lands, where the fog is rising, you can't walk a hundred
paces without finding a field on which one of our
forefathers didn't toil. . . . There were shepherds,
cowherds, woodmen, charcoal-burners. My old man
knew their names rather far back. . . . But I've forgotten 'em! . . . Yet look here, little one! . . . that
don't stop my heart from being with 'em in the peace
their poor souls enjoy. . . . Ah! they deserve well
their rest. . . . They've toiled hard, if the proverb has
it right: 'The Jacquelinets have made the plain.' That
would mean it's them who've dug the wells, stocked
the ponds, cut the forests and made fields out of thorn-
bushes. Everything before our eyes now is the work
of their hard toil and courage. They're dead now.
The dear bones are at rest. . . . But it's us who're

undergoing the test. . . . And it's mighty hard at the present hour! . . . "

Nono sat down on a flat stone which filled the hollow where the road of the Deux-Rentes crosses that of the Crais. . . . A sudden sadness had slid deep into his heart. . . . He recalled having passed by that very crossing, and having already spoken thus. . . . It was on that glorious day when, sitting beside his sweetheart, his lips were still fresh from the first kisses. . . . In front of him the entire Pays-Bas was in full bloom, and like the vast forests and sacred nature, his heart was overflowing with love.

But while Nono drooped his head under the weight of sorrow, a little hand softly placed itself in his like a bird that lies down in its nest. Nono awoke from his dream. . . . He is not alone in the gray mist of the night: there is someone beside him—exactly as at that time—but it's no longer the same being. . . . At that time, the being was taller, darker, more sprightly; its life was as violent as that of a young eagle. . . . But now it is a child! . . . It is a little darling! . . . And Nono feels spring up again in his withered heart a sentiment which is no longer like his former love, but which is something more reassuring and more tender. . . .

"Little father! . . . " murmured Laurette.

"My child! . . . " whispered Nono.

And he pressed his daughter close to his bosom.

Nono's good resolutions did not last very long, how-

ever. Indeed, the wretched days of sadness and indifference had ended; Nono still remained a gay and
loving father to his daughter; but he continued none
the less to get drunk.

"Oh! that don't matter: I drink only grape brandy
and good wine; no more absinth. With that you last
a long time! . . . It makes you trot a bit sideways,
but it pushes you on a long way along the path of
life. Perhaps it'd be better that I shouldn't drink;
but there's nothing more wretched than having a slop-
ing throat, and mine is so damned steep that the wine
rushes down as if from a precipice! . . . "

At night, after supper, Nono always had a good
pretext for going out to gossip and drink with someone
or other. On coming home, if the little girl was not
yet asleep, he would indulge in long, queer speeches:

"Ah! Laurette! I was happy and I clinked with a
merry heart. . . . But I see you want to hand me
out some nonsense . . . tell me perhaps that all that'll
hardly add to the money of the house. . . . But what
do you want? I must live; and that's how things are
now! . . . Everything is dear; besides, I'm lazy and,
to make things worse, I'm a drunkard! . . . What's
to be done? Ah! in bygone days the winegrower was
more thrifty. With his few rows of vines and his
bit of field, he had enough of everything: wine, corn
and vegetables. He owned a cow, a pig, a mule, a
goat and chickens and rabbits: all these animals were
well stabled in warm sheds. And his house was his
own, too. It was a little hovel, just a mere nook;

but there was happiness within even to the very
shingles of the roof. They never bought anything: the
animal and the soil yielded all that was necessary.
Why, not so long ago, some twenty years or so, every
winegrower had his own cow. . . . In the morning,
the cowherd drove towards the mountain a herd of
forty or fifty beasts. In the evening, the cow returned
to the winegrower's stable and yielded whole pots of
rich, creamy milk. To-day, we buy milk, eggs, bacon
—everything. The housewife of to-day would em-
broider rather than milk a cow. And she needs heaps
of things. She enters a shop and buys a mere trifle:
a lady wraps it up in tissue paper . . . and that's five
francs! . . . But in winter you often don't make so
much in a week! . . . "

CHAPTER VI

ONE night, Nono was brought home hopelessly drunk, with a foot out of joint. Two friends were dragging him up the stairs: below, Grêlé was holding in open arms, Nono's legs; above, Piémontais was pulling at the shoulders. This new friend of Nono's was a little fellow, vehement and loud, with sandy mustache. He explained with exasperation how it all happened, while little Laurette, at the head of the stairs, was holding a lamp in hand and sobbing:

"Don't yell at us little one! . . . Nono didn't drink. . . . He's overcome with fear. He wagered to fight with a bear at a fair. The owner was willing: he let the bear loose; but the bear . . . no. She was frightened and hid under the tables of the café. But Nono also had his share of fright. When the beast was unchained, he didn't say a word, but his snout was more terrifying than the bear's. And then the wine went to his head, and on his way home he tumbled down the cellar and sprained his foot. It's the bear's fault, the dirty beast! . . . Damned monster! . . . "

They put Nono as well as might be in the big bed of the room. Nono let them do with him as they pleased, dropping his head at every movement, as inert as a bundle. He only half got up to wipe, very unconcernedly, his long filthy nose on Piémontais' hand. The latter cried: "You dirty Prussian! . . . Now he's blowing his nose on my hand! . . . "

Nono's accident was not serious; but his drunkenness hit him hard. Only after two days of rest did he regain his normal state; then his eyes were once more awake, fresh and gay. For several days everything surprised him; he seemed to have come from an artless world. He looked smilingly at his daughter who busied herself with the housework; her naïve activity was such that Nono had enough to follow and love her steps and gestures. He did not cease contemplating the brisk little girl, admiring her neat work, which finally made the modest house look pleasant and comfortable.

Ah! she was a true daughter of this Côte d'Or! . . . What a light and marvelous land, what a rose-colored, sunny soil, wherefrom the feminine race has sprung with the fine, vibrant elegance of the shapely vine! . . . Those sprightly women . . . they are the soul of the winegrower's house! . . . They are the spirit of order and life in this countryside! . . . They are the salvation of these soulless regions, where man is gradually returning to the grim darkness of the barbarous ages.

But they, too, must find their duty at home. They must make the home bright and clean, so that even the dead walls will beam with grace and happiness. . . . Only then does their loving, active, agile life become really significant.

Nono's smile gradually disappeared, however. A grim sadness came upon him slowly, and spread over his heart like a great darkness which spreads over the sky. No one could have divined exactly what thoughts arose in the sacred life of his soul, behind those little, pensive eyes; but one night, when little Laurette had gone to bed early, Nono limped over to his neighbor, Catherine, and told her of his sorrows.

The fat woman, sitting near her fireplace, wore merely an underjacket. She displayed unconcernedly her large red neck and her powerful, ruddy chest.

" . . . Ah! my poor fellow!" said she, "you can truly say you've a good daughter! . . . If it's only for that, if it's only for having given you that little one . . . you ought to bless your wife! . . . "

"Oh! . . . bless!" replied Nono placidly, "that's asking too much. Let's leave that to the priests. It's their business to dig in the air. And every time they raise their paws in the air—it's five francs! They get something for it! I have to pay. Let others bless my wife! . . .

"But that's not the question, Catherine. . . . These three weeks that I'm unable to go out I've seen things! . . . I've watched the little martyr at every moment of the day! She's only as big as a shovel and she's already dying of misery! She's frail and delicate as a leaf, and she's constantly hopping about on her little legs! . . . And she fills me up with grub till my belly is full, and I have nothing to do but sleep. . . . How can that little being stand it all? And this has been

going on for more than a year! Ever since there's no
mother in the house, the beds have been made and
the meals ready for me. And I never wondered who's
doing it all. . . . And where does she get all those
delicacies? Catherine, there are days when there's
chicken, eggs and cream; not a day passes by without
a bit of fresh meat! . . . Where does it all come
from? Who pays for it? . . . The money of the
house? . . . The savings I put at the bottom of beer
mugs and wine jugs? . . .

"Ah! the poor little one thinks I can't guess it, when
she makes up an excuse to go out. . . . She says she's
going to church, for a walk, or to your house. . . .
Poor child! . . . I'm sure she goes out to do little
jobs, don't she? Ah! look at her: she's only that
high, and she only has skin and bones! . . . That's
what I've been doing while I was blinded by my sorrow! . . . This little martyr who was feeding me
. . . who still trembled in my presence three weeks
ago . . . that's my daughter, my Laurette, my little
blonde darling! . . . "

"Look here, Nono! Don't let yourself go in that
way! Yes, I know: your heart's been burdened for
a long time with bitter sorrow! . . . "

"You can well say so, Catherine: it's bitter sorrow."

"These tears had to come; they've been kept back
a long time—since Nénette left, eh?"

"Yes, you're right. . . . Oh! I wasn't made for
such an affliction! . . . With one blow I was robbed
of my only hope, my only love in the world! . . . And

that left me a degraded man! . . . And I still suffer
from it every moment of the day! Ah! shame is something that can be eaten cold, and which never satisfies
hunger. . . . When once you're put to this bitter food,
you must eat of it constantly, till your teeth are used
up and you croak! . . .

"Oh! Catherine! It hasn't killed me, but it's done
worse! . . . You'll say I should've remained erect and
faced it like a man. But what can you do when you're
felled? . . . I've crouched down like a coward. . . .
I've turned to drink; I've become the butt of the
village. . . . That's bereft me of all: my spirit, my
ideas, my love, and of the little common sense of a
winegrower I had. And yet, Catherine, don't you think
it's partly my fault?"

"Ah! what misery! the poor unhappy child! . . . "

"But what do you think? It's not the daughter;
I'm talking of the mother. . . . "

"I know. I know."

"Well, do you pity her? You're perhaps right.
. . . "

Nono said no more. Both neighbors were looking
in silence at the red flames of the fireplace. They were
reflecting without saying a word. At last, Nono spoke
in that sharp, brisk tone with which he dissimulated
his sorrow.

"Catherine, there are days when I pity her too. It's
stupid, but it's true. . . . That creature destroyed my
life. She brought upon me ruin, despair . . . worse
than fire and death! Well, think as you like; but I

don't curse her; at least not enough; not as I ought
to if I had a bit of courage! . . . "

"Oh! poor children! I saw you both very unhappy!
. . . "

"What did you see? . . . Tell me? . . . "

"Oh! What shall I say? . . . Oh! the poor victim!
. . . "

"The poor victim, you say? And what about me!
What am I if that harlot is a victim? . . . "

"Come, Nono! don't use such words! . . . Besides,
you're saying it against your will. Don't be afraid of
being a good Christian, for we're alone and nobody
will laugh. And she . . . she's perhaps dead by now.
. . . "

"Ah! that's possible. . . . By heavens! perhaps
she's indeed dead. . . . And we're talking of her as
of a being alive and brisk; perhaps she ain't more
than a poor buried creature! . . . And we want her
to square accounts! Anyhow, it ain't my fault."

"Ah! If she had been let alone, she wouldn't have
left on her own account. But she had no peace! You
should've defended her, my friend, not thrust her
aside; kept her near you without being rough. . . .
And then you should've seen things clearly! . . . "

"Yes, I see what you mean. . . . It's my stupidity
that forced her to leave. . . . I didn't know of her
doings. I was the idiot a woman leaves; the cuckold
who's so thick that a woman don't even care to be
unfaithful to him. . . .

"Go on! ain't that so?"

"I didn't say so."

"You didn't say so; but you thought so. Oh! I know it, believe me! . . . The entire village talks like that, and you can't get one over on me! . . . But look here, Catherine! . . . Do you see the bright flames of the fire, there, in front of us? Well, as certain as we're here alone in the night, so certain is it that I had of my wife, of her sins, of that fate which was hanging over both of us, a knowledge as clear as this rising flame! . . . I thought my heart would break! . . . I've borne on my shoulders a heavy cross of misery. The unfortunate can raise their cross so that people can see and help 'em; but I bore it hidden away on my naked skin! . . . I've played the fool while my heart was bleeding quietly like a broken fountain which loses its water. . . . Ah! my love was like a poisoned water, a water almost more cursed than that of the spring of Ensonge which drips dry on the height of our cemetery and waters our dead! . . . Look at me, Catherine! You never saw me so. Look at these trembling hands. . . .

"I said to myself: 'If I look as if I know the truth, I must do one of two things: kick her out or leave. But one is like the other; I'd lose all my happiness upon earth. I can't do it.' You understand: I didn't want to pass for a man without honor; nor did I want to lose the terrible happiness of having her near my eyes . . . not far from my heart. . . . Since I couldn't be stronger, or a coward, I had to play the fool, the idiot who sees nothing, who has sand in

his eyes. . . . And how I acted my part! That woman
scorned me all the more! 'Blockhead!' she called me
when she left. She didn't see clearly into my soul.
. . . She left with bitter contempt for me. Did I
really deserve it? . . .

"Never, upon earth, will the being I loved tell me
the truth which will raise my spirits a bit. She'll ever
see me such as I seemed to her, a very low creature!
. . . And yet, it wasn't through taste and nature that
I had sunk so low; but I remained there with indignation, out of pure sacrifice, with a shuddering heart!
. . . Ah yes! I might've done something else; but for
that I would have had to be young with the spirit
and grace of a happy lover, and I was but a poor
winegrower wornout with work. . . . The last morning, on waking up, I found that same Nénette kneeling
at the foot of my bed. Her face was pale, as if
covered with the dust of the earth and the ashes of
penitence. She raised towards me her dark, tender
eyes. And what've I done: I threw the sheet over her!
. . . Well, I've thrown the shroud over a corpse! . . .

"What can you expect? . . . The heart-felt words
of despair hadn't come! And then, I soon saw that
I was alone in this world. Everybody jeered at me.
I became, then, a wretched beast and a vile drunkard:
you mustn't blame me for it! . . . You're crying,
Catherine! . . . You mustn't cry; at least, not on my
account. . . . But where is she . . . she . . . the
poor child as you said a while ago? . . .

"Ah! the unhappy woman! What have the men

made of her? Oh! those blackguards! . . . They
haven't done her much good! A man don't look wicked
perhaps; but he's rotten to the core. He jokes and
laughs with you; he clinks with you in the café; he
becomes big-hearted, tender and a good fellow. . . .
And behind all that gentleness and gayety, there's a
being that's worse than a jackal, who would devour
the dead if they were good to eat and not full of
earth! . . .

"Ah! when he looks about him, it ain't a road or
light he's seeking; but, trembling with rage, he's seeking a helpless victim to attack. However, he's often
afraid and dares not; then, he crouches in a cowardly
little corner and rages with envy, or else he revenges
himself with his sneering mockery. . . . Seemingly,
he's the king of good fellows; but he's a coward who
secretly never stops hating. His soul is full of
murders impossible to commit, thefts too difficult to
carry out, inward hatred and powerless evil. . . . His
heart, his love and his faith are all full of this gall,
venom and rancor! . . . Catherine! . . . They've
carried off my helpmate! . . . But where? . . . "

"There's no news, my poor fellow."

"None at all?"

"No."

"And yet Renardin had written here. . . . "

"About eight months ago he wrote; but it was to
sell his property."

"Yes, I know."

"And now that everything is sold, what's left of

his money? Undoubtedly nothing. Besides, when he left everything was already mortgaged and spent. . . ."

"Ah! the money is nothing. . . . But what did he do with her? Look here! I'll tell you something, but don't laugh. . . . I think she's thinking of us. . . . Do you know, Catherine? I'm sure her gaze cuts through the dark night and comes towards us, towards this house beneath the spreading vines, towards this stone bench under the rose-bush. . . . There's where we loved so tenderly in the evening. Her arm was around my neck, her little hand held on to my coat; and I pressed her against my bosom, caressing her gently like a little bird. . . . She was such a little darling . . . so frail in everything! . . . I felt her tremble over a trifle. . . . And now, at this very moment, the little one is perhaps alone amidst the terrors of this world! . . . Her young terrified heart is perhaps ever trembling. . . . Oh! what misery!

" . . . But if some good idea should strike her! . . . that she should come! . . . Let her come back quickly! . . . If the little one and me, on coming home, should find her one evening sitting on the bench under the rose-bush! . . . Well, we surely wouldn't leave her there. . . . "

CHAPTER VII

FROM that time forward a truly pleasant and peaceful life began once more for them. The father and child agreed not to leave each other any more. In the morning, Nono went to his vines, while the little one did her housework. In the afternoon, they walked down together towards the fields of the plain and the little garden of the Marais. Most of the good folks of the country were glad to see the long, light, flat cart pass by, going along slowly on the road of the Crais across the vines, where Nono and his daughter, sitting near each other like an old peaceful couple, smiled to all comers and looked at everything. Around them was now spring with its gay awaking of the early bees, or autumn with its dim sky and last crimson beauties of the year. Even winter had a charm with its roads reddened by a cold sun. . . .

Sitting next to each other, the father and child savored the very delight of living. And it seemed to Nono that he had never really loved. Near the child with her soul still uncontaminated, the soul of Nono regained its artlessness, its naïve and great-hearted kindness. By dint of talking to each other, they finally came to understand things in the same manner, as if they were of the same age. They spoke the same

language, using simple, wholesome words, simple and
wholesome like the grass of the fields. But underneath these insufficient words, there vibrated the limpid
and eternal sentiments, which are the air and sky to
the souls of beings.

In the Marais, while her father was tilling the soil,
Laurette gathered food for the rabbits; or she picked
fresh vegetables, shelled the peas, or dried the beans.
Often, too, she would sit on the side of the ditch or
on the flat part of the cart and read her school books.
When Nono was tired he would come and sit down
beside her; and then she would read aloud. The read-
ing being over, Nono would make the following
reflections:

"Well, my Laurette, is your story finished? . . .
It's a little sad; but there's a reason. And this sadness
quite agrees with us. . . . While listening to you, my
child, I thought of many things; and now I feel better
than ever I did. I said to myself· 'The universe with
its countries and peoples is as peaceful as this glade
of the Marais and the eyes of my good child.' But
that's a comparison taken from on high with the daring eyes of charity: For it's of no avail to take a
close view. It's like this village of Gevrey! . . . Look
at it, yonder, at the foot of the hill, lying among the
vines, below the brushwood and the forest, with all
its chimneys inclining! . . . You'd imagine on seeing
it from afar, a pure nook of nature where men dwell
tenderly in peace. Well! you only have to poke your

nose into that dwelling and that peace, and you're bitten worse than in a nest of hornets! . . . "

"Ah! Papa! . . . " said the child wtih a shy smile. "Did my story teach you this fine lesson? . . . Well, teach me something in turn! . . . "

"Yes, my child! . . . Look here! I'm going to teach you a very good thing. There's something fine in the air, my little girl. Do you see the little green buds which are opening on the branches of this hazel tree? Do you see the little yellow pussies that are hanging from the branches of the willow? Do you see yonder the beautiful chestnut color of the woods? The leaves ain't far off; spring is coming."

"Spring? . . . Papa! . . . "

"Oh! You can't think otherwise. No matter who'd feel this west wind coming from the mountain, light as a slow friendly step, no matter who'd feel it would say: 'Tis the lovely season that's coming! . . . ' "

At times Nono can hardly hear, but a beloved voice aids his gaze and soothes his dream. . . . His eyes are fixed in front of him; he perceives those forests, gloomy in the deep silence, the pensive depths of the horizon, the last gray stubble, the dark plowed lands, the glossy plains where the green corn glitters, and afar off the peaceful undulating hills beneath the clouded sky of March. . . . To the west, he perceives the mountain, cutting through the sky from north to south, setting up along the west its rugged wall whence unfolds, from the sky to the plain, the old winding

roads upon which men journey. And Nono lets his
soul wander on the road where man wends his way,
in the distance, farther than the poplars aligned along
the Mansouse, farther than the silvery willows of
Boise. . . . And Nono's love burgeons like the wide
expanse where beings breathe, and where life quivers.
. . .

"Little one! . . . The world is large! . . . My old
man who had been in Africa hadn't seen all yet."

"Africa? . . . Did grandfather see Africa?"

"Little one, he went through the whole of Africa
pursuing the Kabyls. 'I've found nothing worth speaking about,' he'd say. And he was right; for indeed
there ain't a country without good people and fertile
land about 'em."

"Father, where's the good land here?"

"My child, it's difficult to say. If, by good land
you mean the yielding of vegetables, corn or fodder,
no land is better than Le Pays-Bas; but La Côte is
the true ornament of France! It alone has really the
right to the vine; for the vine don't agree with every
soil. In the land of the mountaineer, you must be
as cunning as he to have dared to use the vine. But
you'll say that Le Pays-Bas plants even between its
ponds. . . . Ah! it's base! . . . "

"Well, papa, are you glad to be a winegrower?
. . . "

"Ah! little one! . . . There's much to say on that
matter. On the Côte, the land is good, but life ain't
worth much, and winegrowing ain't worth nothing at

all. First of all, the work ain't honest: it's wild and
brutal. And then the vine is nervous. Ah! it ain't
got the good-will nor the submission of good land.
. . . The vine blooms there where it pleases, very
often crosswise, and yields fruit also when it likes!
It freezes for no reason at all; and dies without anyone knowing why! If it's smoked, it's burnt! If you
don't smoke it, it gets the green sickness! Dress it
two days too late, and the day's gone by for this
headstrong vine! Three days of too much rain, and
the wine has a foul taste! Three days too little, and
the taste is dry! The wretched thing even has luxuri-
ous diseases. It has a worse collection than a good
hospital. . . . If it'd only be gone in a decent way,
and frankly, we'd be through with it! we'd plant wheat
and raise cattle! . . . But no! . . . It must ruin us
first! Ah! it's knavish!

" . . . And we winegrowers, just see how we live
in hovels! . . . And the owners of the vineyards
shout: 'Dig ditches. . . . ' But there's more certainty
in the fields. The work is agreeable and peaceful.
. . . "

"Papa! . . . " asked Laurette, "when are we going
to see the mountains? . . . "

"Ah! that's right! my Laurette! . . . There's a
mountaineer to whom we must pay a visit. I'll take
you there some day, with the mule and cart. Once
we pass the rocks, you'll see a fine country, somewhat
rugged. . . . But we've been gossiping for more than

an hour. That's what you really call resting at four
o'clock."

"Nono," said Catherine, one day, "now your
Laurette will soon be fourteen. . . . Aren't you thinking of having her learn some trade?"

"Ah!" replied Nono, scratching his head with his
cap. "Ah! you're quite right! . . . I'm thinking of
it. . . . I often say to myself that she's too frail to
struggle with the soil, for the soil wears a person
out pretty quickly. Meantime, I let things go, because
her company gives me new courage and I find everything good and beautiful upon earth. . . . But that
won't make her earn her bread. You're right! She's
too delicate to till the soil. . . . But she must have
some trade. Now what is she going to say about
the matter?"

"Indeed, it's she who spoke to me of it. She knows
she must have a trade, but she didn't dare to talk to
you about it. She has some notion: she has a liking
for sewing. . . . "

"Well, she'll indeed make a good dressmaker! But
you arrange it with her, because it's out of my line.
I can drive the mule, bring provisions, handle the vats.
. . . As to the affairs of women, I hardly know anything about 'em."

The apprenticeship of Laurette lasted three years.
After this she·found that she was a grown-up young
lady. Her years had not passed in vain; she was in

full bloom, as lovely as a lily. In the afternoon, when
her housework was done and when the young girls
had dressed up, she would walk through the streets
clad in a gray skirt with two flounces, an apron with
embroidered flowers, a white waist and a velvet bow
in her hair. She takes big steps and feels embarrassed
and coquettish. At times, with a decided and haughty
movement she raises her thin face with its pensive
bold eyes; at other times, having become timid again,
she lowers her head sideways and seems to watch her
deliberate steps. . . . But she is very delicate. . . .
Her heavy blond hair, apparently, is the only thing
about her that shows vigor. She is annoyed when
people look at her; her head turns away with nervous
grace. . . . Her bright, sharp face, whose cheeks are
like wild little apples, seems ever ready to flee. . . .
But each one who gazes on these modest eyebrows,
this charming round forehead and these blue eyes,
divines the soul of the maiden singing like a rippling
spring—a spring that is pure, without sand or cress,
warbling like a bird—the mirror of the light and love
of a wide sky! . . .

Sometimes, however, when at home, sitting near the
window, Laurette stops sewing. . . . She bends her
slender body; she droops her beautiful blond head;
her soft eyes open wide and gaze on nothing, and seem
to reach to some unknown region. . . . Like a peasant
woman, but gracefully, Laurette rests her closed,
veined hands on her patent-leather belt. Thus bent
and attentive, one would say that she is listening to

some call—the strange and soft call of an unknown voice! . . . It is then that, like an unworthy passer-by who defiles the spring where the birds drank, love—and artless love, shattered by iniquity and falsehood, comes to thrust its poison into the loyal destiny.

CHAPTER VIII

A GLOOM has spread over Nono's house. . . . Since
the end of July, he has not seen his daughter smile.
In vain would he at times say to her:

"My child! . . . my dear child! I don't want to
know your secret. . . . No, my little darling! . . . If
someone is forsaking you, let him do it: your father
will never forsake you! . . . "

To that plea, as to every other one, Laurette makes
no reply. Her look is gloomy. The pale little face
terrifies the father, and he remains speechless. . . .
He is waiting for the hour to come when she will
speak comforting words that pardon and soothe.

. . . And now the grapes-gathering is over, and
the grapes are already in the vats. . . . The wine
press is in Nono's yard, and the winegrowers must
have their habitual feast: the indispensable jugged
rabbit, the roast leg of mutton and the raw sausage.
"Let's take good care of our folks," said Nono. "A
peasant's saffron-cake is no feast for a gamekeeper!"

Laurette is also doing her share. In order to be
able to help at the wine press, she has installed her
kitchen in a simple, small room in the yard, which,
in spite of its window and shutters, is only used as a
general storeroom.

The stamping in the vats has filled already two-

thirds of the casks; the wine-press will furnish the
pressed wine.   It is an old, heavy apparatus with a
horizontal screw which lengthens or shortens the frame
according to the amount of grapes to be pressed.   Nono
did not have a great quantity; his vines hardly yielded
six large casks; he, therefore, needed comparatively
little help.   It is customary, however, for neighbors
to assist one another; and it often happens that friends
at odds forget their differences and join in the vintage
festival.   Flon-Flon, Briquet and Flammêche did not
fail, in consequence, to make their appearance.   The
past few years have made Flon-Flon still more flushed
and stout; Briquet, on the other hand, has become
darker and more withered.

"Come now, friends! . . . the place is ready: bring
the planks!" cries Nono, standing in the frame, among
the boards red like those of a guillotine.   In order not
to delay the going and coming of the men, Laurette
takes the planks and hands them to her father.   Nono
takes them and places them so as to level the mass of
grapes and stems which is rising under his feet.   But
now and then Nono is somewhat late, and Laurette,
waiting for her father to take the plank from her
hands, remains holding it in the air.   The frail young
girl bends under the weight; her raised arms make
her waist rise beneath the arm-pits.

On seeing this young body bending backwards, thus
displaying its full grace, a vulgar notion crosses Flon-
Flon's mind. . . . "Flon-Flon! . . . not a bad fellow," people say, "but a banterer at everything."   He

approaches the young girl, in his boorish fashion, and pats her heartily like an old friend: "Well, curly-headed beauty! . . . When will the recruit arrive? . . . "

. . . The scene was quickly over. Laurette, startled by this sudden attack, drops her plank which falls into the frame. Flon-Flon, frightened, sees her shudder and grow pale; all the grim sorrow heaped up in her heart these last three months rises and chokes her. . . . She can barely run to the kitchen and shut herself up. But behind the closed shutters, the window remaining open, one can hear her sob bitterly.

. . . Nono springs up, his arms dangling at his side, and turns his long bewildered face in every direction: "Come! Laurette! what's the matter? . . . What's the matter? . . . Laurette? . . . "

His friends do not need much more to arouse their gayety. . . . There they are, splitting their sides with laughter in front of Nono, who watches them, with furious eyes, roll on the ground with joy.

For a long time this was one of the standing jokes of the region; for many years the exclamation of agony uttered by the father was to remain one of the insinuating phrases of La Côte; and there was not a prank played without someone adding slyly, to encourage laughter: "Come! what's the matter. . . Laurette! . . . " But this is the embellished story: as a matter of fact, the incident was not as farcical as tradition would have it, for those who laugh at Nono to his face do not laugh long.

"Look here! . . . Are you through? Do you want a blow, Briquet, to help you split your sides? . . . And you too, the rest of you? That's enough! . . . "

And Nono, standing in his dark long apron, hard as sheetiron, rose in the frame of the press like a tall black devil. But his serious, hard face had nothing burlesque about it: they all became silent and suddenly pretended to be busy, for they all knew the man. Nono was no dupe this time. Standing as erect as possible, his body emerging vigorous from behind the parapet of red scales, he shouted:

"You pack of blackguards! . . . You ain't men, nor beasts, you're worse than death! . . . You ain't bold enough to play the part of Satan! . . . You've a liking for the job, but your blood is too cowardly! . . . Poor, little, trembling knave . . . dirty cowards . . . you daren't hardly laugh with ease but at the despair of an old man and a child! . . . Look here! Damn you! You laughed at me heartily at one time! My despair at being a betrayed husband made your sides split! . . . I let that pass. But this time I'm going to protect my child! You'll be as dumb and peaceful as a sheaf of corn or I'll make your fiendish blood and your wretched souls ferment in the mud. . . . You understand, don't you? . . . Yes? . . . All right then! . . . And now, a little more heart! . . . Let's fill up the frame, hurry there! . . . "

The three men hurried without saying a word, and started once more to carry the planks. Nono soon filled the frame of the press; now he only had to cover the top, and then support it with cross-pieces.

"Here we are, friends!" said Nono as he forced down with a blow of the hammer the last iron wedge. "The frame has its full load; let's push the wheel now."

However, standing on the platform of the press, Nono put his hand to his forehead and raised his head. He uttered a feeble cry of distress: "Ah! poor little one."

Behind the shutters, the sobbing gradually grew fainter: "Ah! my poor little child! I've guessed almost everything a long time ago. I didn't dare say a word. I didn't dare take her in my arms, kiss her, or rock her. But let her know that she'll not be abandoned. There's someone near her who's to her at the same time a father and a mother, and who's ready, if it must be so, to be a good grandfather too. . . . I still love her, I'm still sorry for having been unkind to her, I'm still thankful to her for her kindness. . . . I've a great respect for her, and her misfortune of to-day can't change anything. . . . Ah! I want her to hear my voice behind the shutters! Listen, she ain't crying now! Does my child hear me?"

And turning towards the vintners who were waiting somewhat embarrassed: "Look here! Once I hurt her face with a blow of the fist. It was on a mad night. That's my crime. But what has she done? She had faith in another being! . . . What a pity! . . . But get to it, friends. Come on, push ahead, eh?"

From the platform, Nono set the wheel agoing with much vigor, and it forced the screw down with a loud squeak. Then, when it started to press the planks down, the four men seized the pegs of the wheel; the eight arms thrust in all directions and pulled at it. The huge blood-red press soon forced the planks down, and the wine began to stream into the vat with the murmur of a large spring.

When the work is done, the vintners have nothing else to do but to cross their hands under their bibs. As they were thus sitting and resting, Flon-Flon walked over to Nono and in an embarrassed but gay and cordial voice said:

"I said some stupid things a while ago without meaning any harm. I don't want you to be unhappy. Your daughter is a good girl."

"I understand. You're a goodhearted fellow, I know it. You see now that it's wrong to jeer at these poor girls who're with child. My poor Laurette didn't even dare go out to buy sugar or bread. Ah! she was suffering much, and you just added a bit. What wrong has she done? Where's the crime? She's a victim, and she can remain in the house: She'll remain honest, and if the child comes I'll support it."

"Ah! in certain houses of the bourgeois and in the castles of the nobility they'd surely be very much embarrassed if the young lady was secretly with child. But we can't make a great fuss, crush the unfortunate with the air of merciless bigots, and repeat that honor exists only among people with large incomes! Us poor devils are too poor to be hypocrites. . . . And then, why be frightened? Because a little one is budding? . . . We're upset as if one dear to us were going to die! But it's just the opposite; I accept it willingly.

"Ah! he's come without the mayor having had his say. . . . But I don't like to listen to that crank: he married me, like a heartless creature between two thrusts of the spade, and of what use was it? . . . The curé didn't have his say? Perhaps his master on high, the father of all the innocent, has had more to say about it, and not in gibberish Latin. That's how it is, I tell you. . . . But let's take two or three more turns at the wheel."

When that was done, Briquet decided to give his opinion on the matter.

"You're no doubt right, Nono; but if the fellow wanted to marry, perhaps you ought to consider it. For you know that the curés don't like to baptize bastards nor are they eager to administer the communion, nor marry 'em."

"Well! the curés won't put it down on their registers, that's all! . . . Why worry about their scribbling? The Eternal Father don't agree with 'em in the final reckoning. Why, they're cheating Him. Besides, when the curés have brayed 'Magnificat,' they think they've done their share."

But Flon-Flon, who was sorry, wanted to say something serious: "Yes, all that is true, but when one works for somebody else, it's a bother to have a bastard child."

"That's right. I know that there are bourgeois houses who've already refused my daughter work. But the bourgeois of to-day are a fine lot! . . . "

"To be sure!" exclaimed Briquet vehemently. "We ain't become a Republic for nothing. What can indeed be done with those pigs? They walk through the streets well done up with healthy faces, and fresh, red lips. They hold their curved noses out and their drawn-in chins over their collars; they walk on their toes hardly touching the ground with their heels; and they look as if they hated to tread on the same soil with us. The women are still worse. They're different goods—they're powdered, polished, varnished and done up to their spleens: they look so sugary and affected that they hardly dare walk, see and hear. Everything disgusts 'em: the road, the air and the sun. . . . I wonder how they dare eat the same bread we eat, and do things like all other mortals."

"The old folks," said the sad Nono quietly, "were better than that. I've known some with beards, good fellows, who sat peacefully in their gigs with pipes in their mouths. In fact, everything I see now displeases me. I've become spiteful, and I'm disgusted with many a man—with 'em, with you, with myself, with everybody. But with my daughter . . . with my Laurette. . . . Oh no! . . . never!"

CHAPTER IX

ELEVEN months later, one afternoon in August, Nono was watering his little garden in the back of the yard, when a tall mountaineer appeared.

"Ah! it's you, mountaineer?" said Nono calmly.

"Yes."

"We haven't seen you in a long time."

"I was in prison."

"Ah! . . . Why?"

"I was caught in the Collonges woods."

"Ah! you poach? That's all right. That's the kind of prison that only dishonors the government."

"You're watering the spinach seed-beds?"

"I'm watering the seed-beds, and I'm watering the flowers."

"The flowers?"

"Yes. . . . I'm going to transplant 'em on a grave."

"Ah! . . . "

"But I've finished. We're going to have our four o'clock bite."

When the two men were at the table and they had started to eat the sausage, Nono said: "Mountaineer! My daughter liked you very much. She knew that you played your part in her life. You used to

169

sell her the charcoal. . . . You won't sell her any more. You looked for her a while ago. . . . You won't find her."

The mountaineer did not answer. He held the sausage in his hand, and he cut a piece off with his knife.

"Yes, my friend, a great misfortune has befallen me."

And Nono began to tell his sad story.

"But before the occasion of bitter sorrow, this little one was for me a great joy. Because of her, I blessed life, a life, which has only brought me misfortune. Ah! our happiness was destroyed when she took to sewing. The poor child wasn't strong, and I was afraid that the work of the soil would be too hard for her frail and graceful body. Ah! the soil is wretched and knavish: you must strike at it hard before you can get anything out of it. I, therefore, had her placed as an apprentice with Mlle. Gaudry, who is homely but of good character and clever at her work. To-day, she's married to a mountaineer by the name of Dabain of B'evy. This girl taught our Laurette very well; at seventeen she worked for people by the day or did sewing at home. But it's hard work, no matter what they say; for my Laurette killed her chest by being always bent over her needle and thread.

"Ah! no suffering and no shame was spared that little being! You can guess the story. In the midst of the gay harvest season, I had suddenly noticed that she had changed very much. Of that dear and beautiful girl, there remained only a pale face and ashy-gray eyes. Oh! it didn't take me long to understand the mystery. I wanted to talk tenderly to her; but I couldn't find nothing to say, nothing to soothe a downtrodden soul.

"One day, however, while making wine, my bitterness provoked me and forced me to speak in the best way I could. But what can you say and do, when you see a village of five hundred hearths delight in the misfortune of a girl? The entire region was wrangling for the death of my daughter! Each of their jeering smiles made my child take another step to her grave! In this struggle against a wicked world, I wasn't the strongest. She didn't even dare go out for milk. She would wait for the night, the darkness that hides what is shameful. Besides, she lost her work; the bourgeois sent her away, and the winegrowers laughed at her.

"After the child was born, she fell sick. Indeed, she only rose from her childbed to lie down again on her deathbed. She had some relief for a few weeks, however. Poor Laurette attended, then, to her duties as mother. She seemed to have forgotten her regard for other people. She would feed her darling baby in anybody's presence.

"At times I'd take her with me to breathe the fresh air of the fields. But she'd already become so delicate, so thin! . . . Ah! I wasn't at all easy on looking at those shining eyes, gazing at I know not what. She hardly ever spoke to me. She just answered me.

Why, she seemed to keep all her love for her child. Sometimes she'd raise her eyes towards me as if to say: 'I'm forgetting you, father.' And I'd answer stupidly perhaps: 'Yes, my child, do it!'

"When she'd nurse her baby, she'd shake her head with nervous movements of despair; and she didn't take her eyes off the little darling, almost lost in the blanket, who'd hold, with tiny fingers, her breast. With her fingertips, as delicate as blades of grass, Laurette'd squeeze her breast so tenderly that it seemed to give at once all the milk and all the love of the mother. On seeing this, my broken heart only brought tears to my eyes; and I'd go to the garret and weep bitterly.

"I've told you that she cared no more about people; but they tried very hard to win her attention, and would always look slyly at her. She didn't mind it. On her pale face, tired of this world, there was an expression that terrified me. You could read on it the terrible resignation to everything, to life as well as to death.

"One afternoon in April, she went with me to breathe the air and see the sun for the last time. We went down in the mule's gig. 'Come, my little dar-ling,' I said to her. 'The April sun won't hurt you.' Alas! it hurt her as much as possible. On our way back she spat blood on the dust of the road.

"My Laurette was, to see no more the fields and the sun. We took her baby away from her breast. The doctor had threatened to do it, but didn't. Then

one day he said: 'No more!' The neighbors took care
of the baby, then they came to look after my daughter.
The work of the vineyards was at its height, but I
remained near my child as much as possible. On June
23rd, I was obliged to be out all afternoon; on coming
home in the evening I found the doctor near my
daughter. I was very much surprised when he told
me she wouldn't pull through the night. She was very
sick. In her delirium she called for her mother. Suddenly, she looked at us, seeking among us. And then,
she—so quiet, so resigned—began to shout vehemently
and insult us. She wanted something that was impossible, my friend! . . .

" . . . Ah! I feel better when I talk to you. My
child is dead eight weeks, and this is the first time
I've spoken of her at length. To whom can I speak?
. . . My friend of the mountain, you see before you
a strong man. People weep much upon earth; few
wipe the sweat off their foreheads with their fingers.
This is the sweat of the soul. These tears do me
no good. It seems to me that the longer I live the
harder is my sorrow. It's sinking into me and
burning my inner being. Listen, let it last till my
death! Let me die quick with my grief still keen. But
what, ain't there the baby? When the neighbors will
wean her, who'll take care of her . . . if I ain't here
no more?"

Nono was silent. He sat and thought with his body
leaning forward, his elbow on his knee and his hand

over his eyes. The mountaineer closed his knife with a sharp click, and Nono raised his head.

"Have you eaten as much as you want of the sausage?

"Well, you must drink another glass, and here's to you! . . . "

"Ah! my friend!" said Nono putting down his glass. "It ain't easy to do your duty in this world. But how far did I get in my sad story? Ah! I was telling you of that terrible night! Well, an idea occurred to me. I ran to Piémontais, and I told him quick what he must do, what I expected of him . . . the sad comedy we had to play. We had to give the little one her last consolation on earth: make her believe that her mother was still alive and was coming to see her. I come home and wait. I don't wait a long time. My man comes in; but on seeing the little one on her bed he began to cry and moan. . . . He wept bitterly because he saw my poor child leaving this world. . . . 'Yes!' he cried at last. 'I met Nénette in the streets of Dijon! She was well; by heavens! even fat. . . . She was looking at a show-window of pipes when I met her. . . . She asked about you, little one. I told her that you were a little sick, but getting better. . . . Well, she's coming to see you to-morrow morning. To-morrow morning, by heavens! with the coach of La Côte! . . . " Poor Laurette, with her eyes wide open, stared at him with her very soul, drawing in great agony from that direction her last breath, as if he had brought her life. She asked:

"'Mamma! . . . where is she? . . . Tell me quickly!'

"Why, at Dijon.'

"'In what part?'

"'In what part? . . . Yes, that's right . . . in what part? . . . Well, she's at the Porte d'Ouche. Besides, I've been there: street, number. . . . I know everything. I would bring you there with my eyes closed. . . . '

"'Ah! . . . ' sighed my dying darling. 'Ah! what good news! Oh! yes! . . . To-morrow, then? . . . To-morrow morning, be sure it's not in the evening, eh? . . . '

"And then she added, after gasping for breath: 'I'll be gone then.'

"Hearing this, Piémontais at once ran to the staircase and disappeared. Then Catherine tried to save the situation: 'Don't prepare anything, Nono. I'll make Nénette's bed to-morrow. . . . I'll bring the linen and the mattress. . . . She'll sleep here, in her daughter's room. . . . '

"Laurette moved her head on her pillow from left to right. She seemed to say no. But what did she exactly mean? . . . I don't know. The dear couldn't speak. She gasped for air, and kept pulling at the sheet. Then, I told them all to leave, for I wanted to remain alone with my daughter during the last few moments of her life. She was suffering and moaning.

I bent my head and wept. Hearing no noise, I looked at her and saw her dear blond head motionless, and her two eyes riveted on me; they were big and wide open, with an understanding of life which terrified me! . . . She stretched out her arms to me. . . . 'Raise me a little, little father,' she said. I raised her somewhat on her pillow. 'Hold me, little father! . . . That's right. . . . Let me look at you a last time.' She put her limp arms on my shoulders and her face was near mine.

" 'Papa! . . . I'm causing you much sorrow, ain't I? . . . But I don't do it on purpose. My papa . . . you loved me a great deal. My soul is going away full of your love.'

"Oh! it's true then, my Laurette? . . . You want to leave me? . . . What's going to become of me all alone? . . .

" 'Poor papa! . . . I'm going away through my shame, do you see? . . . '

"Through shame? little victim! . . . Oh no! . . . The angels of heaven are calling you! . . .

" 'Oh! I don't know!' she said shaking her head in doubt and crying . . . yes . . . crying. Oh! what terrible tears to see! . . .

"Dear little angel! . . . Ah! what a sad life you've had! You've had few happy days and little luck! . . .

" 'Oh no! I wasn't lucky. . . . ' And she added in a soft voice, her head falling sideways on her shoulder. 'Oh no! not lucky, not at all! . . . '

"Yes, my poor child: no luck and no happiness.

" 'Who's going to love you now, little father? Oh! how good of you! . . . That man who came to speak to me of my mother! . . . You wanted to let me depart with that hope! . . . Thanks! little father! . . . for you called that man. . . . ' I had no more courage. . . . I couldn't deny it longer. . . . I motioned yes.

" 'Yes! I knew it,' she continued in her poor soft voice. 'But one day, it'll be true, my papa. Mamma'll come back. Let her find forgiveness . . . open arms! You'll talk to her of me, won't you?'

"These were the words of my daughter. She was exhausted and I laid her down. I covered her shoulders with the sheet. She looked as if asleep. She even seemed to breathe more quietly. . . . That lasted a while. I even wondered if a miracle wouldn't happen before my eyes. Suddenly she got up and threw the sheet back. 'Ah yes!' she cried. And she sprang out of bed. I ran to her, and she was already sitting on the edge of the bed. Oh! what a terrible look in her eyes: it wasn't life or death but worse!

" 'I want to go there,' she cried.

" 'Where,' my child?

" 'To Dijon, to mamma. Oh! I know where! I know! . . . I'm going there! . . . Let me! . . . ' I held her back; she pushed me away with great force.

" 'Well, my child, we'll go there. . . . But wait a moment. . . . "

" 'No. Let me! . . . . . . I'm going there. . . . '

" "But it's dark, my child! . . . It's the middle of the night. ·ı œ ıɔ.'

" 'Night? . . No! . . . It's a lie . . . a lie! . . . ' she shouted, but so loud that no human voice could be more piercing! . . .

" 'A lie! . . . Yes. . . . Everything you tell me is a lie! . . . Oh! . . . ' Here she calms herself a little and looks at me. 'Oh! Jean! . ;. . My dear love! . . . My Jeannot! . . . little Jeannot! . . . Oh! what did you make of me? . . . What did you do?'

" 'My child . ̤ . it's me! It's your father!' She looks at me and recognizes me. And quietly she tells me: 'Papa, I'm going to mamma.' And I answer: 'Yes, my child, we're going together, in the gig; there's just time to hitch up the mule and we depart. . . . '

" 'Hurry.'

" 'Yes. But lie down for a while. . . . That's right. I'm going down to hitch up.'

"Then I pretended to go out. But I stopped at the door. I listened. . . . I heard no noise. . . . I come back to the bed. . . . I saw at once that I couldn't take my child on the stony roads of this earth, but must wait like a Christian for God's moment, and close her poor eyes."

CHAPTER X

"Ain't you got a little brandy to drink?" said the mountaineer, who was smoking his short pipe.

Nono awoke from his dream: "Why, sure! . . . Poor friend! By heavens! I keep on dreaming and I leave you here with nothing more to drink, and without even offering you a dram! . . . Let's drink it quickly."

And when they had swallowed the brandy, Nono continued: "Yes my friend, I've had a sad spring. But we'll have a good wine harvest. The vintages of '96 and '97 were bad; but the '98'll be good."

"You've indeed had a great deal of sorrow," said the mountaineer; "you ought to be righted in some way."

"Ah! mountaineer! You know, I can't believe that this'll be the end of the love between my daughter and me. I'll tell you something that you'll no doubt think strange: I wasn't in despair when I followed my daughter's coffin. And while I was taking my child to the grave, I looked at the sun, the fields, and the vines. . . . It seemed to me they were the ornaments of the just. No, I think my daughter hasn't utterly disappeared; but there's near me a dear shadow. . . . I think that after death the soul comes to the beings

179

who've lived through it. . . . But what can I tell you?
My words can't explain what I feel."

Saying this, Nono raised his eyes and lifted his arms
somewhat, as if he wished to grasp in the air the
incomprehensible words of the great mystery. Alas!
many others have raised towards them useless hands
and ineffectual arms, ever since the day that man
first here below came stooping and seeking.

"Another would say; I don't know. But let it never
happen to you that you put your child in her shroud.
She wasn't very heavy; about half a hundred weight!
. . . That's what twenty-one years of life had left of
her. She only asked to pass through the paths of life
and of this world like others, smiling and working;
but the first steps were already cut off. . . . Look
here! I'm not a weakling; I'm rather a brutal fellow.
But when I covered forever the face of my child,
I rose saying with all my heart: 'I hand her over
to someone more powerful and more just than men.'
Don't you think so?"

"Oh! you know I'm a man of the woods, and I
can cut my trees well enough; but of these things I
know very little. . . . "

"All right. But look here, if there ain't a supreme
God who looks after our dead children when they can
no more love us, there ain't no use living, unless it be
to plant potatoes and dress the vines. . . . And yet,
how uncertain 'tis! . . . The last terrible words of
my daughter! . . . The look of doubt she had! . . .
Ah! what can we say? What can we think? People

say, the world is large. Not enough, since there 'd be
nowhere the true rest of the living, or even of the
dead. For theirs 'd be the same as that of the stone
or rock which has never loved! . . . "

"Oh! . . . If you've done your duty, you've nothing against yourself, and don't bother too much about
the rest."

"My duty! . . . To be sure, I think I've done it.
My old man used to tell me at times queer things.
They were never very clear; but after a great deal
of round about talk concerning the life of former
postmen, he always ended by telling me that I was
a fool. And yet my old man was wrong. After all,
I'm richer than him. At times I stop and look back
at my poor panting life with its two loves, the one
destroyed by dishonor and the other by death. . . .
Well, I'd almost say! 'I ain't sorry for nothing!' At
certain moments I feel he's very near me. And when
he reaches my heart, I no longer despair and say to
myself: 'My Laurette is in good hands.' Besides, I
can well say that I've the tranquil soul of an honest
man. I suffer indeed; but we're here to suffer. We
must always suffer somewhere, whether it be in this
world or the other. Suffering is everywhere, it awaits
us on all sides."

The peaceful assurance that Nono did not always
find in his heart came to him from elsewhere. To
calm a troubled soul, there is nothing more effective
than the inexpressive smile of a poor baby. Nono's

happiest moments were, indeed, when the neighbors brought him his little Catherine, asleep in her swaddling clothes. The good woman, who was her godmother, also acted as her mother. It was understood that later on, when the infant should have been weaned, Nono would take her back in his charge.

"I've had a great misfortune in losing my daughter," said Nono. "But something worse might've happened to me: I might've remained alone upon earth; as it is, when my daughter was gone I had only to bend over her little old cradle and find another one, who put her tiny fingers in my face and pulled at my mustache."

Nono worked courageously at his vines and small fields. By dint of always living out of doors, he was gradually won back by the peaceful silence of the fields. It is not in vain that nature spreads before man from the plain to the mountain her immense seasons. . . . In his little garden of the Marais, Nono found once more all the sweetness of former autumns. But it was especially in the mowing that Nono's heart gladdened, when the sun rose bright and smiled upon nature, when the woods had the glowing purity of a fresh morning. Nono slept very little, and at times he would even come to his fields at daybreak, when, beneath the osiers and willows, the troubled vapors of the still waters rise. They sway without lifting from the earth, like the vague light of a dream. Their feet of white satin walk among the reeds and wild mint.

. . . In the early part of October, heavy rains suddenly began to fall; and as soon as they had ceased, the mists appeared with their drooping masses. The plowmen then began their sowing. The naked soil, flattened by the roller, was already waiting for the time when the young corn would sprout; a little farther, the dark plowed lands still lay in even rows. Man was everywhere; one saw him in the distance scarcely moving along the fields. The willows, the osiers and the green slopes spread along the ditches at the bottom of which the rising waters flowed. In the forest the work of winter began; the woodcutter attacked the woods with his ax, and, near him, the charcoal-seller built in silence.

But for Nono is also come this melancholy wind of autumn, which severs the leaves and strips the branches. Before the dying forests and the bare soil, Nono, with his head in his hands was sitting and dreaming. His little red eyes look up towards the clouded expanse, towards the timeless distance where the roads of men have their origin. He looks back on his past: the veil rises and the numberless days of the bygone years which have weighed him down in silence pass before him. Like the thin mist which rose from the ditch, all the phantoms of former days come forth. They continue to rise from the eternal earth, their arms full of caresses . . . flowers of a past spring, the love of a former day.

And now the winter has come with its pitiful gloom, and its frost covering the roads. But the joys and hardships of the seasons, which pass over a soil that dies, do not matter to Nono. His primitive soul has risen to the heights where alone there is light. Solitary at home, in the deep silence of the long evenings, he listens in peace: he listens attentively without despair, and yet there is no other noise but that of the wind in the dry branches and on the pointed roofs. But he is not listening to the wind without. It is his torn and tender soul which yearns toward the unknown wind, to that merciful breath which is ever present, which moves us more and more here below, and which gradually invites to itself the living and the dead.

. . . Only those hear it who have the soul of Nono . . . those who gently raise their heads above the lowly sorrow of this world and listen in peace . . . those who in life await death.

PART III

CHAPTER I

SEVERAL years have elapsed. . . .

On a rainy afternoon of last September, the wine-growers of the neighborhood were sitting and talking at a table in the Café Caillot.

"What are we going to have now?"

"Well, as Nono says: a good absinth with a golden edge."

"Nono is a good sot now."

"There ain't a worse one: he's never sober."

"Ah! Nono! a jolly fellow, always in good spirits. Well, I like him better like that than the way he was eight years ago, after the death of his daughter. Why, he wasn't a man: he was a preacher. He'd poison us with stories which smelt of the candle and the preaching at a cemetery. . . . "

"Ah! . . . " said Grêlé in his hoarse, weakened voice, "I can still see this Nono, on an April morning, preaching to me in the open field: 'We ain't the sons of the sand and the rocks. . . . We're the children of Heaven. . . . ' And he shook his finger under my nose, holding out to me his long face of an old Pater-

noster. . . . But friends, look! there's our customer!
. . . "

Sitting near the window, the big good-for-nothing
raised a corner of the curtain:

"Yes! . . . He comes right on top of us. . . . He's
full! We'll have a good laugh!"

"None of your jokes, eh?" cried Briquet. "You
know him: when he's drunk, you must let him blab,
otherwise he gets angry, and fells you with a blow
of his cap, for he keeps the fist inside. Mind you
now, eh?"

The door opened; Nono entered slowly, holding out
his long, bewildered face. The entire pack yelped in
chorus:

"Here's Nicolas! . . . Hurrah! Here's Nicolas!
. . . Nono! . . . Old pal! . . . Old pal!"

Nono listened, still standing with his hand behind
him on the knob of the door. It was still the old
Nono, but with deeper wrinkles, gray hair and a hag-
gard look.

"Well, you pack of knaves! you're gay! You gang
of drunkards! you drink like choristers, and yet you
sing false."

"Ah! oh! . . . here you already have his compli-
ments! . . . Nono, what'll you have? . . . "

"At once, quickly, a little absinth. Annette, fix it
up nicely: something well stuffed and thick; make it
a good roguish absinth, silky like the bristles of a
pig. Go ahead, Annette! You fat wench, get a move
on you, I'm in a hurry. . . . But just wait a minute,

Annette. . . . My pretty child . . . one question
. . . only one question: Baby mine! how goes it
with your love affairs? . . . No! no! you mustn't
slap. . . . That's how I like a woman, you see!
She must be nice and plump like you—a good
substantial armful. None of your scrawny weeping skeletons for me. The young men are fond
of you, I'll be bound—aren't they now. Confess! . . . Ho there! ho there! . . . No fighting
here! . . . Confound you, don't scratch me, you
little vixen. . . .

"Look here, friends! 'Tis the day for long speeches.
I see you there at your tables, gloomy like the dark
rains, sour like farmers, with wretched little glasses
like the ones they serve in the field—except to the
sentinel! . . . Sentinel, don't fire: there are only
ghosts before you! But ain't there no spirit, nor thirst
among you creatures there! We'll see. We're going
to line up some good bottles; absinth as strong as a
good guard and bitters as lively as a bombardment.
To-day, friends, it's the day of great thirst and long
speeches: I've got crowds to convince, and the baffled
universe will hear us speak of it. But first of all.
. . ."

And Nono stopped and raised his hands as if to
bless. . . .

"How goes it . . . with . . . with your families?"

"Very well, Nono. How's yours?"

"Very well."

"And how's that Catherine? Is she well? And still well-behaved, to be sure?"

"Oh! . . . well-behaved? That's a question. To be truthful, that creature hardly gives me much pleasure. There ain't here a worse shrew. And besides, she ain't easy to handle. She lords it over you all the time:

" 'Nono, do this! . . . Nono, do that! . . . ' And when I tell her sometimes: 'But you who order about others so well, why don't you do something, too?' Well, instead of doing it she runs out in the street like a dogged wretch. I didn't have much satisfaction from that little creature. . . . I didn't think it'd come to this, some time ago."

"Do you know, that it's me who first announced the coming of this little one in the Baraques?"

"That's right," replied Nono.

"And this wag there got after me! Oh! like a real hungry wolf!"

"Yes, you're right there again; I was taken unawares."

"Oh Nono!" said all at the table. "Nono! Nono! It's mean what you've done. Poor Flon-Flon! Nono, find something to cheer him up a bit. . . . "

"I'll tell you what! I'll pay for some good wine. I say so, and I don't go back on my word. We're going to drink a glass to the Republic, and let the entire bourgeois croak!"

This idea made Briquet jump up:

"The Bourgeois! . . . One of these days, we're go-

ing to send 'em to dress the vines in their turn.   It's
been long enough ours.   And that's not all: the land
and the vines must belong to the municipality.   I feel
strong enough to be a State winegrower."

"Ah! upon my faith!" replied Nono placidly, "this
bourgeoisie is a rotten lot.   There ain't a single beast
among 'em who'd hand me a bit of work in winter.
Do you see that! . . . Not one of 'em wants to give
me anything declaring as an excuse that in the last
two or three years I've become too much of a
drunkard."

"Do you see that!" the chorus continued plain-
tively.

"Yes . . . as for them, have they blood red enough
to be good drunkards? They're a disgusted lot. Nothing's good for 'em: neither vines, vintage, nor sun.
They must have water, like a fog. To play the clever
ones, they buy expensive water, mineral water, in
which rocks are steeped. A pack of blackguards! In
the meantime we can't sell our wine! Besides, everything disgusts 'em. They breathe the air as if it was
medicine. And when they eat a good piece of meat,
all juicy, they suck at it between their teeth like
licorice. . . . We'd like to eat meat if we had it. But
we ain't. I haven't eaten meat in four years."

"But what do you do when you kill your pig?"

"Then I eat pork; but pork ain't meat."

"He eats so much of it that he don't eat bread for
two weeks."

"Ah! you can well say that I treat myself to it!

But at other times, when I don't buy any meat, at least I buy some fat. For I'm just as clever as any of you, and I know that vegetables well cooked in fat is better than lean meat. We're often obliged, however, to eat dry bread and imagine that the crumb is the sauce and the crust some dainty game. Seasoned with a good idea like this, the piece of bread becomes a real treat.

"But after the drought of this summer, what are we going to eat this winter? . . . What do you say there, eh? No beans, no cabbage, almost no potatoes; and the little we have is going to dry up, if we have no rain. Ah! it'll be wretched. There'll be wine you say. It's to be seen. But admit it. We have to wait for the vintage. But the wine merchants wait for us too. And now they all sit in automobiles and stare at us, laughing as they see us swallow with great respect their dust and struggle there for famine prices. . . . And we must live a whole year on it! Do what you will: it's twelve months and four seasons you've got to pull through, with a gang of ravenous creatures who watch every mouthful you eat. Besides, there's this pack here, ready to drink everything a man earns. Ah! you'd make fine pigs: you've got big snouts and you don't do a damn thing!"

"And what about you, Nono?"

"Oh! me! I'm worse than all of you, believe me! I'm attacking you, and yet there ain't a bigger blackguard than me in the village. . . . I ain't worth much, I ain't even perhaps worth this miserable Flon-Flon

who's looking at me and laughing. My friends . . .
my poor friends . . . you're laughing! . . . Oh!
don't laugh . . . You've here before you an unhappy
man, a man whose soul is shattered, and on account
of whom there's a wretched woman who's dragging
her sorrow from place to place. . . . Poor little
Nénette! . . . Where is she? Tell me, in Dijon?
They all tell me she's now back in Dijon. I hear it
so often that there must be some truth in it. She's
in Dijon then? . . . Ah! if you've seen her, tell me
whether she's still young . . . whether she still gads
about, singing all the time . . . whether she still has
her childlike voice and eyes. . . . Tell me how she is
exactly. . . .

"The poor child was very nice when one knew how
to handle her. And what did I do, I kicked her out!
That was quickly done: a few hasty words . . . and
then out! The door banged behind her; and at once,
three beautiful lives were torn to pieces: hers . . .
hardly good; mine . . . wretched; that of our child
. . . worse than anything.

"You're laughing to your heart's content! You're
waiting until I get drunk enough to tell you my woes.
That's your great pleasure: to see tears. . . . Well,
look at 'em! . . . Ah! you think I don't guess it? Of
course I do. You think I'm stupid? Stupid. . . . I
am; but not too much. I'm just enough: not too
much, and not too little. Just enough to be an honest
man, and not rob anybody. But you? . . . What are
you, come out with it? . . . Are you Christians? . . .

No! . . . And you're right in saying there ain't no
God, nor an Eternal Soul. And the socialist municipal
committee was quite right in deciding that in a good
Republic, the soul must croak with the rest of the
body. But what will the Eternal Father indeed do
with your souls? It's quite a commodity to keep fresh
for all eternity! Can you see Flon-Flon clad as a
pure spirit in a corner of Paradise, and the knave
answering 'Halleluja' when they ask him the price of
wines! . . . We all live under the same banner of
cruelty and debauchery. After our death, if there's
someone above, among the stars, let's not call him!
. . . If there's an owner of the universe, let him look
after his business! . . . There's nothing to be gained
by showing him the thread of our souls.

"Ah! I haven't always said that. But now, through
being with you, I've reached the very point of disgust
and despair. You're neither men, nor beasts. What
else will you have me tell you? I'm shouting at you
the terrible truth! You're all rotten beggars! And
if one of you budges, I'll break his jaw. . . . Let no
one budge! It's understood, eh? All right. The thing's
done! . . . And I'm going. . . . I'm going. . . . "

CHAPTER II

WHEN Nono had left, there was a hubbub in the café. A one-eyed shepherd, who was drinking alone, exclaimed: "He's great, that customer!"

"That's the man!" asserted Grêlé. "He's of pure juice, no sugar and no mixing!"

Briquet, very drunk, squeaked: "My friends! That was a fine scene. I laughed to my heart's content. But I laughed within."

"A good precaution, friend."

"What do you mean there, you fool?"

But Grêlé continued to roll in silence his eternal cigarette. This calm indifference exasperated the little fellow, grown old and rancorous.

"You big blackguard! You're done for. It's good for you. Spit with blood! . . . spit! . . . You big hop-pole soaked in pig's blood; soon you won't be seen hanging about in the streets squinting with your knavish eyes. You can laugh: You'll soon be with the worms. So go ahead and croak at once."

"Oh! Oh!" exclaimed the shepherd, "the man who was here a while ago was funnier than you."

"You'd soon have enough of him," said Flon-Flon, "for he's always the same idiot and the same blabber."

"That's nothing. I'd like to follow him for a day."

Grêlé, who had lost nothing of his waggish assurance, moistened his cigarette with a brisk movement of the tongue, closed it against his lip and began: "Friend, if you want to follow Nono for a whole day, you must be up before the chickens."

"Before the chickens, but not before the shepherds."

"Before all beasts, chickens and shepherds included, there ain't a morning when Nono ain't up, peering about as early as two o'clock: 'Ah! by heavens! I've let the day come. And to think that I wanted to put up a potful of soup!' Thereupon he opens the shutter and pokes his nose out into the dark night: 'No! The dawn ain't come yet. God's still sifting his grain. But never mind, I'll go down and take a turn in the yard.' "

"In the yard! . . . At that hour! . . . But what can he be doing there?"

"He roams about. He goes and chats with the mule, from without, through the door. 'Here you are, you little blackguard. Sleep a bit.' Then the donkey begins to bray. 'Keep quiet, you little rogue, see that you ain't a little rogue, eh?' And desperate: 'Shut up, rogue! You're waking up all the neighbors. There, here's a beet-root . . . shut up!' All of a sudden a notion runs through our chap; he's going to count his rabbits: 'Bless me! they're all there!' He watches 'em caper about, gets hold of the mother rabbit; caresses its white belly: 'Oh! she's blooming fat! the beasts are lucky; they can grow fat on grass. A belly like this among us 'd cost a great deal!' But now he's at it, so he goes to pay his pig a visit. He caresses its udder and scratches its belly. You can well imagine whether the pig is in good humor on waking. But

Nono also gets angry: 'What do you think! It wanted to bite me. You damned brute! I'll get square with you when I'll salt you!'

Finally, after having roamed about everywhere, enraged the animals, gaped at the moon, listened to the dogs, the trains, the frogs, and after having foretold the weather . . . he goes upstairs again. He wakes his little girl: 'Do you know, little one, it's already time to put the pot of soup on the fire?' Little Catherine naturally sends him away. 'Ah! so that's how 'tis,' cries Nono. 'I can't say a word this morning without being called down! Well, I'll have nothing to do with nobody! I'm going to drink a glass and have my breakfast alone.' And now our man's off to the cellar with two bottles under his arm. That's how his day of drinking starts. . . . All day long he's always near the cellar, inviting the passers-by to help him drink his wine and listen to his endless speeches.'

"Shepherd! . . . That's the man. . . . Is it surprising, then, that, with such a creature about, all the people of this café are become drunken louts!"

They all laughed; but Flon-Flon protested: "He's exaggerating, this Grêlé. There ain't a worse lout than him!"

"Do I exaggerate?"

"Oh! Why sure! . . . Besides, did you hear Nono put those questions to his mule?"

"I didn't hear the questions, but I heard the answers, for the mule is solid when it comes to braying. 'And then Nono tells me a lot of things. He and me are chums."

"You ain't hard to please, because he's a great donkey himself."

"Old man, you don't always say that! When you have some produce to take in, you're glad to find the man and the donkey and hardly pay 'em. And there's more than one here who can laugh at the innocent fellow, but still better use him for nothing."

"But let him ask to be paid! And besides," concluded Flon-Flon " . . . there's no pity for lame ducks."

But there is another Nono besides the waggish fellow who diverts people. That Nono is born and dies every day. He lives but for several hours, during which he works at his vines and fields and walks along the paths pensively. Here he is in his field of the Marais, this Nono, who only last night, in the café, made his chums laugh so heartily. Here he is, amidst the fields and swaying grass, sitting wrapped in thought at the edge of a ditch, his long legs stretched out on the wild mint and the reeds. . . . Here he is with his constant dream.

. . . At the bottom of the ditch still breathes a little spring that is feebly rippling. All around Nono there is deep solitude. Man is far off with his heart monstrously indifferent. Here, in the Marais, are only things that remain inoffensive after great hardships: stretches of dry land, dead gardens and Nono's soul, full of misery.

CHAPTER III

THE following Sunday, on the approach of evening, a man of Brochon met Nono on the road to the station. Nono was wandering along the slope of the road; he gesticulated and talked to himself. The man listened:

" . . . But in all good justice, it's him who should've married her.. . . And then, mind that! . . ."

Nono shook his finger with the grotesque solemnity of a drunkard. His body swayed forward, over-balanced by drink.

" . . . Mind that! . . . she'd 've been Madame Renardin. There's no doubt about that: Madame Renardin. I insist upon it. . . . And then, let's follow it up closely! . . . Madame Renardin we've said, eh? . . . And where'd I come in? . . . Ah! that's the real question. I don't want to brag, but I could've played a much prouder part than they think in the village. . . . But who'd 've been the betrayed husband? Not me. Quite the contrary; I'd 've been the cunning fellow. . . . But you'll say: 'A good cuckold and a bad widower are on a par.' . . . And here we agree. That was my idea from the very beginning. . . . "

"What are you raving about? . . . This sounds like

a buffoon's speech! You're drunk, my friend!" said
the man from Brochon.

Nono was accused often enough of being a
drunkard; but this time he took it tragically.

"Ah! . . . Ah yes! My friend, you've queer ideas.
You mean to say that I'm drunk! You've a strange
way of reasoning. Look for once into the white of
my eye. . . . Hm! . . . Drunk, me! . . . Poor fool!
. . . Why, I didn't take a dram. How can I be drunk?
Unless the air have some spirits I don't see with what
I could've got drunk. And then, listen, my friend.
Drunk. . . . I can't be. I ain't. . . . I ain't . . .
that ends it. . . . But there's something that makes
my soul and body writhe terribly. . . . But listen and
answer my question: That Nénette, ain't she a
wretched creature? . . . Think of it . . . to come
back to Dijon, a stone's throw from here! . . . Ain't
that enough to demoralize you too? . . . I say it's
knavish! She's more of a criminal than Satan! . . .
Not Satan when he's off his job, but Satan when
he's in the fight, hard at work. Yes it's the trick of
a rascal. For you know how she's departed from
here. She didn't leave in a very fine way. Why come
back to Dijon, then? . . . right near my house. . . .
Oh! that's the way of a Judas! I can't forgive it. . . .
Oh! don't try to calm me . . . leave me alone!"

"My friend, let's admit you ain't drunk, and that
it's cold water that's gone to your head. But if you
ain't drunk, you're mighty cracked."

"Yes, I'm a little cracked. There's indeed some-

thing gnawing at me within that's driving me mad.
Listen: there, in the station café, when I stopped to
have a drink, I learnt just now a simple and terrible
thing. I met there two men: a fireman and a machinist
both of 'em with a railway locomotive. And the fireman, who's a man with a remarkable mind, and who
has received an education . . . where do you think
he lives, my friend . . . where? . . . In Dijon, same
street, same house, same floor as Renardin and that
woman . . . who bears my name! In the eyes of the
law, my friend, she's Jeanne Jacquelinet. . . . For
there was no divorce; too poor for that; too stupid.
. . . Jeanne Jacquelinet, do you hear? . . . Call her
by that name, and she'll answer . . . she'll dare to
answer. In the eyes of the law, she's that; but in
my eyes she ain't Jeanne. Jeanne was a little curly
head, a clever thing; but a loyal and loving darling.
She ain't Jacquelinet neither. . . . Oh no! It's a good
name, borne for centuries by a fine family. Then,
she ain't neither Jeanne nor Jacquelinet. What is she
then? . . . She ain't a being; she ain't a daughter
of the soil. But she's a daughter of Satan; she's a
demon who was bored, and who's come to poach
secretly."

Nono was standing in the middle of the road. His
lanky body was reeling, as he threatened imaginary
adversaries with his raised arm. In his eyes, sickly
and shrunken, there was a faint wandering look. His
inexpressive face was drawn with agony. . . . The
man pitied him.

"Come, my friend Nono, Nono of Les Baraques of Gevrey, let's go to the village together. Let's go, I say. Give me your arm."

But Nono freed himself violently with a push of his shoulder; and his arm stretched out, gnashing his teeth, he went on, stressing each word with wild energy:

" . . . She has murdered twice: she was the murderess of her daughter, Laurette! . . . My proof is yonder, halfway up the hill, in the cemetery of Ensonge. . . . That's one. . . . But she murdered again! she has killed my mind. And now, you look at me with pity, eh? Who made of me this brute that I am? Not my mother . . . not my father. It's her betrayal . . . a betrayal well planted! . . . There, bang! . . . and Nono's a cuckold! . . . And there are people who think it's funny! . . .

"Ah yes! The man who's talking to you has perhaps drunk a bit after all, without realizing it. But there's something else. To get to such a state of sottishness, you must be helped. I was helped. I was given a good hand. Believe me, there's drunkenness, but there's sorrow too! Let go, my friend! go your own way! But listen to this one thing. I had pardoned the creature who's done all that. Indeed, I'd got to believe that she'd suffered for it. I'd got to love her again. Twenty years with a Renardin is a serious penitence, thought I. When she'll return, I'll say to her simply this: 'I don't ask you where you come from, Nénette. For me, you've just lost your

way, and you're tired. During my stay alone, I didn't
let my friendship die; therefore, here's your old home
. . . rest here.'

"Instead of that, my friend, here she is in a narrow
street, fourth floor, right near here! It's a house of
revelry and debauchery: she's there! . . . She's there,
nicely curled and done up, like a real harlot! She
makes money—she's providing for herself—the cursed
creature! . . . But walk on. Don't look at a man
who's crying. . . . Go your own way. . . . "

"Come, come, my poor fellow! Don't cry so."

"Right in Dijon, my friend! And perhaps they'll
be in Gevrey to-morrow! . . . Ah! how miserable I
am! When thinking of her, I saw her wretched and
repentant, and my heart'd open and be ready to re-
ceive her again. Instead of that, there's a slut ready
for the first comer. . . . Ugh! don't speak to me of
that woman: she's a Prussian! . . . "

"Come now! calm yourself. Go home. Do you
hear? . . . You must go home!"

"Hey there! Don't use that tone of command, for
you're running into danger. . . . I've lived, and I've
suffered. My heart's torn to pieces by something worse
than death. Therefore, shut up! . . . Here are these
two criminals in Dijon. Who'll stop 'em from coming
to Gevrey? And then can you imagine? . . . Suppose I meet on the road the two traitors of my life!
Suppose I meet, by mere chance, that woman who
lived in my house, who's loved me when in my arms,
who's given me a child! . . . That ain't possible. I

tell you there'll be a tragedy here. Tell it to the village. Don't hide nothing. A tragedy! . . . yes, a tragedy! . . . I'll have her life . . . her skin. Ah! a beautiful skin: the skin of a harlot! . . . "

Nono however, gradually grew calmer. On approaching the village, he no longer uttered a word. His companion was talking now, and Nono was listening meekly to the remonstrance of his friend. To hear better, Nono bent somewhat his long body and with his arms dangling he had his usual bewildered air. He approved everything the man told him by nodding his head with such admiration that it made him stagger.

" . . . Yes, my poor fellow, they're jeering at you. . . . They've turned your head with that story of Renardin. . . . They've invented it so as to laugh at you. . . . I can't say your wife ain't in Dijon. It seems that she's indeed there; but as to her being rich, that's quite another matter. . . . And as to Renardin . . . that one I know where to find. . . . "

"Ah! . . . Where? . . . "

"You'll find him on the Plombières Road . . . in the madhouse. I've an unhappy brother there, as you know; but Renardin is also there. . . . "

"Then he got the notion of losing his mind?"

"A strong notion indeed; they needed four men to hold him down!"

"Oh! what an idea! . . . Ah! he's mad! . . . Very good. Oh! how I'd like to see him break his teeth!

. . . Let's go and spread the good news in the village. . . . "

"You better remain quiet. . . . "

"But so many people ask me for news about my old wife. That'd be a good way of telling 'em."

"Come, my poor Jacquelinet! Don't talk so much about your wife, and stop being a fool. Pretend not to care for her when they talk to you about her; they'd let you alone if they'd see that you don't think any more of your wife. . . . "

The good man from Brochon gave him still other but similar counsels. When the two new friends were about to separate, Nono grasped his companion's hands and shook them with the touching tenderness of a drunkard:

"Friend! . . . Although you're from Brochon, you're a kind fellow and a good adviser. Besides, I know and I love your town. But there's a thing I reproach you with: you never come to make me treat you to a bite and a drink at four o'clock! . . . Ah! that's knavish! . . . "

CHAPTER IV

Nono had, indeed promised to simulate indifference; but events were stronger than his resolutions. The Sunday which followed his meeting with the man from Brochon, another man from La Jeannotte brought some news which put Nono in a great flurry. This man was a poor creature who tried to get all kinds of odd jobs in order to be able to feed his lazy wife. He had just worked at Dijon in a tannery, where he had seen Renardin and Nénette. They went to fetch Nono in great haste. They plied this "Jean-jean," as the man from La Jeannotte was called, with questions; but they had to wrench every word from him, for he was one of those who never hurry. His weak voice, that of a poor fellow resigned to his fate, did not utter one word louder than the other. This especially exasperated Nono.

"By heavens! . . . but how did this damned Renardin look?"

"Ah! I don't know. He looked like everybody else. . . . He looked like a man who's sitting . . . who is calm. . . . He was watching us work. . . . That amused him. . . . "

"But ain't he mad no more? Ain't he no more at Chartreux? . . . "

"Ah! he was there a while . . . not very long. The doctor of the madmen declared him to be a drunkard; but he was a rotten doctor. Renardin told us that he was merely a little nervous from the noise of a smithy next door to him. They let him go. . . . But his chest began to bother him, and he had to go to the hospital."

"They put him out of the hospital, didn't they? I tell you there ain't a place upon earth where they'd want to keep that blackguard longer than three days. . . . "

"Oh no! Oh no!" Jeanjean quietly protested. "If he left the hospital it's because he wanted to. They're dogs in that hospital, it seems, Renardin told us all about it. 'When there's a poor corpse,' he said, 'that can't hardly defend himself, the sawbones come with their tools; and they begin to cut him up as if he were some salad.' He got out. . . . He did well. He was too honest to remain there. . . . "

"Too honest! . . . " shouted Nono, "that one too honest! His only regret was not to be able to tell two lies at the same time. But at least one followed the other."

"Oh! you mustn't talk that way. . . . We like him. We used to see him sit quietly on his steps and look at us, and so we got to talk to him. He often spoke of Gevrey and of his old business as a hog dealer. That's how I knew who he was. I told him what I knew of him. Oh! he didn't hide a thing. . . . 'Yes. . . . I was somewhat of a knave,' said he. 'What

could I do? Those sluttish women were all after me;
and now because I've tried to please 'em all, I'm done
for!' Then he'd begin to cough and spit; and his
wife'd bring him something to drink which he sipped
seated on the steps."

"His wife! . . . But by heavens! she ain't his
wife!" protested Nono violently.

"That's what I've been telling the others. But they
wouldn't believe me when I told 'em she was married to Jacquelinet at Gevrey."

"Ah! And why should they've believed you? You
little idiot! Do you fancy for a moment that a little
wench like that has the right to my name just as if
I'd made her? . . . What an idea to go about braying
that she's called 'Jacquelinet!'"

They calmed Nono.

"To be sure, I don't give a hang. But ain't I right?
I've been waiting for news these twenty years, and
now a ninny like this must be the one to bring it so
stupidly!"

"Don't get angry, Jacquelinet," went on the peaceful Jeanjean. "The others didn't believe me when I
told 'em she was the wife of another man. 'Go on,'
they answered. 'If she wasn't his wife, nailed to him
by the mayor and the curé . . . do you think she'd
keep on nursing a dying man who treats her like a
dog? She's unhappily married and a poor miserable
woman . . . that's all.'"

"Ah!" asked Nono. . . . "Does that blackguard by
chance beat her too?"

"Not exactly. . . . But he told her a thing or two."

"What did he say?"

"Why I don't know. . . . I didn't pay any attention. . . . However, I remember we once laughed heartily. He had just sworn at her violently: 'Get out of here! Clear out, you old flea!' he shouted to her. And he calls a young apprentice: 'Hey there! Parigot la Crotte! there's twenty sous: go and fetch me another wife.' But the boy ain't stupid, he said: 'Oh! for that price I can fetch even two. Only, how do you like 'em? . . . Thin. . . . Fat . . . or just mixed? . . . '

" 'Fat ones! by heavens! . . . I've been twenty years with a bony wretch! . . . I've enough! Now I want a real change!' We . . . oh! we laughed! . . ."

"Oh! what a pity!" said Nono sadly. "The woman must've looked unhappy, eh?"

"Oh! I don't know. . . . She didn't look happy . . . after that!"

"But look here! she didn't say anything? . . . She didn't fight? . . . For I know her: she's very sensitive about what she's told."

"Upon my faith, what do you want, I don't remember! And then, you'll see for yourself, because you're going perhaps to see 'em soon right here in the village. . . . "

"What? . . . What are you saying?"

"Yes, Renardin told me he'll ask to be taken into the hospital here. I think he's had this in mind for a long time; only shame held him back. But now he's nothing to lose. 'Yes,' he said to me, 'I can't croak here in the hands of the butchers. I'd like to die in my village.' And he spoke of sending a request to the Council."

Old Voisin, municipal councilor of Les Baraques, was present. They questioned him: "Is the thing possible?"

"But why not? After all, he was born here. Only, he'll have to come at his own expense."

The matter was discussed at great length.

"Ah!" said Nono. "Ah! you're going to think I'm hard hearted. If it was for others, I'd say: 'Hitch up the donkey, and let's go and fetch the two unhappy children of the village.' But for them . . . no! Those two beings have brought too much misery upon me in my life!"

"Yes! I'll do this! . . . No! I'll do that! . . . " said Nono. Indeed, he incessantly made different resolutions. At times, he would yield to his weakness and sermonize naïvely: "Let that poor creature who's done you no ill alone! . . . She's nursing a dying man: it's her duty. . . . She's an unfortunate woman. . . . That's all. . . . Go your own way."

When in another mood, heated up by some vile creature of the village, Nono would shout angrily: "Ha! the slut! . . . She was shamefaced enough to come back to the village! . . . The Town Council had the heart to let two such rogues return to the com-

mune, and shelter 'em for nothing in our hospital—
especially to keep one to nurse the other! . . . There
was a carriage and a coachman to bring us that from
Dijon! . . . "

In vain did the kind Catherine, his confidential and
excellent friend, try to calm him: "Oh! . . . None
of that talk! . . . She's worn out, you say! . . . But
worn out from what? . . . Not from digging, anyhow! . . . "

Catherine then related to him what she had learned
of Nénette's pitiful existence. These last nineteen
years Nénette was earning, by hard and honest toil,
a wretched livelihood. She got up at two in the morning every day, and did all that her tiring business of
second-hand clothes dealer exacted.

But Nono did not relent: "Oh! . . . Oh! . . .
Second-hand clothes dealer! . . . And what next?
. . . That was only by mere chance. All those town
trades which are carried on with a cart are for useless
and lazy people! . . . Let those carters try and dig
the soil! . . . Oh yes! . . . If they were given land
just as they get a writing set! . . . But so long as
it's necessary to work the land with bent back and
sinews—they'll keep away! . . . "

On another day, Nono, less vehement and more
moved, did not hide from Catherine that he was very
much irritated.

"Catherine! . . . Listen. . . . I tell you frankly,
but don't repeat it: I had some hope.. . . . For a

whole week I've been by the hospital again and again,
with the mule, three or four times a day. . . . They've
seen us, haven't they . . . Well, not one word came
from there to say to us: 'Forgive me!' or else: 'Come!'
Not one word! . . . Not a look! . . . I got nothing!
. . . Nothing budged for me in that house, where
there's all my hate and all my love! . . . It's worse
than a morgue for me. Well, they really don't give
a rap about me! . . . "

And Nono complained of the cruelty of destiny:
"Catherine! now I ain't got the right to hate her, nor
to forgive her. . . . That's what I've come to! . . .
She don't want to know me. She denies me more
than if I was dead! I never thought I could suffer so
much! . . . Never did I think that God'd be so nasty
to me! . . . No, never. . . . I never would've
thought that of Him! . . . "

What was bound to happen took place. One evening, Nono was walking home from the Marais. He
was going up the Avenue de la Gare, almost hidden
beneath the tops of the faded lime trees. Through
the vines, the scattered frail peach and round cherry-
trees gently yielded to the blowing fresh wind their
frilled leaves. La Côte, where the darkness was
mingled with smoke and vapor, was taking on the
life of the night; and, on the waste lands of the sum-
mits, the grayish curves of the roads lay like arms
bent by fatigue.

The little mule was jogging along; and Nono let

him keep up his ancient gait. "My best companion,"
said Nono. "He gnashes his teeth like a tiger, but
he ain't arrogant, and he has a warm heart, too."
Indeed, did not this companion alone remain faithful
to Nono? Life had passed like a scorching summer;
and a belated appeasing wind was blowing now on a
withered soul and on faded days. At the square of
Les Baraques, there is the bustle of the housewives
who come for their bread, the winegrowers who are
going home, the children who are driving cattle from
the pastures. The women who dress the vines have
taken their hoods off; and under their arms, rolled up
in a green linen apron, they are carrying the straw
they picked up on the way. One can scent the odors
of the hay-stacks and the stables.

And Nono, at the very end of the long cart, looks
at the goers and comers, from the height of his eternal
innocence. He soliloquizes, according to his wont,
on the different persons he happens to notice.

"Oh! little sluttish Poincenotte! Hardly fifteen years,
and already gossiping at the fountains! . . . Ah!
that's youth! . . . That little blackguard Pierrot, he
won't drive his cows aside to let me pass! . . . Poor
old Carbasse: it's nice of him to grow old that way,
for he's got a good daughter who loves him. . . .
But why the deuce did she marry a quill-driver who
figures the gas in town? It's always the same story:
they don't like to milk cows. . . . Ah! . . . But
who's that one there? . . . Our Catherine seems to
talk kindly to her. . . . Who's that? . . . Can that

be? . . . No! . . . But . . . anyhow . . . ain't   it
that Nénette who's coming back from the errands she
does for the hospital, eh? Oh no! confound it! . . .
I was afraid. . . . But I've never seen that wretched
specter."

The flat car was gradually advancing, so that Nono
was able to contemplate the face of the poor woman.
But he could not exactly give a name to the sorry-
looking person. No, she had not the features of a
face he recognized—that wan complexion, those woolly
cheeks, that curly head with the plait above . . . that
masculine nose. . . . "And in spite of that," said
Nono to himself, "she don't look so bad with her
big vicar's nose. . . . And yet she has an air that
I know. . . . Where the deuce have I seen her? . . .
Ain't she from Morey? . . . Oh! I know her . . .
there are poor eyes for you! . . . I say! . . . I say!
. . . ''

Suddenly, his heart contracted: Great God! . . .
The eyes that the woman raised towards him still had
the fire of youth! . . .

"Yes, that's how I recognized her, my poor Catherine. She looked at me with eyes that still sparkled
the way they did at fifteen. . . . That's her, believe
me! . . . I   recognized   her. . . . Where   others
would've seen the old age and misery in her thin body,
I've seen something that ain't herself . . . the way she
moves, the eyes, the youthful way of hers that I still
love. . . . "

"Don't cry, my poor Jacquot," says Catherine. She calms him with kind words, offers him a dram to raise his spirits, and makes him sit down. She has brought him to her house, for no sooner did this poor, innocent Nono descend from his cart than he wanted to run after his Nénette! . . . "I've something to tell her . . . a parting word from her daughter. . . . Look here, don't run away . . . wretch! . . . " Then Catherine had taken hold of his arm, and led him off by sheer force, staggering and raving.

And now that Nono is calm, he gives vent to his feelings. "Oh! Catherine! . . . How one can age, and how one can change! . . . I've known her when she was a mere buttercup; and now to find her so! . . . He, at least had warned me: I'd guessed who he was, when I saw him the day before yesterday, through the bars of the hospital, bleeding and fleshless as though flayed. . . . As soon as I saw him, I had a name for him. . . . But death calls him louder than me; therefore I've no more grudge against him. . . . But she, the wretched woman! . . . Nobody'd warned me. . . . Can one age that way! . . . Did you know her in her youth? . . . One afternoon, we were making hay together in the Riguad meadow. . . . But no, I can't tell you that: it'd tear my heart to pieces! . . . "

"The poor woman's not happy," interrupted Catherine. "She's paid dearly. . . . She told me her life. . . . Oh! how she had suffered! . . . The scoundrel'd beat her with all his might. . . . But she's been feeding him these eighteen years. . . . "

"Ah! don't tell me more. . . . Be quiet! . . . Oh misery! . . . Oh my Catherine! that's a sad life. The night when the poor child wanted to die,' I should've let her do her will. . . . For see what the wind from Dijon brings back to us after nineteen years! . . . Oh Catherine! I knew that buttercup! . . . Catherine, listen, I'm going to tell you something that I oughtn't to tell you; but you know . . . the one who didn't get her caresses when she was twenty . . . who didn't hear her that night, when we loved, murmur 'Jacquot' . . . don't know what passion there can be in the life of a man. . . . Do you remember her in her youth? . . . Any good man who'd 've seen her'd 've said: 'She goes right to my heart and soul.' "

"Come, come, my Nono . . . have a little courage!"

"What do you mean? . . . It's stupid. . . . Why of course I will. I don't need none. I've nothing to do with that woman, and if any should brag me about her I'll tell him to go hang himself. No, I've nothing to say to the woman. . . . I needn't see her. . . . The despair that takes hold of me don't come from her. . . . It's from my daughter, it's from myself . . . it's from all of us here below who struggle under this empty sky and the burden of our years, without even a poor God to give us a bit of justice. . . . Look here! I've worked myself to death at thirty acres of vines and three acres of fields during forty-seven years! . . . Now I say there ain't justice! . . .

There's nothing . . . nothing but the wretched vines and a rotten universe . . . a great nothingness burned by a worthless sun . . . misfortune for honest people . . . and good luck for knaves! . . .

"Just look at the weather we're having! . . . You think such a drought ain't disgusting! . . . What can I do? I'm going to fill my vats with water anyhow. . . . You'll say it's a bit soon. But what's the use of waiting? We must get ready to gather in the grapes, even when there's no rain coming. But it's unfortunate. Indeed, tell me: A grape having come without being moistened by a sprinkle of rain . . . a grape that hasn't felt the sweetness of dew . . . can that grape be a true offspring of the earth? . . . No. . . . Remember what I foretell, Catherine: If the rain that softens don't come . . . that wine'll be as bitter as a bastard."

When Nono had returned to his yard, his neighbors questioned him: "Well! it seems that you've again seen your little wife to-day? . . . Has she changed? . . ."

And he answered placidly:

"Pshaw! . . . Yes. . . . She's changed indeed . . . to tell the truth, a woman changes quickly. Sometimes a few turns of the moon is enough: she loses a tooth in front . . . her eyes sink in . . . you thought you had a fine goose; but you only have an old chicken."

CHAPTER V

On September 20th the rain that Nono longed for came. Beneath the gentle showers, the fields grew animate with a scarcely perceptible whispering of swollen earth, rising grass and trembling roots. One scented the musk of the ripe grapes. The harvest was quickly begun. Nono started his carting, and between whiles he did his sowing too.

But when the grapes were gathered in and the sowing done, the hour of Renardin's destiny sounded. On a calm and melancholy afternoon in October, he who for forty-seven years had devoted his life to wickedness was summoned to his account peacefully, even like the good.

The following day, a priest came for the remains. Only one woman, Catherine, and some fifteen men followed in the funeral procession. Nono was among them. The funeral train at first passed through the village, where the wine-presses were already being set up. On the Place des Marronniers the frail still of the alembic was up, and in the yards the red, round casks were arranged in line, and throughout the village there was an intoxicating odor of must.

The funeral train proceeded in silence, from the church to the cemetery, halfway up the hill, among the vines with their red leaves. Above, there were stretches

of fallow land interspersed with irregular thickets of
golden box-trees and azure junipers.   Below, in the
distance beneath the sky, rolled the plain with its narrow paths where, in a thin mist, breathed the life of
a hundred peaceful villages. Everywhere there reigned
the melancholy sweetness of autumn, a sense of the passing year . . . of fleeting time. . . . The priest murmured prayers which entrust the dead to the infinite
mercy of the Almighty. . . .

When it was over, Briquet said quietly to his dreaming companion, "Nono, you mustn't remain like that.
. . . You must also think of our thirst. Come, let's
have some white wine at Tranquetin's. Look here: at
the Thiebaud's they're having their ten o'clock dram.
Sha'n't we have a glass too?"

"Well, go ahead, and have your drink. . . . Let's
cheer up our spirits a bit, for I'm sad."

As was customary, the men who had just been
present at the burial stopped at the café. "Here are
the death-hunters!" the people gayly shouted at them.
They were heartily welcomed; but Briquet carried off
the trophy when he squeaked:

" . . . I tell you. . . . I'd 've bet anything that
our idiot Nono'd be there. . . . But you haven't seen
the funniest thing of all. . . . You've seen him pass
by, yawning, as he followed the funeral train. . . .
But you should've seen him in the yard of the hospital,
with his black cape and his little, flat felt hat, perched
like a butter-cake on top of his big, blinking face!

. . . His affected airs were side-splitting; he stamped his heel to draw himself up; he jogged his head to and fro; and with the big umbrella that he pressed near his heart, he looked just like a perfect ass. . . .

"But listen to this: I got it into my head to cry, 'Hey there! . . . giv' us a hand! . . . ' as we were about to lift the coffin. Oh! he jumped up, all upset, turning his head from side to side, not knowing where to put his umbrella; at last, he decided to put it on the ground, there . . . bang! . . . and, with a tragic air, he runs to us; he gets hold of the coffin with open arms as if he had a great love for it. . . . You should've seen him, then, act the courteous fellow with the dead man, his gaping head resting tenderly on the corner of the box, while both his arms clutched it like a father's hugging his son. . . . We laughed quietly.

" . . . At the cemetery, as the earth was a little in our way, we pushed the coffin rather roughly. 'Be careful!' he cries to us. 'Be careful! Not so hard.' And he stiffened! Then our Carongeot, who ain't cranky and who was holding one of the sides, whispered in his good-natured way: 'Oh! even if we'd shake him up a bit! . . . There's no fuss to be made. . . . Let go, believe me . . . let go and don't hold it back. . . . There . . . now . . . easy . . . That's right. . . . Put it down . . . there! . . . '

"We put the coffin down; we stood up and wiped our foreheads. There were fifteen of us, all old pals, kneeling on the gravel, holding on to a grating and

looking at our dear deceased getting acquainted with
the earth, and listening to our vicar recommending him
in Latin to the Eternal Father.   That little wag of
a vicar, in a long white robe, his small short-sighted
head buried in the mass book, nibbled at bits of prayer
in a sugary fashion; he threw his paws towards the
corpse every once in a while, and mumbled a 'Dominus
vobiscum' and an 'æternum' . . . do you want 'em
. . . have 'em. . . . But it was above all the sight of
Nono that made us chuckle. He drooped sideways his
stupid head, with beneficent eyes; and on that long,
thirsty face, a beautiful, angelic grimace rested. . . .
Oh by heaven! . . . just like a butterfly on a box of
sardines. . . .

   "On leaving the cemetery I tried to talk to him;
but it wasn't possible.   He began to preach: 'Poor
fellow! without knowing it you're passing over the
same pitiful path over which all the dead have passed.'
You can well imagine that I was off in a hurry! . . .
He's to meet us here. . . . We can have rare sport.
. . . Friends, do you catch my idea? . . . Well, if
we know how to handle our idiot without rushing the
thing, if we know how to lead him up to it nicely,
I'll bet you he'll sleep with his old one to-night. She's
at my landlady's now. . . . Catherine is consoling her.
. . . She's leaving to-night for Dijon. . . . Well,
we've got to carry it out.   Only, be careful! . . .
Nono always gets violent at the end of a party."

   "Oh!" said big Jonas peacefully, "let me handle
the ninny."

CHAPTER VI

WHEN Nono entered the café, he found many people and a merry welcome. Big Jonas made him sit
down at his side; and the splendid drunkard leaned
his truculent face towards Nono and blurted out his
sympathy. . . . But it was not necessary to prepare
the dialogue, for Nono, from the start, struck at the
very core of the matter, and Jonas had but to reply.

"You're, indeed, very kind to offer me. . . . But I
really don't want to drink. And yet I'm so sad over
what's happening in these parts. . . . "

"What is happening?"

"Well, it's the way certain people act that don't
please me. When the procession passed by, they
laughed. . . . There ain't nothing to be smart about,
however. Even in a little village like this, death is
death. I'm always sad when I see a poor corpse, and
I say to myself: 'Here's one who'll perhaps never
again celebrate Saint Vincent's day!' "

"Indeed! But there's no reason to mourn Renardin.
He's dead. . . . That's no bad business. Besides, it's
just that it should be him rather than the cow of a
poor man. . . . "

"Ah! it's just!" And Nono shook his head with

the knowing air of one who is well informed on the subject. "Ah! it's just! . . . Well, justice is rot! I don't know what knave was the first one to say: 'Don't touch nothing of mine.' On that account, they've built prisons for those who had nothing, and who nibbled at the hoards of others. That may be one way of seeing; but as to being just, sand and rocks are also just: they don't do harm to those who look for nothing. But we ain't the sons of sand and rocks: we have nothing from 'em. . . . "

"Oh! just listen to this. . . . That's what you call babbling! . . . You're handing us out the ideas of a cobbler! You're off again, you cracked nut, attacking the society that guarantees you an income! . . . "

"Oh! I don't give a hang about society! The government, the authorities, the Bench, the soldier with his helmet or the judge with his round cap—all that, that can do no great good and no great harm. Hail, disease, death—that's at least something to cope with! . . . that can master us! . . . But there's your prefect: he's got all sorts of ribbons on him. . . . Yet to what purpose? . . . Can that creature even mow? . . . Look here: all the dragoon colonels of France, in all their cavalry life, in spite of their stormy temperaments, can't do us one-hundreth part of the harm that good hail can which does nothing more than drum at our windows for ten minutes. . . .

"Ah! I repeat again, it ain't from the capital nor from the prefecture that our real misfortunes come. It ain't the police sergeant who brings 'em in a letter sealed by the mayor. . . . No, no . . . our misfortunes don't come from people. . . . They come from elsewhere. . . . That's an idea that runs through my mind every time I see a person die."

"And where do these misfortunes come from, Nono? Who's that clever Satan who belabors us with his devilish humor in this way? . . . "

"How should I know? . . . I never went up towards the sun. My highest ladder is thirteen feet high, hardly more. To be sure, I can see the starry heaven, but I don't know what's beyond, in the hayloft! . . . "

But a cunning fellow wanted to intervene in order to lead Nono to a more amusing subject:

"All right, let it be so. Let's talk of something else. . . . Let's leave Renardin in peace. . . . Why, what's new in the village besides this, Nono?"

"Well, nothing new. It's even pretty old in this world. There are people always armed to the teeth, shouting: 'Justice! . . . Justice! . . . Let's get revenge! . . . Kill him! . . . ' They've always got some mad virtue in their heads. . . . Their honesty ain't all easy to get on with! . . . A man has to begin with three terrible enemies: poverty, disease and death. Why should we want to add another one? . . . "

"Oh! look here! look here! It seems your Renardin is forever worrying you. . . . "

"It's him . . . it's you . . . it's me . . . it's the fate of all of us upon earth that's worrying me. . . .

While we're reveling here, a poor dead man is alone
yonder, his head on a pillow of marl, with six feet
of gravel for a feather-bed! . . . You're laughing,
eh? . . . Meantime, he's struggling with the worms
of the earth! . . . No other amusement but to let 'em
eat his belly! . . . And we say: 'No pity for a
wounded beast!' No forgiveness neither . . . but
blooming hatred, sprinkled well with gall, and ever
fresh! . . . Such are the men of nowadays: gherkins
pickled in vinegar. . . . "

"But after all, that Renardin. . . . "

"Pooh! . . . But I repeat again: why bear a grudge
against a poor being? . . . Ain't it enough that death
is after him? . . . Look at Piémontais! . . . Look at
Grêlé! . . . Ain't they dead? . . . They're both as
dead as beasts can be! . . . "

Nono gradually grew more and more excited. They
forced him to drink; he drank one glass after another. . . . And to set Nono agoing, big Jonas began in a friendly, scolding tone: "Look here, Nono!
. . . Do you want me to talk to you frankly . . .
there . . . like a friend? . . . Well, people ain't satisfied with your having gone to the funeral. . . . It
wasn't your place. . . . "

"Ah! I know it very well. . . . But, you know, I
went to see him on his death bed, the terrible enemy
of my happiness. . . . And what did I see at hand?
. . . a poor, little red corpse very much worn out.
. . . I've also heard his death-rattle. . . . 'He's going
to choke' they said. And from the road where we

passed by with the mule, I heard the fellow cry in his agony. I said to myself: 'Oh! how dearly he's paying for his death!' Then, my poor friends, on hearing those last cries, it seemed to me that they were the calls to me of someone departing. . . . And I said to myself: 'Jacques! . . . Go there with all your courage. . . . A brother of this earth is calling you. . . . He's your brother Cain, but he's your brother all the same. . . . Go and tell him to leave in peace . . . provided he don't come to torment you again . . . for there was disagreement between you two.' But it was too late; when I came near him, my enemy was dead; the soul which loves and which forgives had fled from him.

"Later, I really didn't decide upon anything; but when the time came, I went to put my cape on. . . . I was buttoning the collar of my shirt, when I saw the vicar and the sexton pass in the street. That fat sexton, old Tapecloches, carried his pot of holy water, swaying it with a bantering air, as if he was going for his four o'clock bite. . . . It didn't please me. . . . And I said to myself: 'That Renardin ain't no more with us, nor with this world. He belongs to another justice now: let's not spoil his business. Indeed, I don't ask of God to be relentless with that unfortunate man, for it's enough simply to be dead. Let Him not be more severe than me who's suffered all my life!' Then to show there was no wrangling on my part, that I really pardoned him, I decided to follow the unfortunate man, and I was there. I took my place at the end of the train, and I did my duty bravely.

" . . . What are you laughing at? I didn't do no harm. But that white wine don't go well at all. I'll have none of it! It scrapes too hard! . . . It's the rottenest knave that ever came out of a cask. . . . It's like a booted gendarme, spurred to the eyebrows, who swoops upon you, his saber between his teeth, down the hill. . . . Confounded bigoted inn-keeper, I'm done for! . . . Hurry there, bring us an absinth. . . . No alcohol lemonade, but real absinth which smells of the Franc-Comtois.

" . . . And now let's reflect. You seem to joke. . . . There ain't a thing to joke about. This morning they've nailed some boards together and put in it a man of forty-seven, who was one of the strongest of the village. Is that a joke? Yes indeed! . . . They say to me: 'You seem to forgive him.' But I can't thrust a bayonet into the belly of a corpse. Look what he is now. Don't ask him anything: he won't say neither 'I was wrong nor I was right.' . . . He'll say nothing at all. . . . Not even the African army, nor the eleven stripes of the Field-Marshals of France will impress him: he won't answer you more than a log will. . . . What can be done then? . . .

"You're laughing. . . . And you there with your alpaca coats . . . you merchants . . . you makers of the poor . . . you're playing at cards instead of buying our wine! . . . Let's drink, then, since we can't sell it! . . . Here's to you! . . . Here's to everybody

. . . to the entire world . . . to the women, in spite of all the trouble they give us! . . . "

Nono was applauded. Briquet rejoiced: "He's got his fill: he's done for. . . . We can get at him now. Great heavens! What a souse! . . . But be careful later on! . . . He makes a bad business of it in the end." . . . Jonas thundered with his sounding voice, and gave vent to comic outbursts of indignation:

"No! Nono, no! . . . I never would've thought it of you. . . . I thought you more frank. . . . You're turning into a bigot. . . . You disgust me. . . . Instead of dealing blows, you act like an angel, or rather like a donkey. You haven't more courage than a spade. Don't you hear everybody jeering when you pass by? . . . "

"My friend . . . my friend. . . . I hardly have the time to hear. . . . I pass by with the mule, carting in the produce of different folk. I look here and there. . . . And I see the simplicity of nature; and I listen to the silence across the fields. That's the silence of the dead: let's not fear it. . . . Besides, the poor dead don't suffer any more our misery, and for them it's always Sunday."

"Well, you big ass, don't whimper longer for your big darling Renardin, since he's quite at ease, comfortably boxed up. . . . My friends! . . . a dram to the health of our dear Renardin, the most peaceful man of the village, sheltered from draughts, with his hands on his belly counting his triumphs, and with

his legs stretched out nursing his swollen veins. . . .
To his health!"

"Damn blackguards! . . . " murmured Nono. . . .
"They've ideas, all the same! . . . I laugh in spite of
myself."

They were happy to see him laugh. The customers
of the café became, little by little, more numerous.
Beneath the low, smoky ceiling, swarms of flies were
buzzing. A mouldy smell of beer and absinth made
the air sour. The merchants were playing at cards;
and the winegrowers of Rue Hante, with glowing
faces, hardly stopped laughing. But there were two
groups of winegrowers who had come for their coffee.
They all beset Nono: hilarious fellows with their
aprons sticky with lees, well fed with sausage and
jugged hare. There were several other lively wags,
a few masons and vineyard owners who also sat
around Nono. They bent towards him their red
drunken faces, each one muttering tender remarks to
the object of their pity:

"Our good Jacques!"

"Saint John the Innocent!"

"Graceful like a filthy snout!"

"Cunning like a sausage. . . . Warm like a hot
pudding. . . . Foxier than a gardener."

"A fine heart with all that!" added Jonas. "The
little darling of the women! . . . A veritable rascal,
I say! . . . But tell us a little . . . now . . . frankly
. . . between friends. . . . How do you find your old
woman? . . . eh? . . . Do tell us! . . . Not good

still . . . for? . . . And he ended his sentence with a pert twinkle.

"Oh!" answered the peaceful Nono. "Don't talk to me of that misery. . . . "

Briquet, overwrought with drunkenness, tossed about the café, struggling from table to table: "I tell you, great heavens! . . . I tell you to-night he's going to sleep with his old woman!"

He shouted so much and so loud that Nono asked him: "Hey? What do you say? . . . Little Briquet! . . . Poor worm! . . . Just because you've the snout of a weasel sprinkled with coal, you'd like to jeer at your master . . . jeer at Nono! . . . Listen to this, friend: Nono with his false clownishness is more clever than you with all your snobbish airs of the dirty knave."

"But listen! It ain't a matter of jeering at you. That's what I hear in the village: 'Nono's wife is back again. She's become a good woman, and she's going to give him choice caresses.' Is there any truth in that?"

"Oh! I see quite well what you're driving at. There are smarter people than me; but there are others who are confoundedly more stupid. That's true. Some say: 'Nono is an idiot.' Poor cobbler! . . . But there's a cunning that's so well rooted in my bones that I often distrust myself; for I know myself: if I'd follow it to the very end, I'd do harm. And those who want to put one over on me, if they'd see the danger, they'd be scared out of their wits. Oh! I ain't the artillery arsenal of the Beaune Road; but I ain't like the morning dew either; and even if I had to confront an iron jaw, I'd put the shivers in him! Oh! I'm not so easy. I wasn't brought up by delicate ladies. Why since the age of twelve, I've been struggling with the Hell of the Earth. For three-fourths of the world are rogues. The greater part of the rest are filth; and the remainder rotten beasts. I say that for you. . . ."

"Hey there! . . . Now you've made him angry," said Jonas looking vexed yet in good humor. "Let this poor Nono alone for a while. Don't bother about 'em, my chum Nono. . . . Let's speak of something else. . . . Why, let's talk politics. . . ."

"Politics! . . . Well, as to politics, I say that this government is rotten. Since I failed to sell my black currants, I've no more confidence."

"Well, what about it? . . . Give us some opinion more definite."

"Well, as to opinion, my great remedy for everything is this: 'Go ahead . . . bourgeois! go ahead . . . and till the soil! I've been digging these forty-three years: I've got enough.' That's true, too! . . . We see those lazy bourgeois swaying their fat heads gracefully as they eat a grape carelessly, while we work at the soil like madmen, hard enough to croak. . . . But as I say . . . let each one till his own bit of land. Ain't I right?"

"Well, my Nono, that's how to organize something to dispossess the bourgeoisie. . . . "

"Oh me! . . . I don't bother no more about anything. . . . "

"Oh! my Nono," continued Jonas, "it's up to you to get at the head of the movement. You're the bright fellow of the village. . . . "

"Me! . . . But I'm just as honest as you," Nono vehemently protested. "You've nothing to say against me. I was a good recruit. I went after the chicks as conscientiously as anybody. . . . I was a soldier for two months and that sharpened my wits. Then I worked hard enough at the vines and fields; and I've carted the produce of many people. . . . That's my life. . . . What have you got against it? . . . You pack of Prussians! . . . You ain't the sons of the old folks! . . . No! . . . No. . . . The old folks were good people; with their little, clean-shaven peaceful faces, they'd go to mass with their bandy legs and with their blouses blowing in the wind. They'd wink their tired eyes; and they'd shake their heads, saying politely 'yes,' each time you talk to them. There was no more falsehood and rancor in 'em than in good bread. . . . Instead of that . . . you! . . . with your swaggering airs, you're all made up of the same paste as Cain! . . . I'm a poor contraband Christian. . . . But you . . . you're all miserly wretches and Judases, and you'd sell the God of heaven and earth for a jug of wine! . . . Look here! You think I can't guess?

. . . that you're trying to string me on? . . . Pack of vermin! . . . Knaves! . . . "

"Be careful! Be careful!" whispered several of the company. "He's becoming nasty."

Jonas courageously risked another remark: "Oh there! . . . Wait a minute, my chum! . . . When one's a coward like you, one's the right to shut up."

"Me, a coward!" yelled Nono.

"That's sure! Did you even have the courage to break Renardin's jaw?"

"But he's dead, you thick pate! . . . Besides, it ain't my fault: he did it. But now he's got to make up with Satan . . . not with me. . . . Let's hope that Satan knows his business! . . . For if I had him there . . . right there . . . in front of me . . . how I'd land on him! . . . The blackguard! Tell me, what harm did I do him? . . . Nothing! . . . Nothing at all! . . . I was a good neighbor: that's all. I didn't do him harm; and he did me a great deal. . . . "

"Oh! not so much! . . . He took your wife away . . . but look here . . . that's how you got rid of her! . . . "

"Indeed, I got rid of her! . . . Ah! if you knew how that slut drove me wild! . . . How she insulted me! . . . If it was now. . . . Oh! how I'd beat her! . . . Great heavens! . . . so that my hands 'd ache! . . . Or rather I'd break her jaw once for all! . . . If I had her . . . ugh! I've such a desire to choke her that it makes my teeth gnash!"

"Well," said Briquet quietly, "don't hold yourself

back, friend! She's at my landlady's. Come at once with me. . . . Come. . . . You'll crack her jaw to your heart's content. . . . Come. . . . "

"Oh! I don't need nobody. . . . I want to do the job after my own fashion, and with a clear head."

"Hey! you big donkey! You've just got to walk three hundred paces . . . just a little way down . . . and you back out! . . . you don't dare! . . . "

"Me! . . . don't dare! . . . "

"No, you don't dare! . . . " shouted the entire café.

"Well, by heavens! I'm going. I'm going to kill her. . . . I swear it before you all. . . . Come along!"

Nono rose and stumbled. They held him back a moment to listen to useful advice: he should find some pretext, for instance, "invite her to have a bite at four o'clock, and, if she refuses . . . get at her and beat her up! . . . "

"Yes I'm going at once!" brayed Nono.

The crowd pushed him out of the café. The gang of drunkards dragged him on towards Les Baraques. He walked along railing:

"Slut! . . . Wretch! . . . You're going to pay! . . . Such a harlot! . . . She's just good to put a knife through and make sausage of! . . . "

CHAPTER VII

THERE was a violent racket on the staircase of Catherine's house; suddenly the door was opened with a heavy blow, Nono was pushed in by many arms, and the door was quickly closed. While his friends were slipping away, Nono, nonplused, stumbling with drunkenness, remained standing in the middle of the mean room. His long emaciated face gaped stupidly at the two women sitting near the window; they looked at him in silence.

"Hail to you!" began Nono at last in a heavy voice, making grotesque gestures with his hand. "Hail to you! . . . Greeting to the company! . . . Ladies! . . . No gentlemen? . . . No? . . . Well, greeting to the women! . . . Honor to the women! . . . Let's say no more 'you set of harlots!'

"Listen to this now. I'm come to invite my former wife to have a dram and bite with me at four o'clock. That's square, eh? . . . What does that slut think of it? . . . She don't want to come? . . . No? . . . She refuses? . . . She thinks it's the four o'clock of a beggar! . . . Damn! . . . What are you looking at me like that for? . . . Do I ask you for anything?"

Catherine, indeed, was regarding him with sadness, His large blue eyes, firmly set in his big red face, told a long tale. She spoke gently to him, with a kindly voice that almost calmed Nono:

"Oh! go away! . . . Go away quick, my poor fellow! . . . Your old friend speaks to you just now with all her heart: it ain't the time for you to come here: go away! . . . Mind me and go home."

"Well, you're right! All right. It's agreed. The business is settled, I'm going. I see there ain't nothing to be done here. But first, you must pay for a glass. Go ahead! Catherine! Pay for a glass and I'm off! . . . Pay! . . . A glass of something to drink, by heavens! . . . Just a glass! . . . No? . . . Ah! . . . She's great, that one! . . . Ah! She's bad, that fat good-for-nothing. . . . She don't seem to understand that I'm thirsty! . . . But it's an easy thing to see. Won't you budge, you fat wretch, and go to the cellar! . . . Eh? . . . Wait a minute! . . . I'll give you some kicks to knock the dust off you! . . . What are you looking at me like that for? I'm going to help you stare at me! . . . You big beasts, haven't you seen me before? . . . No? . . . Look here! there's one who's been with me almost as much as with the rest of the village, and who don't want to recognize me! . . . You drab! . . . I'm angry, indeed, but ain't I right? . . . I came here with good intentions: I didn't want to reproach you with anything. It was only a question of four o'clock. And that's how I'm received! . . . with insults! . . . Low wench! . . . But since it's so, give an account of yourself! . . . First of all, who allowed you to leave my house twenty years ago

in order to become a harlot? . . . Answer! . . . You
can't eh? . . . But give me a drink, Catherine, my
child! . . . Just one glass! . . . I'm of this village.
Look here! you can't refuse me a drink, eh! . . .
Don't look at me like that! . . . I don't like it. . . .
Do you hear me? . . . And you, why do you stare
at me like that? . . . Don't you know me? . . . Well,
I'm Jacquelinet . . . an old husband of yours. . . .
You miserable madwoman, it's no use looking at me
with pitiful eyes! . . . It won't take now! . . . All
that's passed. . . . No weeping scenes! . . . I came
to tell you that I've had enough of it, and clear out.
. . . Don't count on my help! . . . Fancy that! she
thinks she can be a slut for nineteen years, and then
come home and peacefully begin over again! . . . Oh!
you can't do it with me! . . . Keep right on, don't
stop here! . . . "

"Goodness! . . . Goodness! . . . " said Catherine
bursting into tears. "My God! Listen to that! . . .
Oh! the wretched man! . . . Every word you're saying is a crime! . . . "

"Ho there! . . .A crime? . . . Do you want to
preach to me . . . you . . . a woman without education! . . . Go on! my wits are sharper than yours!
. . . My old man, who was a sly fox, has left me
his malice. . . . Remember that!"

"But, Nono . . . my poor man . . . in spite of
your drunkenness, do look at this unhappy woman!
. . . Haven't you no pity?"

Nono then looked, in silence, at the poor woman.

He gazed at the slender, wrinkled body, at the fleshless neck with its crumpled skin, at the drawn old face, and at those sunken eyes whose glances showed but humble submission to fate. . . . Shame overcame him. . . .

"Ah! Ah!" said he somewhat perplexed. "What do you want me to look at? . . . That woman there?" He made some evasive gestures. "To be sure, she's hardly .plump. She ain't as appetizing to look at as a lion's cub. She's changed. I don't bear her no grudge: tell her that . . . I can't say any more! . . ."

Catherine took Nénette's hands, and sitting beside her and leaning towards her, she spoke with loving ardor. But Nénette shook her head with an air of doubt and distress in reply to everything Catherine said:

"No, Jeanne, no. . . . I'm not going to take back what I told you a while ago when we were alone. The poor man . . . don't judge him from what he's saying now. He ain't aware of it. He's as innocent of what he says as a child in swaddling clothes. Believe me, at heart he's the same, good old Jacquot. . . . But what can you expect? . . . They've made him pitilessly drunk, those wretches! . . . "

"Oh! . . . " protested Nono. "One must be as stupid as you to talk of my drunkenness. Everybody knows that I can stand a lot of wine, and that I can drink without stopping."

And he added shaking his finger in his remonstrant

and apt manner: "Rather say that it's the drunkards of the village who envy me because I can beat 'em all! . . . And you, pack of beggars, you think you can see when I'm drunk, but you don't see whenever I'm thirsty. But I'm tired of standing up. . . . I'll sit down with the permission of both of you. . . . It's good to act the clerk, that is to have your seat on a chair. . . . "

Catherine continued to talk to Nénette without paying any attention to the innocent Nono. But Nono, who was listening, answered nevertheless:

" . . . Believe me, my poor Jeanne, there are worse drunkards than him, for drunkenness ain't a vice. . . . There's more sorrow than drink in it, and he needs very little to put him in this state. . . . "

"Oh! look at the idiot! . . . She's going to say soon that I get drunk merely by smelling the leaf of a vine! . . . "

" . . . Besides, it's a blessing for him to be drunk: he don't see his misery. . . . "

"Misery? . . . I had it. I needed someone behind me. . . . First of all, we must admit that in the vineyard nothing can replace the hand of a woman. . . . "

" . . . Yes, weep, my poor Jeanne, for you don't know how unhappy and forsaken Nono was! . . . "

"Forsaken? . . . not as much as you think! . . . In the village I still found a good deal of friendship. . . . They liked to make me talk. . . . As a matter of fact, reasoning is my strong point."

"Oh look here!" said Catherine with a sudden impatience. "Can't you be quiet, you poor fool?"

Nono grew angry: "Shut up! . . . Me! . . . You want to make me shut up! . . . It ain't so easy! . . . The revolutions and the barricades of Paris gave us the right to talk when we please. . . . And you'd like to upset a right that the Republic is proud to uphold! . . . First of all, who's the elector? the true Frenchman? . . . Of the three who're here, who is the one who's served in the fourth of the 3rd, of the 27th at Dijon? . . . Eh? . . . You fat insolent creature! . . . She's just good enough to comb some dirty bristles, and she'd like to attack the freedom of speech of Frenchmen. . . . Come now! . . . None of your caresses! . . . I don't give a rap about 'em."

"My friend! my poor fellow! . . . " said Catherine, pleading with Nono. "What an ill luck to see you in such a state to-day! . . . "

Her tone moved Nono: "Well, what do you want? I didn't mean to hurt you. You were insolent. . . . I objected to it: now we're square. But don't cry. What do you want. You seem to laugh at me, and think me drunk! . . . I don't hate anything so much as that."

"No, my boy, no! . . . We don't want to tell you you're drunk, but you lack your usual good sense. You're not so bad; there, don't talk! . . . For, without wanting to do so, you've made this poor woman very miserable. . . . She looks most unhappy, don't she? . . . "

"Yes, she looks as if she hadn't much luck. . . . Besides they've said so."

"Don't insult her, but pity her: she has suffered a great deal upon earth, believe me."

On hearing that, Nénette covered her face with both hands.

"Oh!" said Nono, "I don't say no."

They were all silent. The evening was gradually approaching, and it had already begun to grow dark. Nono was sitting with his long legs bent beneath his chair. He was trying to keep in the background, making himself humble and small, so that he was no more than a poor, long back pitifully bent, and a shaking head. Then, after a protracted silence, he murmured in his pensive and drowsy musing:

"Yes . . . yes . . . a wretched day! . . . Believe me, I understand it. . . . I'm not stupid. . . . A regrettable day for everybody. I see it now. I should 've had some regard. . . . That woman's in distress. . . . Well, after all, it's her companion they've buried. . . . Death is pitiless. . . . But what can I do about it? . . . Mourn too? . . . Yes. . . . I'm mourning . . . tell it to her . . . don't hide it from her. . . . "

"Oh! poor fool!" interrupted Catherine. "As to mourning, the unhappy woman has simply ended her martyrdom."

"Ah! indeed! . . . who'd 've thought it. . . . You think, then, that he made her suffer. . . . Yes, that's right, you already mentioned it to me; and I've thought

of it, too. For that blackguard was always heedless
. . . a mad knave. . . . ”

“Let him rest in peace!” muttered Catherine.

“Yes. . . . Yes. . . . I hear him. . . . Leave that
alone! . . . But what’s the matter with me? . . .
Something’s gnawing at me. . . . Why, Catherine,
suppose you give me something to eat. . . . I’m very
hungry. Look here! I’m so hungry that I could eat
a bear!”

Catherine hastened to fetch him some bread and
sausage. Nono took his time, however. He opened
his knife slowly, and cut a slice of sausage and a
piece of bread. He ate slowly, putting some bits of
sausage on his bread and pushing it carelessly into
his mouth with his thumb.

“Hey there! go on and eat too!” said Nono.

Catherine pointed him out to Nénette.

“Do you see him, this poor man hasn’t eaten perhaps for two days!”

“Oh!” agreed Nono, “I really don’t know. And yet
we had some soup two or three days ago. To be sure,
I’m not fat. . . . ”

Catherine persuaded Nénette to eat too: “You must
have some strength if you want to walk to Dijon.”

“She’s decided to go back?” asked Nono.

“This very night.”

“Oh! look here! . . . I’m not hungry now. . . .
But why go away so soon!”

“To-morrow morning she must be at Binges to get
the onions and celery they’re keeping for her.”

"Won't the onions and celery be sorted out again!
You oughtn't to bank on 'em too much, and to leave
us on that account . . . poor woman!"

"Oh! they won't sort 'em again, for I've seen to it.
I was even lucky: they took my stock before the first
storm."

These were the first words uttered by Nénette since
Nono had entered. This broken voice dulled by
trembling hoarseness—could this really be that of his
former companion? Nono looked at the poor woman.
Had he, indeed, seen her! . . . Had he seen on that
wan meager face, the honest and loyal wrinkles of
hard work! Had he especially seen that absolutely
resigned look, which says that her duty upon earth
was accomplished . . . accomplished in hardship . . .
but accomplished all the same in spite of everything
. . . "through the iniquities of man . . . under the
trials of God."

"Your work is hard, ain't it?"

"At times."

"Do you get your stock at Dijon or from the farmers
of Saone?"

"I go twice a week to Auxonne."

"Ah! imagine! twice a week! . . . "

"Oh! it's a good market. I've seen tomatoes there
for less than a sou a pound."

"Indeed!"

"One year I brought back in baskets on my arms
one thousand three hundred pounds of celery and

tomatoes, and I made more than a sou and a half a pound."

"Oh! that celery! . . . those tomatoes! . . . one thousand three hundred pounds on one's arms! . . . Poor woman! . . . That must 've been heavy! . . . It brings tears to my eyes even now. . . . Let's hope the winter won't be too severe. . . . But something is the matter with me; I feel sick. . . . "

"Do you want a little wine?" asked Catherine.

"Oh! indeed no! . . . Leave me alone with your wine. . . . You, too, 'd like to get me drunk? . . . Don't you think I ain't drunk enough yet? The truth is that I ain't worthy to drink a glass of wine. To give a rascal of my sort wine is to offend the sun and the earth, the father and mother of the wines of La Côte! Listen! . . . I'm ashamed of myself! . . . By heavens! for a trifle I'd destroy my vines and replant with nothing but barley. . . .

"Ah! that's so! . . . I understand what I've just done! . . . Loaded like a pig, I've come here to make a full show of my shame! . . . And I didn't have a word of pity for that poor woman! . . . That poor woman . . . why it's our Jeanne . . . hey, Catherine? . . . Let her not cry, because it breaks my heart to see her cry. . . . She don't look rich. . . . I've hardly no money. . . . Tell her I've some cabbage. She can sell it and have a little money. . . . Catherine, tell her to go in peace; I've no hatred for her. . . . "

"My friend, I've told her. . . . She knows it already."

"Ah! . . . Well, to be frank, the feeling I have for her, deep down in my heart, can be called friendship. . . . Tell her that too. . . . "

"My friend, I've told her that too."

"Well, if you've told her everything, I'll be going now. . . . I'm going then. . . . But, my Catherine, just one minute. . . . I beg of you one minute. . . . If you only knew how bad I feel! . . They've made me drunk, those blackguards! . . . I'm ashamed of what I might 've said to you. . . . But forgive me, because, you see, the nonsense I've said comes from a madness and sorrow that's without a name! . . .

"Let me look. . . . That woman is our little Jeanne . . . ain't she? . . . Poor girl. . . . Look at her, Catherine . . . her face says: 'Pity me. . . . ' Her tears are looking at me. . . . They seem to say: 'Forgive me.' Well, listen to this, Jeanne: don't ask that I forgive you, because I've done it long ago. . . . Indeed, for long I've had no bitter feeling against you. You see, little Laurette once kissed me very hard; and something burst within me: it made my soul humble, and I've forgiven you with a willing heart. . . .

"But don't cry like that, Jeanne! . . . Jeanne Jacquelinet, do you hear me? . . . I don't know how to name you. . . . Oh! that's right . . . show me your dear face. . . . Oh! in spite of all, how young your eyes still are! . . .

"But go on! . . . Go away quick, my child! . . .

The man you see before you is a miserable drunkard. Go away, my child! It's you who came in my youth with your little pale face? . . . You had no business to leave me: I ain't as bad as all that. . . . I recognize you. . . . Go away quick. . . . The Nono of your love is now the good-for-nothing drunkard of the Baraques. . ... . He's now the butt of the village. . ... . Go away! . . .

"But before we part once for all, let me look at you with friendship. . . . And then forgive me for having let you go that day. . . . Twenty years of wretched life have been inflicted on you for the crime; but the remorse I feel still has all its leaves and roots. . . .

"Go! . . . go in peace . . . little Jeanne! . . . That was a wretched day for you! It made me unworthy of you! . . . Go then! . . . But some day if your heart prompts you . . . go up to the staircase of our house without fear . . . and try the knob as if you were entering your own house. . . . Once you've passed the door . . . above the cupboard you'll see a photograph. . . . It's our Laurette . . . our angel. . . . After you left, her eyes were quite like your dear ones. . . . Did you know it? . . . "

Nénette hid her face in her hands streaming with tears. . . . She sobbed, all her body trembled. . . . Catherine turned her back, and affected to break some fagots to light her fire. . ... . Nono was standing and waiting. . . .

Suddenly, Nénette rose and walked to the door without saying a word. . . .

"Don't go too far!" said Nono softly. . . And he took hold of her arm. . . .

From the corner of the balcony, Catherine looked down the street discreetly. . . . There was no passer-by. The stones were washed by the rain. Above the red brick roofs, cutting into the white space, the platanes made delicate angles with their strange leaves. . . . The night had descended from the mountain, bringing with it the perfume of the oaks; it was everywhere now, a universal friend to the eyes of dreamers. . . . Catherine was watching Nono lead Nénette . . . both walking side by side . . . approaching their house . . . entering it. . . .

CHAPTER VIII

WHEN Nono and Nénette had entered, Nono closed the door of the landing to the street and waited to let his companion catch her breath. They remained there, in the dark, at the foot of the staircase, when suddenly the door opened and little Catherine's school bag struck against Nono's legs. The little girl rushed in and was about to run off; but Nono caught her wrist and held her back. She raised her arm to ward off a blow, hiding under the bent arm her small, stubborn face. She looked with terror at the two standing in front of her.

"Listen, my little Catherine," said Nono, "listen to me for a minute. . . . "

The gentleness of Nono's voice reassured the child; and she tried to escape.

"Let me go, let me go, I tell you! . . . The children are waiting for me." And her frail, little fingers sought to free themselves from Nono's grasp.

"My darling . . . little darling . . . listen! You see this woman? . . . Well, she's the mamma of your mamma . . . of your dear mamma."

But the angered child began to struggle and stamp her feet: "I want to go. . . . I want to go."

Nono in turn grew angry: "Go on, wretch! . . . Clear out!"

The little girl ran off, and Nono banged the door.

The husband and wife were again alone in the dark. Without saying a word Nono climbed the wooden staircase. But nobody followed him. . . . He stopped. . . .

"Are you coming up, Jeanne?"

No one answered him. He walked down the stairs and was seeking with his hands. . . . Nénette had remained below, sitting on the first step; she was weeping noiselessly.

"Come! my Jeanne. Let's go up to our house."

"I can't," muttered a weak voice mingled with tears.

"You can't? . . . And why?"

Nénette did not answer.

"It's the little one who repelled you? . . . Tell me? . . . Eh? . . . Answer! . . . Well, if that's so . . . wife, here's your duty before you. You've seen the forsaken child. . . . If you know your duty, do it at once: the child needs you. . . . "

Nénettte did not move.

"Poor woman, what's stopping you? . . . Answer! . . . Eh? . . . "

Nono was waiting in vain for a reply. . . . He then put his hands tenderly on the bony shoulders:

"Well, all right! . . . Look here, I'm going to tell you something which will make you decide. I didn't want to tell you this, because I hoped to see you come

back to me of your own free will. But since it ain't
so . . . listen, wife: it's me who came to seek you.
I'd gone to Catherine with an idea: to make up with
you. . . . To get up a little courage I'd drunk a bit.
. . . But one glass leads to another, and I'd had too
much. . . . But now . . . look: I'm holding out my
arms. . . . Jeanne! . . . Now, as in former days, it's
the same arms which love you, which are opening out
for you. . . . Come! It's me who's pleading! . . .
Come up! . . . "

On hearing this, Nénette began to sob, holding her
head in her hands. Nono sat down beside her; he
put his arm about her waist and pressed her to him
tenderly, and he spoke, bending over her as over a
cradle:

"There's something else? . . . Eh? Poor mother!
. . . Dear wife! . . . Call her, that dear daughter!
. . . "

"Yes. . . . Yes. . . . Jacques. . . . There's a little
martyr who lived upstairs . . . who died there. . . .
I killed her. . . . I don't want to go up there . . . no,
I can't! . . . "

"Wife! stop! . . . Stop your sobbing, and don't
feel so miserable! . . . Let her come and see, indeed,
the one who foretold and pardoned! . . . She's the
only one who has a right to be your judge. Listen!
your call's been heard. . . . I've seen her breathe her
last. . . . I speak in her name. . . . Your daughter
lived and died without hatred for you. On her deathbed, she pleaded for you. . . . I love her too much

to belie her. . . . Therefore, I tell you come up. . . .
Come up! . . . Follow me! . . . Follow me slowly:
there's perhaps a little phantom preceding us with a
friendly spirit. . . . You remember: the stairs ain't
steep. . . . That's right! . . . Don't slip. . . . Get
hold of my hand. . . . That's right! . . . That's fine!
. . . Now we're up! . . . "

Having reached the stair-head, Nono opened the
door. They both entered. It was agreeably somber
in the poor dwelling. The night deepened, and its
shadows like pious memories knelt at the foot of each
lowly object. . . . Nono showed to Nénette a little
faded frame that was hanging on the wall:

"Here's her little photograph. . . . A man who happened to have a stall at the fair thought her so neat
and pretty that he took her photograph, out of sheer
pleasure, as he said, for very little money. . . . That
and her soul is all that remains here. . . . You're
kneeling, wife! . . . Then I'll leave you for a while.
. . . "

When Nénette stood up, she stared at the poor
dwelling with it's mouldering plaster. From the black
beams of the ceiling were hanging chains of onions,
garlic and dented sausages; certain plants were drying
there with their roots in the air. In the corner, between the chimney and the window, there was a heap
of dry wood, vine-branches and broken props. The
kneader was full of rags and rusty pieces of iron.
. . . Could this be the dwelling of former years?

. . . whose walls were freshly plastered? . . . which was adorned with bright colors? . . . which was beaming like upright eyes? And yet Nénette found again in this sullied house the smell of sour bread, the aroma of chicory and of dry earth, which is the odor common in a winegrower's dwelling. And in spite of all, by still more subtle signs, Nénette found once more the past and recognized her home.

She was sitting, her body bent and her head in her hands; she was gradually surrounded by the soft shadow of the evening. In her inmost soul the aged woman sees a more degrading and grimmer gloom than the darkness about her. She plunges into that pitiful night which is the horizon of our souls, which veils our past and our despair, which makes us forget our bygone days of sorrow.

But what is this presence? . . . Is it a hovering soul which moves about in the dark, lowly dwelling? . . . An immaterial phantom seems to deepen the silence and the musing of souls in distress. It slips into their revery, caresses them with the awkward tenderness of a blind person who no longer sees yet searches. Then, imperious it hails them forthwith to the most bitter remorse; it descends to the abyss to absolve them, as though a divine visitor should stoop, to raise us from our sinful state.

Nono came in, but Nénette retained her pensive attitude. At first, the poor big fellow was very much embarrassed. He scratched his head, shook his long face, and, as if he were taking a decisive step, said:

"Well, I'm going to make the fire."

When the fire blazed up, Nono made another attempt to begin a conversation: "That's a fine fire." Nénette nodded yes, but she answered without having heard anything. Sunk in her chair, her elbow on her knee, her cheek resting on her clenched fist, she was gazing and dreaming. The flame shone on her thin worn face.

"That wood," said Nono, coming back to his idea. "That wood is excellent. It's the best kind of wood; it burns well."

"Yes."

"Oak ain't as good as they say. A piece of oak never made the stove red."

Nénette nodded her assent, and Nono continued:

"However, ash wood blazes perhaps better than any other kind. . . . But do you know? . . . It ain't so much the kind of wood which matters: you must know what forest to choose."

Nénette did not say anything, and Nono continued to explain: "It's the same with wood as it is with the vine. We hear people speak of different vines: 'It's on marl. . . . It's on sand. . . . ' And they yield two kinds of wines, the one a very dry wine and the other a very weak wine. But the forest also obtains from its soil a kind of temperament, and perhaps a more marked one, for it has a still wilder humor. . . . Remark that the mountain woods ain't as good as people

think. . . . But look here, you ain't listening to me.
. . . Talk to me a little. . . . I'm the only one
talking."

"What do you want me to tell you?"

"But say a few words to me . . . a few words of
affection. . . . "

"Oh! . . . what shall I say? . . . "

"Poor woman! You've forgotten that language."

"Yes."

Her voice was cold and indifferent. She sank in
gloomy dejection.

"Perhaps I was a bit rough a while ago."

"No."

"My Nénette! Look here! Is it really you? . . . in
body and soul? . . . Why yes, it's you . . . yes,
you're the old love of my youth and the consolation
I'm waiting for. . . . Say to me a few words of
affection that'll reassure me, and let me feel that I
ain't forsaken . . . that I've got near me my companion. . . . You don't want to say anything? . . .
You hardly understand me? . . . Am I the only one
here who feels our old friendship? . . . But you refuse to hear me?"

"Oh no!"

"Well, I'll let you alone for a while, till your good
heart'll feel again your old affection for me. Besides,
I've something good to do: I'm going to put up a
nice pot of soup. Let's make first of all a good fire."

Nono threw some fagots into the fire, and the little
burning twigs began to crackle and leap in every direc-

tion. Some of them jumped to where Nénette was sitting; she bent down and with her finger-tips quickly threw them back into the fire. Then, out of habit as housewife, she gathered the little sprays about the fireplace and also threw them into the fire again. The tongs were near her; she took them to stir the fire; and, with the little broom that was lying in the corner, she cleaned the square tiles of the hearth. Her old habits led her on still further. After the hearth-stone, she swept the floor near it, and finally the entire room. Then she began to dust the furniture, doing unconsciously and in the same diligent way her work of former days, when she had been a young housewife.

Nono was watching her.

"Well," said he, "I'm going to get the bacon and the vegetables. Only since you're sweeping, I'll open the window a bit. Now I'll tell you one thing: You find the house perhaps a little in disorder. It's a little topsy-turvy, for I'm a bad duster and not much of a sweeper; and indeed, to tell the truth, I spend so much time in removing the coaldust from the vines, that I don't care about the bit I see at home. Now there's also this! I don't like to make the beds, and I've always left 'em to good fortune. But she ain't much of a mattress-maker, for the little one and me have slept in hard beds. I don't care about myself, for I've got big bones as hard as stones. But is the little one well or not? . . . I don't know: she don't say anything. At all events, you can look after your bed; but you know more about it than me. . . . I'm leaving you. . . . "

"Ah! indeed! . . . " said Nono, when he returned. "That's right, wife! . . . It's about time! . . . That's what you call well-made beds. . . . But this little dwelling's beginning to look like something: we're going to be here like princes."

Nénette was tucking in the big bed. She had beaten and rearranged both beds well; the wretched mattress of little Catherine had become a real bed, clean, neat and pleasant to look at beneath the carefully spread quilt.

Without giving herself time to breathe, Nénette sat down beside Nono, and both of them peeled the vegetables. Nono was chatting. Each time that he threw a peeled potato into the pail of water he raised his head briskly and remarked with satisfaction:

"They're good potatoes. They come from Champfrans. They're rare this year."

"That's true. I've got much trouble finding 'em."

"And do you know? . . . With these last rains, they're beginning to get bad, and we'll have to dig 'em up quick. But I've some fine vegetables."

"Yes. I saw 'em the other day at Gerberois. They're very fine."

"Oh yes! Now the drought was driving me to despair; but the soil's so fat and fertile that they sprang up in no time."

"Did you do your sowing?"

"Yes. I've even struck it right. I took advantage of the rains during the vintage season. Everybody was busy with his casks; but I took care to look after my good fields a bit. It's a good thing to have wine; but what feeds the pig, the mule and the people? . . . It ain't the delicate plant that fattens those who're dressed in silk! . . . And the grapes can be heavy: it ain't them as fill the bellies of the cows! . . . "

But suddenly voices cried in the street: "Nono! Nono!"

"Listen: they're calling."

"Nono! Nono! . . . " repeated the unknown voices. Nono rose, went and opened the window and shouted in the darkness: "Who's there? . . . Who's calling? . . . "

A group of men appeared in the shadows, and yelled together: "Is your love-making all right?"

Nono closed the window, returned and sat down.

"I thought so: it's the blackguards. It's nothing."

It was sufficient, however. Nono tried in vain to take up the conversation again. . . . Nénette no longer listened to him!

"But I don't feel like talking. . . . I'm talking, and you don't even hear me!"

"Oh no! poor, dear man! . . . Oh no! I don't hear you."

She dropped her head and peeled her potatoes.

"Come, Nénette, what's the matter with you? . . . Just because some low knaves 've come to bray, you're almost in despair.   But the howl of a beast mustn't frighten a soul. . . . "

"Oh! my friend, it's not for me that I'm in despair."

"It's for me?"

"Oh yes! poor friend! . . . They're going to jeer enough!   They're going to mock . . . in these Baraques! . . . in these shops! . . . "

"Then to please the people, to have a reputation among the shopkeepers and respect in the Baraques, I must fire some bullets in your face! . . . Ah yes! . . . that's what you've come to! . . . "

"Oh! my poor friend! . . . But I'm a wretch broken-hearted with shame! . . . "

"Come now! . . . Come now! . . . "

"My friend! . . . My Jacquot! . . . "

"Come, Come! . . . don't sob like that, and let me talk: I ain't even put a word in. . . . But what do you want me to do? . . . I can't hate you, since I love you. . . . But tell me, little one! . . . why didn't you come sooner, since you were so unhappy?"

"Come back here! . . . Bring my shame to my daughter! . . . to my Laurette! . . . Oh no, never! But how? . . . how can you forgive me . . . my Jacquot? . . . "

"Forgive you? . . . It's no great task to do that: all men are the sons of forgiveness. . . . But listen my poor little one: had I had, that morning when you left, just a bit of brains and a little courage . . . both of us'd 've been saved . . . my child! . . . A mere trifle . . . my Nénette . . . it was a matter of a mere

nothing . . . and I'd have called you back . . . **and**
we'd 've remained friends for life! But they've en-
slaved both of our existences in barbarous **chains**
forged on **a** beastly anvil. . . . We've had our **fill of**
suffering: we've nothing to be proud of. . . .

"And besides, do you know? Each one's his **own**
way of acting. . . . To me poor devil . . . my justice is my good heart. . . . But there's a holy justice
that'd reproach me for having played the pretentious
fellow, for having affected his air and imitated his
voice. . . . Listen: He who sees and hears . . . instead of laughing at our poor love, will ask us **one**
day for a loyal account, well weighed and measured.
. . . We'll be much perplexed. . . . But the shameful
are His preferred children. . . . He who had Judas
against Him don't seek his friends among those
who've the respect of shopkeepers and the credit of
merchants; but he looks underneath the wrongs.
. . .

"It seems to me you told me that you'**d** go at times
to Binges. . . . "

"Yes, my friend. . . . "

"I know those regions. I've carted wine there. And
it's strange to see how the land changes once you've
passed Dijon. As soon as you go to the left of Arc,
towards the Beires, you see hop-gardens. . . . For
hop is the chief product of that region, hey?"

"Yes; they also raise cattle."

"Yes, and even big cattle! Especially near Mirebeau,
ain't it so?"

"Near Mirebeau . . . near Pontailler . . . yes. But near Groy, it's no more."

"Ah yes! . . . the plain of Groy! . . . yonder! . . . there's fine wheat and fine corn! . . . But the people are headstrong. . . . It already resembles Prussia . . . that region. . . . "

CHAPTER IX

LITTLE Catherine, weary of running about the streets, at last decided, somewhat late, to come home. She found the table set, and the husband and wife sitting near the fireplace. Nono was speaking of the vines and crops, and compared the different soils and their yield. The little one, without paying any attention to the new guest, sat down and noisily asked for her soup.

"But, little rascal, can't you let people talk a bit? . . . No? . . . We've many things to say to each other, your grandma and me! . . . She's your grandma . . . that woman. You don't care, eh? Oh! little beast! . . . That's how this little one is, my poor woman: she cares about nothing but tricks and pranks. A nasty little thing!"

"Why, no. The poor child's hungry, that's all. We must put the bread in the soup. Besides, the soup is done."

Nono was comfortably seated with his back to the fire, warming the palms of his hands which he crossed behind the back of his chair; his long legs were crossed beneath him. He was calmly watching Nénette bustle about, getting supper ready. There was a wholesome

odor of fresh cabbage and cooked bacon in the house.
He smiled contentedly, happy to be near the fire like
a master at rest, watching his wife, go, come, and
move about like the mistress of the house, with the
smiling placidity of his eternal innocence. . . .

"What was I telling you? . . . Oh yes! . . . We
were talking of wine. . . . Do you know at present our
greatest difficulty is not to be able to sell the wine.
The Parisians, the townfolks and the foreigners all
buy the wretched wine of the South which is a cursed
drink that costs too much if you don't get it for nothing, and if you ain't paid to drink it.

"And then there's another thing that's doing us
great harm, that's killing us: it's the manufacture of
wine. The soil and the sun are without work, and
so the winegrower. The miserable chemists 've done
us a great wrong: think of 'em manufacturing wine!
First of all they get up their laboratory: empty casks,
jars of chemicals, little tubes of poison and big bags
of brown sugar. . . . Then they pump water over it;
and after a farcical fermentation you've got wine!
. . . It's the vintage of the new century. And while
those rogues draw their Chambertin from the well,
we must work at the vines like slaves; and the wine
we get from nature after a struggle of ten months
with the soil and the sun, ain't good . . . it seems!
The merchant from Bercy who tastes it says: 'That's
sewer water. . . . I prefer the manufactured stuff.'
Do you think that is just? . . . "

Meantime the bread was put in the soup. Nénette

served the child; then Nono helped himself to a plateful.

"Well," said Nono to his wife, "eat your soup, too."

"I'm going to," replied Nénette. But she placed on the table the dish of vegetables and bacon, and at once began to look after the dishes and pots. From time to time she would stop working in order to watch the robust little girl eat. Catherine was calmly and slowly swallowing big mouthfuls. The old oil lamp lit up the room, cast on the three faces its soft light and spread on the wall its faint, yellow glimmers.

Little Catherine broke the silence: "Tell me, Nono . . . who's that woman? . . . "

Nénette at once put out her arms, and in a voice choked by tears said:

"My child . . . she's your grandma . . . or rather she's a mamma to love you! . . . Do you want me, my darling?" And the pitiful face drooped and tried to smile.

Catherine did not answer. She continued to eat her soup with the discreet slowness of a sedate little person. While eating, she riveted her eyes gravely on the two aged beings who were contemplating her with tenderness.

"My poor woman," said Nono, "what are you telling her? Ah! you want to be her mamma! . . . She don't care a hang, I say! . . . She ain't missing a single mouthful. But look here . . . why don't you eat? . . . By heavens! I'm going to get angry! Now your soup is cold! It was a simple matter to eat it

hot. . . . But I'm going to take another little piece
of bacon. . . . It's very fine bacon. . . . It's much
better than the bacon of the belly. . . . "

And Nono began to look for a choice piece in the
dish.

"Ah! . . . my Nénette, you can't imagine how
happy I'm now!"

Nénette was not listening. She was eating; but she
watched the child closely all the time. Catherine had
finished her soup, and she was fidgeting on her chair,
playing with her spoon in her mouth. Suddenly, she
came back to her idea: "Say, Nono, is that woman
going to stay here always?"

The child's tone was so pert that the husband and
wife could not refrain from laughing. The little one
watched them laugh with some distrust.

"She sometimes makes remarks that are very
funny." Then turning to the child, Nono shouted:
"You wicked little wretch! . . . Does it bother you
to see that woman remain here?"

"Yes."

"It's too bad, because she's going to remain here
anyhow. Little fool, she was in this house before
you. . . . "

"Leave her alone," said Nénette, "she'll get used
to me soon."

"Just look at her! It's no use talking, she ain't
very loving. It ain't in her nature. . . . She's never
kissed me."

"Oh yes, my friend, but you don't remember. You're going to kiss us, ain't you, my darling? . . . "

"No. . . . You smell too bad. You smell like an old woman. Where did you get that old woman, Nono? . . . If she robs you, it'll serve you right."

"Listen to that! . . . Where the devil does she get her ideas? . . . The reasoning of the wretch ain't so bad! . . . " And Nono continued, turning to the child: "Won't you shut up, you wicked creature! Here's this martyr who's here to make your soup, wash your dishes and make your bed . . . who don't even take time to breathe and eat . . . and you want to kick her out! . . . You're nasty! . . . You ain't bigger than a four-pound loaf, and you're already sharper-tongued than a bailiff! . . .

"Speaking of a bailiff, my poor woman, I'm hardly rich. That's my great crime. The good days of our youth are no more. Two days before Michaelmas, they almost seized my property: the bailiff had a grudge against me. I just had time to run to the notary. And now we're fixed with a mortgage on the house! . . . We'll have to look out and keep our eyes open, for we can't fall asleep when a notary begins to lay his claws on us. . . .

"Besides, I owe about one hundred francs at the Café Caillot, which is also a nuisance. I haven't paid for my wood; and I must buy twenty bundles of props. It's true, I've got some wine to sell; but I owe money right and left. . . . Ah! but the most troublesome fel-

low of all is the miller of Barges, who's a mad, low
knave. . . .

"And yet I've done all I could: in Gratte-Paille,
I've planted potatoes; in Gerberois I've planted dis-
ettes; in la Ramonée there were some fallow fields
and I've planted barley; and then I've my wheat in
Boise, where the soil is very good. You see, after
all I didn't waste my time, and I managed to do my
utmost. But it's poverty anyhow, poverty taken with
a good will, that's all."

Nénette was removing the cloth from the table while
listening to Nono's gossip.

"What can you expect, my poor man! . . . I've seen
much worse misery, believe me! . . . We must have
courage. . . . We'll have it. . . . "

"Courage? . . . Oh! it ain't that that we lack. But
I'm afraid of many things."

"Why no, my friend."

"Wife! I know what I'm talking about. The soil's
in very bad state. At one time, a Spanish clover lasted
twelve years; now, it's doing well if it lasts five years.
The soil is getting exhausted; it's dying underneath
our feet.

"It's the fault of the fertilizers. They manage
to produce one harvest; but it's like a fire of straw,
and then . . . there's nothing left."

Nono shook his head with a knowing air: "There's
something else too.

"Yes, it's true, we no longer manure the fields.
We've abused the heavy yields; we want too many

beets. And then, at one time, the fields weren't always cultivated; but now they've no rest.

"That's very true; but there's still something else. Look at the countryside: the springs are disappearing. I remember the time when every village of La Côte had its large brook. Now La Côte is drier than a hoof. My old man announced that the phylloxera was coming. He didn't use the right word, but he foretold the thing: the vines are dying and all's going to ruin. There's something deadly gradually rising beneath us: our grandchildren'll see the thing grow up. Wife! we're tending towards dire happenings. But enough . . . it's a subject that terrifies me. Let's speak of something else. . . . "

"My poor man! You mustn't talk so: you'll make people think you've lost your reason. Poor dear man! . . . "

Meantime Catherine had fallen asleep on the edge of the table. . . . Nénette was staring at her.

"The child must be put to bed," she said.

"Oh! she'll go to bed alone. At night I've enough of my own affairs, without bothering about her."

"Since I'm here, I can just as well put her to bed."

Nénette was looking a long time at that little, plump, round face, which was resting peacefully, with her cheeks on her hands. She was looking at that mouth with its open lips, fresh like a cherry cut in two. Catherine was no longer the wild, reckless child of a moment ago; and Nénette was trying to discover in the child's graceful slumber, some of the dear features of her own daughter. Hesitatingly, she turned to her former duties. She began by undressing the child. Catherine did not wake, but muttered some indistinct words. Nénette took her up in her arms, and the sleeping child put her arm around her grandma's neck.

"Ah! ah!" said Nono, "now she's caressing you. If she was up . . . she'd caress you! . . . yes! . . . with her nails! . . . But after all there's a way of getting round children, and that ain't the business of men. I tried sometimes, and I was always pushed back. You've tamed her at once! . . . "

While Nono was holding the lamp, Nénette carried the child to bed. She arranged the bolster, threw back the blanket and straightened and tucked in the sheet. After these little attentions, the child's dimpled, pink, sweet face looked as if she were in swaddling clothes. Nénette stood and contemplated the peaceful slumber of the child whom she had henceforth the right to love.

"Ah! the clock's already struck nine," said Nono. "Do you want to come with me? I'm going to take my nightly turn in the yard to see if all the animals are asleep, and if there's no fire in the hay-loft."

CHAPTER X

Nono lit his lantern, and the husband and wife walked down into the yard. They first entered the stable of the mule. Nono caressed his snout and opened his lips. The mule kept quiet; but he raised and shook his head like a goat, wagged his tail and gnashed his teeth, which were as large as dominoes.

"He's become as hard to please as an old maid. He has his manias and notions, and nothing can make him waver. Why, he's more headstrong than a charcoal-burner. You can't get him, for instance, to cross a puddle, no matter how small, for all the beets in the world. When he sees one, he backs up, and then he advances very slowly, putting down his little hoofs on dry spots, with the little steps and airs of a damsel who's afraid of dirt. He's funny to look at! . . . Hey there! . . . rogue! . . . There ain't a worse knave than this little beast! . . . Eh? Sonny! . . . "

While talking, Nono stooped down towards the donkey, and patted his dusty back amiably.

"Hey! you're satisfied, little rogue! . . . That's our old friend, Jeanne. He's got a good many years. People say: 'A donkey lives thirty years, no more.' Now this one's long passed thirty, and I say that a donkey lives much longer, and can even outlive a man.

267

Look at him! If after my death he meets with some-one who's almost after his fashion, and with whom he can agree . . . he'll pull through his hundred years without muttering a word! . . . But come over and look at him, Jeanne."

Nénette approached, and caressed the back of the ill-humored donkey. But the ungrateful mule suddenly began to snort.

"Hey there! ruffian! . . . Be a little polite. . . . He surely recognizes you, however. Only he ain't a noisy creature, and he don't like people to bother about him. Do you know what he says to himself: 'That's all right. . . . Don't make such a fuss!' He's right. If you wasn't here, he'd bray at me, with his nose in the air like a cavalry trumpet. But seeing you, he's a little embarrassed. Why, he's as timid as a child. But he's a rogue, too! . . . Look how solid he is! . . . four little legs of a dog to carry the belly of a cow! . . . Ah! knave! . . . Give him a beetroot. Let him see you give it, so that he'll know you. He smells it, he won't trust a soul. No matter what you give him, he must sniff at it from all sides. . . . Ah! he's getting at it. Listen to his teeth working! . . . Heavens! how they gnash! . . . His dentist'll croak with rage, and gnash his own teeth! . . .

"Do you want to see the rabbits? . . . Here they are, the little four-paws. They think we're going to give 'em some grass. . . . "

Under the faint glimmer of the lantern, they saw the rabbits huddled together like little gray balls at the bottom of the trellis. There was a heap of fleecy, silken backs, on which long horn-like ears were reclining. Their little snouts, nostrils and whiskers were pricked in the air towards the two human faces that were amiably watching them.

"Do you see 'em! . . . They're of the last brood . . . and how fat! . . . They ain't worrying much. . . ."

"I'm not going to show you the pig: that'd be too stupid . . . and besides I ain't got one. You're laughing, my poor woman! I'm so happy! You see that I'm still the same simple fellow. . . . Nono the gossip, not cunning, and hardly rich! . . . I've hardly improved, eh? . . . You're crying . . . now? There's no reason, believe me. . . . "

They walked out of the stable. The night was clear and bright with moonlight. In the sky hung low the incomplete face of a strange yet expressive moon. . . . And Nénette recognized in that pale light all the places of her youth . . . the yard . . . the cottages . . . the lowly and touching objects. . . . And in her soul, a ray of light rose above the ruins and penetrated her misery. . . .

The husband and wife clasped each other in silence. . . .

"Let's go up, Jeanne," Nono said at last.

She did not answer. He waited a moment . . . then he continued tenderly: "My wife . . . you mustn't cry. We can't remain here, it's getting chilly. Let's go to bed."

. . . They walked upstairs, but they did not go to bed. They sat down, and stirred the fire. Then Nono began to talk. The sound of his dull, hollow voice was made less monotonous by the cheerful accompaniment of the crackling fire. Nono trod back over the path of time, penetrating far into his cruel past. . . . And Nénette listened with all her soul, while from underneath her closed lids tears rolled down noiselessly. When Nono heard a sob, he would stop; but she said to him: "Go on . . . go on . . . I'm weeping, but it's doing me good." And he shook his head, on hearing this, in his habitual, resigned, good-natured manner.

" . . . She'd go away in the morning, slowly clambering up the road alone on her way to school. . . .

"Sunday morning she'd laugh like a child, and animate with her graceful work the whole house. . . .

" . . . On seeing her, anybody could divine her pure heart and noble soul. . . .

" . . . The little one and me lived all these years hand in hand. . . . "

"It was on Candlemas-day that she gave her heart away. He inspired her with faith by talking of pity. He spoke to her of you and me, and told her he'd find you and bring you back. 'The butcher business is a good one,' he'd say, 'I'll make money for all of you. . . . '

" . . . She went with all her courage, and knocked at the door of that bitter house. But someone 'd already taken his place. He'd left the village. . . . He never came back. . . .

" . . . One journey leads to another; but the little one'd gone on the long journey. . . . Ah! she suffered so much!"

Suddenly, Nono placed his hand on Nénette's shoulder, and in a strong, spirited tone said: "Wife! she asked for you continually. . . . When she saw that her end was coming, that it was her last night, that she would never see the dawn . . . then she called for you louder than ever.

"Well, do you know what we did? . . . We made believe that we'd heard from you. . . . Someone came up and told her he'd seen you. . . . But when we remained alone together for the last time, with despair in our eyes. . . . I had to confess sobbing my falsehood. . . . And then it was she who gave me true news; she rose for the last time, she spoke of you, and the miracle happened. It's as true as I'm talking to you, she pointed out with her drooping head the place where you're sitting now, and she said you'd come back! . . .

"Wife! I lived with that hope, and my hope wasn't in vain. There's her deathbed before which I learnt my lesson. Wife! what I learnt that night I'm repeating to-day in my own way. So you see all we can do is to continue on our path here below, going hand in hand. . . . Yes, my Jeannette, that's right! . . . Come to my heart. . . . Weep in my arms. . . . Oh! the dear kisses! . . . "

"Jacquot! . . . Forgive me! Forgive me! . . . "

"Come, be quiet: you'll wake the little one!"

"Forgive   me! . . . Jacquot! . . . Laurette! . . . Oh! my friend! . . . "

"Come now, don't scream! . . . Come, you mustn't cry, because we've everything to make us happy: the little one, wood in the wood-stack, bacon in the salting-tub, wine in the cellar . . . besides all that, we can love each other, and in a lasting and supreme way which was unknown to us in the time of our kisses. . . . For be sure, it ain't in vain that we've suffered."

THE END

www.ingramcontent.com/pod-product-compliance
Lightning Source LLC
Chambersburg PA
CBHW020649030726
47498CB00002B/433